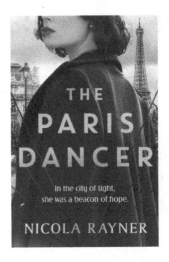

In the city of light,
she was a beacon of hope.

NICOLA RAYNER

CW00548657

yasmeen.doogue-khan@headofzeus.com
+44 (0)20 3940 7186

Sales •
sales@headofzeus.com

A heart-wrenching and unforgettable story of courage, friendship and resistance, inspired by the incredible true story of a Jewish ballroom dancer in Paris during WWII.

Paris, 1938. Annie Mayer arrives in France with dreams of becoming a ballerina. But when the war reaches Paris, she's forced to keep her Jewish heritage a secret. Then a fellow dancer offers her a lifeline: a ballroom partnership that gives her a new identity. Together, Annie and her partner captivate audiences across occupied Europe, using her newfound fame and alias to aid the Resistance.

New York, 2012. Miriam, haunted by her past, travels from London to New York to settle her great-aunt Esther's estate. Among Esther's belongings, she discovers notebooks detailing a secret family history and the story of a brave dancer who risked everything to help Jewish families during the war.

As Miriam uncovers Esther's life in Europe, she realises the story has been left for her to finish. Grappling with loss and the possibility of new love, Miriam must find the strength to reconcile her past and embrace her future.

NICOLA RAYNER, born in South Wales, is a novelist
and dance writer based in London. She is the author
of *The Girl Before You*, which was picked by the
Observer as a debut to look out for in 2019, optioned
for television and translated into multiple languages.
Her second novel, *You and Me*, was published by Avon,
HarperCollins, in 2020. In her day job as a journalist,
Nicola has written about dance for almost two decades,
cutting her teeth on the tango section of *Time Out*
Buenos Aires. She edited the magazine *Dance Today*
from 2010 to 2015 and worked as assistant editor of
Dancing Times, the UK's leading dance publication,
from 2019 until 2022. She continues to dance
everything from ballroom to breakdance, with varying
degrees of finesse. You can find her on Instagram @
nicolaraynerwrites and on X
@nico1aryaner.

THE PARIS DANCER

Nicola Rayner

An Aria Book

First published in the UK in 2025 by Head of Zeus,
part of Bloomsbury Publishing Plc

9 7 5 3 1 2 4 6 8

A catalogue record for this book is available from the British Library.

ISBN (PB): 9781837931828
ISBN (E): 9781837931781

Printed and bound in Great Britain by CPI Group (UK) Ltd, Croydon CR0 4YY

Head of Zeus
5–8 Hardwick Street
London EC1R 4RG

WWW.HEADOFZEUS.COM

The Paris Dancer

For my parents who danced beautifully together,
for Jason who learned to dance for me,
and in loving memory of Olav
who played the music

Prologue

Almost seven decades later, I still think of your face squashed up on the pillow next to mine in the mornings. You couldn't bear to see those early hours of the day slip by. "Wake up," you used to whisper. "You're wasting it."

Deep in the bowels of the musty theatre – a place daylight never reached – we could hear the noise of the occupied city. The curt demand, "*Aufmachen! Sofort!*" A human cry, protestations of innocence, a shriek of fear. Sounds that left me wide awake, my heart thrumming in the darkness. Waiting until they came for us.

You were right: there is never enough time. Even if you live to your nineties. I'm careful not to waste those early hours now. I'm careful not to waste any of it. But I don't know whether I'll be granted the time to finish what I started here. And I don't know if you ever forgave me. If I'll ever forgive myself.

I

Nothing too sad, nothing too frightening. That's Mim's rule for films now, especially when flying. She's learned to be careful – you never know what's out there to ambush you. *Stupid.* She berates herself. Stupid to watch something like that. What was she thinking? And now they've come on too quickly: sobs that feel like they could choke her. Ugly-crying, Frankie called it. Ugly-crying on her own in the dark, seven miles above the ground, while everyone else in the plane sleeps around her, with their smug little eye masks and shoulder cushions. Their neat and tidy lives.

The grief, when it's like this, feels as if it could drown her. It could drag her under. Mim pushes up the flap of the window. There's nothing out there but darkness. *It's a metaphor*, she tells herself, and snaps it shut again.

A hand, outstretched. A tissue. Mim looks at its owner. There's a spare seat between them. He's been sleeping for

5

most of the flight and they've barely interacted, even when she had to clamber over him to get to the bathroom. His face without the eye mask is a pleasant surprise. He's her age – in his thirties, perhaps. Or maybe a little younger. Nerdy handsome. Messy dark hair. Trendy dark-rimmed glasses.

"If we were in a 1940s film, this would be a crisp white handkerchief." He glances apologetically at the scrunched up paper napkin.

Mim peers at the tissue. "There's a smear of chicken korma on it." She wipes her face hastily with her hands. "Chicken or beef."

A blush spreads across his handsome face and he folds the tissue away. "That worked better in my head – it's never like the movies, is it?"

"It's OK," Mim finds she's smiling, despite herself. "I'm no good on 1940s films, anyway," she adds. "*Breakfast at Tiffany's* is my favourite old movie."

It had been Frankie's too. They'd watch it together on hungover Sunday afternoons, weeping self-indulgent tears at that final scene in the rain, laughing and crying at the furious wet cat.

"That's the 1960s." The guy grins. A nice smile. There's something sweetly boyish about him. And he's wearing braces, Mim notices. She's always had a weakness for braces. "Far too late for me."

"Sorry," she says, though she's not sure what she's apologising for: her tears, perhaps, or being ungracious about the tissue. "I have a case of the mean reds – you'd know what that meant if you'd seen *Breakfast at Tiffany's*."

When she'd queued for the loo earlier, she'd tried her

hardest not to look at the emergency exit. It did something funny to her, made her wonder what it would feel like to push up the lever holding the door closed. Would anyone stop her? Would the door fly open? Would the suction of air feel like an enormous hoover, pulling her out into the sky?

"I get more emotional when I fly," the young man agrees. "Especially when I have a drink." He glances ruefully at a couple of Bacardi miniatures tucked in the seat pocket in front of him. "Though technically it wasn't drinking alone," he adds. "You were right next to me."

"I don't drink any more." Mim used to be smoother at this – idle chitchat, shooting the breeze – but she can't remember how she did it. Booze helped.

"Well," he says, "it doesn't help with heartbreak."

For a moment, she wants to correct him, but what better word is there for what she's going through?

"Is that why you're running away to New York?" he asks. "Or are you skipping the build-up to the Olympics in London?"

"I'm not really the sporty type." She smiles. "And who says I'm running away?"

"You don't sound American."

"I'm" – she hesitates – "between things. That sounds better than unemployed, doesn't it?"

"Sure," he grins. "I'm between things too. At least for the summer."

"My great-aunt died recently." Mim fishes her water bottle out of the seat pocket and takes a sip. "I'm going to sort out her paperwork. Partly because I'm a writer too and partly because..." She takes a breath. *My family don't know what to do with me.* The words come into her head, but she won't say them aloud to this handsome stranger. "My older sister, Abi, has two small children," she says instead. "So she's got her hands full."

It's the kind of phrase Abi might have used herself. "Can you just do it, Mim? I've got my hands full here."

And, without warning, she is ambushed by a memory. Being on the phone to Abi. Her mobile sandwiched between her shoulder and ear, rolling her eyes at Frankie on the sofa opposite. Desperate to get her sister off the phone so she can get back to her best friend and the bottle of wine they're sharing.

"Anyway," she returns to the present, to the aeroplane, the handsome stranger next to her, "I'm…"

"Between things," he finishes with a smile.

"That's right." She nods. It's good to be with someone who doesn't seem to judge her for being unemployed. "What about you?"

"I'm a dancer. I'm spending a summer in New York to check out the scene there. It's the mothership – especially for swing dancers. Where it all started."

Mim frowns. "I can't picture swing dance."

"Have you seen *Hellzapoppin'*? That's one from the 1940s – there's a great swing dance scene in it."

She shakes her head. "Sorry, I'm useless. The closest I've got to the 1940s is going to Casablancas in Brighton. A jazz club," she adds by way of explanation. "Kind of. I think we were dancing to the 'Macarena' last time we were there."

"The 'Macarena'?" He pulls a pained face. "No, no, no."

"Is it so bad?" she laughs.

"I just think dance used to be more romantic," he says. "The ballroom hold. Flying across the room in someone else's arms. When I had a bad day as a kid, my mum would let me drag a duvet downstairs and make a den on the sofa, where I'd watch Fred and Ginger. I used to try to teach the guys at History Club my favourite pieces of choreography."

"History Club." Mim suppresses a giggle. "How did that go?"

"Well, there were only three of us, so we had to double up…" He smiles. "I was probably doing that while you were learning the complex choreography to the 'Macarena.'"

"Thank you," Mim says, "for acknowledging its complexity."

"What kind of dancing do you like now?"

"Actually, I don't really go out much these days." She reaches for her water again, but largely to give herself something to do."

"Not even at Casablancas?" When he smiles a dimple appears on his right cheek.

"No." Mim's gaze slides away from him. She doesn't want to think of Brighton – she shouldn't have brought it up. "Things moved on."

There's a moment or two of silence between them. And then the guy looks at his watch. "I don't know if you heard, but they've actually found a cure for heartbreak."

Not this kind, she thinks.

"Yeah, it took them a while, but it turns out it's been with us all along. Or since 1952." He leans forward, lowers his voice to a whisper. "*Singin' in the Rain*."

"Is that a fact?" She remembers watching it on one of their hungover Sundays – Gene Kelly swinging around lamp-posts and splashing in puddles. She's reasonably sure *that's* not going to help.

He leans forward. "I've got good news for you – they have it on the plane." He taps the little screen in front of him with a finger. "So, what do you say we plug in and watch it together? And if you don't feel better afterwards, I'll give you your money back."

"Fine." Mim is smiling again. "You're lucky we're not sitting in business class."

*

"I was right?" checks her new friend almost two hours later. "It *is* a cure, isn't it?"

They are sitting side by side now, eating a pre-landing meal together like old friends. Mim peels the lid from her fruit salad and spears a piece of anaemic-looking melon with a plastic fork. She wants to say something witty and cutting, but it's funny: her face feels more relaxed. She is smiling. "It wasn't so bad."

"Wasn't so bad? The best film ever made?" He hits his palm on his forehead.

She reaches out and touches his shoulder, just the lightest contact. His shirt still looks fresh and clean, as if he has stepped out of one of those old-fashioned films, where the men are handsome and everything is safe.

"It was actually quite... good," she says. "Quite funny. And the dancing – even as someone who doesn't know what she's talking about – I can appreciate it's something else."

His face flushes with enthusiasm. "When I watch 'Good Mornin'' at home, I have to stand up for that moment when the three of them dance over the sofa," he says. "It's too exciting to watch sitting down."

She wonders for a moment if there's a woman next to him on that sofa and feels an odd pang of jealousy. That's how it begins – a feeling of possessorship. Is that a word? She can't remember. Anyway, maybe it's just his mum. Is that better or worse? Mim feels a small flare of curiosity. What would it be like to reach over and touch him again? How would it feel to start over as someone else?

"Did you teach that routine to the guys at History Club?" she checks.

He nods solemnly. "Of course. And to 'Moses Supposes' – that's one you can try sitting down." He begins to tap out the rhythm of the song on his tray, making his empty glass and cup jump up and down. "Moses-supposes-his-toeses-are-roses."

"Could you stop that?" a woman in front of them snaps. Just a sliver of her face is visible between the seats – red cheeks, eye mask pushed up on her head.

Chastised, he sits back and taps the rhythm quietly on his lap like a naughty schoolboy. "But-Moses-supposes-erroneously."

"Well, my toeses aren't roses." Mim smirks.

"Not yet," he says. "Maybe they'd bloom if you came out dancing with me."

Mim lets the invitation hang there, unsure how to respond. She's conscious of the flicker between them. Easier to snuff it out than watch it be extinguished in some other way. She can't look at his hopeful face. And then, mercifully, she's saved by the Tannoy telling them that they're about to begin their descent.

She feels a wave of sadness at the missed opportunity, as she folds away her tray and adjusts her seat to upright. She knows how it goes: the plane will land and everyone on it will unclick their seatbelts just as soon as they can and get to their feet to grab their hand luggage, despite tutting attendants telling them to sit.

Then you wait, all sticky and dry-eyed and bloated, and file awkwardly out of the plane, and one of you, on the way out, says, "Have a good trip." Or "Good luck with that project." And maybe – if you're lucky – you give one another a rueful smile and then you each go on your way.

It's a cliché, anyway, she tells herself. Meeting someone on a Transatlantic flight. What does she think this is? One of those old-fashioned romances he seems to like so much?

Except, things don't play out as she anticipates. He waits for her as they get off the plane, and they make their way through border control together.

"What are you up to tonight?" he asks as they wait by the luggage carousel with the rest of the bleary-eyed crowd.

"I don't know," Mim says. "I need to get some sleep – and I don't know what kind of state the flat is going to be in. It might need some tidying. Esther was a heavy smoker and she had cats, so it wasn't the most hygienic place." She sighs. "Not that it ever bothered me."

A memory of the chaos of the apartment bubbles up. There were always brimming ashtrays and the reek of cat urine – that much was true – but then there was the warmth with which Esther would greet you whenever you knocked on the door to her bedroom. She would look delighted as she glanced up from her desk and she would say Mim's name with such pleasure in her lovely husky voice, which had never lost its French accent. "Miriam." No one said her name quite like that. Mim always knew she was Esther's favourite. But she had no idea why.

"What about you?" she asks. "What will you do?"

"Nap, shower, a few beers with my pal Augustine. And

then out dancing tonight, of course." A beat. "You're welcome to come with me."

"I told you I don't really dance any more," she says. She needs to be clear about what she can offer. Or can't. No point in stringing such a sweet person along.

"You *don't* dance," he says.

"That's right."

"Most people say they *can't* dance – not that they don't."

A wave of weariness washes over her. She doesn't want to have to explain herself – *can't, don't, won't*. It's too late for all of this: flirting and new beginnings. It doesn't lead anywhere good – this fluttery feeling. She knows that now. All she wants to do is sleep. There is no way she's going out dancing tonight.

"I'm sorry," she says. She'd guess that she's just a few years older than him, but in that moment it feels like a lot more. "I don't have your energy."

And there it is – perfect timing for once – her case on the conveyor belt: easy to spot with one wonky wheel held together by yellow tape. She steps forward to claim it.

"All the best in New York." She offers her hand for him to shake. "Thank you for the tissue. And for *Singin' in the Rain*."

His boyish face falls a little. "I never asked your name."

"It's Miriam," she says. "But everyone calls me Mim."

"I'm Lucky."

His name suits him. "Happy-go-lucky." She smiles.

"That's right," he agrees. She could be kidding herself but he doesn't seem to have shaken off the disappointment.

She only allows herself to turn around once as she walks away and, when she does, his gaze is still on her. Caught watching, he breaks into a smile and mimes the "Macarena" arms at her. It's goofy, but oddly graceful, even when he circles his hips and jumps to change direction. Lucky moves as if he knows where every part of his body is. He's not scattered and discombobulated like Mim. It's unnerving. Attractive.

She shakes her head, still smiling as she walks away. The broken wheel on her case makes a terrible din. *It's a metaphor*, she tells herself. No point dreaming of new beginnings while her past is still rattling behind her.

2

You're the queen of self-sabotage. Frankie's voice turns up in her head in the taxi queue.

Self-protection, Miriam tells her. *It's not the same.*

She inches the broken case a little closer to the family in front of her. Just five more in the queue, then it'll be her turn. She's too tired to read or to listen to music, so it'll have to be this instead – conducting an argument in her head.

Whatever. He was nice. Frankie sounds cross with her.

Too nice for me?

I didn't say that. Frankie sighs. *You should let your mum know you've landed, by the way. She'll be worrying.*

You never used to be this responsible…

Silence. Frankie is sulking.

A child in the queue shouts with delight at the sight of the yellow taxis. You never forget your first time in New York. At the front, a harried-looking man in a suit gets into his cab. Four to go. It's still muggy, long after the sun has gone down. Surely only a mad person would come to New York in the summer.

Mim fishes out her phone to message her mum.

You could go back. Frankie returns. *You could say you've changed your mind – that you* do *want to go dancing after all.*

But I don't. Mim swallows, glares at the ground. *I only want to dance if I can go with you.*

She's going to cry again. The grief is always worse when she's tired.

A hand on her shoulder. Someone is shaking her gently. "Miriam. Mim." Lucky, looking flustered and a bit sweaty. The woman behind her in the queue is tutting, thinking he's cutting in.

"I'm sorry, Madam, I'll just be a minute." He flashes the woman a dimpled smile, which seems to melt her froideur, and turns to Mim. "Look, I know you're sad at the moment," he begins. "But will you let me help with this one small thing – to find the right dance for you?" He takes a breath. "The way we dance at weddings and parties – that's just one kind – and it's great, I'm not knocking it. Or the 'Macarena.'" He grins. "But there are so many ways to dance. There's ballet. Or tango. Or salsa. Or Lindy hop. Give dance another chance" – he smiles at the rhyme – "because I believe there will be one for you. Truly."

"Truly?" Miriam teases. But he's sweet, this sweaty eager boy. She thinks of him planning his speech as he paced across JFK to find her. "You didn't tell me you knew the 'Macarena,'" she says. "You actually dance it quite well." The family in front of her start to get into their yellow taxi.

They don't have much time.

"Well, a gentleman shouldn't reveal all of his talents immediately." He touches her arm, just the gentlest brush of his fingers. "So, how about it? Could I have your number?"

The car with the family begins to pull away. The next cab is hers. "Where to?" asks the driver – round and portly, with a bald head and bristling moustache.

"Brooklyn Heights," Mim tells him, as he puts her case into the boot. She fishes out a receipt from her wallet and scrawls her number on it for Lucky.

"Here you go." He passes her his business card and waits at the taxi rank to wave her off.

That was cute, Frankie tells her, in the car.

Wasn't it? Mim turns the card over in her hand. It says, *Lucky García – Swing Dancer*, in Art Deco lettering with a trail of footprints swirling around his name.

"Brooklyn Heights, did you say?" the taxi driver checks.

"That's right." She leans back in the car seat and closes her eyes. "Grace Court."

"Nice area."

"I haven't visited for years."

"Are you seeing family?"

"Kind of," she says, tired of all the questions. "It was my great-aunt's place."

"She'll be pleased to see you." He's missed the past tense, is blundering on, regardless.

"I doubt that somehow," she tells him. "She's dead."

This manages to kill the conversation for the rest of the journey. Mim pushes Lucky's card deep into one of the pockets on her backpack and zips it up. She looks out for familiar landmarks lit by streetlights – the café they went to as kids, the neighbourhood bookshop. Strange to be back here without her family, without her mother fretting about the kind of state Esther's flat might be in, without her sister by her side telling her things. Growing up, they used to visit Esther every few years, but the trips had become less frequent in adulthood. Her great-aunt rarely travelled to Europe and as far back as Mim's bat mitzvah she'd stopped coming altogether, because she and Grandma weren't speaking. Mim's grandmother had been there, of course, looking immaculate as always, but Mim missed Esther that day. She wonders if the sisters ever made up.

It hits her afresh that there will be no Esther in the flat. No Esther answering the door in her Katharine Hepburn slacks, a cigarette burning in her fingers. She feels guilty for a moment – she is six months too late for the funeral. For meeting Esther's friends. For finding out more about her life. She should have asked more questions; she should have paid more attention. It's yet another thing, in a very long list, that it's too late to do.

The taxi driver still hasn't forgiven her by the time he pulls up outside the luxurious apartment block that towers over the neighbouring brownstones. He's grumpy as he retrieves her case from the boot, and Mim feels bad – he was only trying to make conversation. She hitches her small backpack on to her shoulders and pulls the case behind her to the front door, its broken wheel rattling.

Just for a moment she experiences the prickling sensation of someone watching her. She glances up and spots a blurred face looking down at her from a lit window high up in the block, but the person steps back as soon as he or she has been seen and the light in that room snaps off.

In the lobby, she feels scruffy and inadequate, but the doorman greets her like an old friend, giving her the key and a set of instructions for the flat, and insisting on helping her to the lift with the luggage.

As she puts the key in the lock of Esther's apartment and nudges open the door, she almost hears her great-aunt's voice, saying, "Miriam."

But the feeling shifts once she's inside. It's so different now, without Esther. It has been cleaned up – no brimming ashtrays, and only the faintest smell of smoke. *What happened to the cats?* Mim wonders suddenly. She never asked.

She makes her way to Esther's bedroom, where her great-aunt used to write with her desk pressed up against the enormous window, enjoying one of the most coveted views in New York – the Lower Manhattan skyline, Governors Island and, beyond it, the Statue of Liberty. A tiny figure from this distance.

As a child, standing by her great-aunt's desk, Mim had peered at the green copper lady who held a torch high above her head.

"She was a gift from France," Esther told her. "She used to make me feel less homesick when I first came here. I promised myself that, when I made my fortune, I'd buy a place with a view of her. Do you know what it says on her pedestal?"

Mim shook her head.

"Give me your tired, your poor," Esther said, "Your huddled masses yearning to breathe free." She took the binoculars from Mim and looked at the statue again herself.

"It meant, for us, for my sister and me, that we were safe. I'll never take that for granted: we got out in time. Not everyone was so lucky."

"And then Grandma found Grandpa here?" Mim checked.

"That's right," Esther said.

"And what about you?"

"I found myself. Which is just as good."

Mim nodded, unconvinced. Everyone knew that happy endings always came in the form of another person.

Now, she sighs, and pulls the curtains closed. She climbs into Esther's old bed, which someone – maybe the same person who cleaned the flat – has kindly made up for her. Understanding has come too late – you can't know how much it means to find yourself, it occurs to her as she drifts off, until you've lost yourself first.

As she dozes, her drifting mind shuffles through the day. The emergency exit on the plane. The rattle of the broken wheel. Three people with linked arms dancing over a sofa.

*

For a moment, Mim doesn't know where she is. She thinks she's back at her old flat in Brighton. She nearly calls out to Frankie, but then it comes back, as it always does.

She's here, in New York – the city's artificial light leaking through the edges of the curtains. A siren. Distant traffic. She checks her phone. It's just after four. Even on New York time, she has still managed to wake at this dreaded hour. She was woken by the usual dream. Her hair clings to her sweaty neck, her arms are still stuck to her sides.

She shakes herself and swings her legs off the bed, fumbling for a lamp. It's always better with the light on. Useless, she knows, to try to get back to sleep. She's alert now – the sorrow in her is strongest at this time, running through her like an electrical current. What does her mum always advise? Get up, do something, make yourself some tea.

A few minutes later, she is cradling her hot drink, pacing the room. Esther's desk is the only place in the disinfected apartment that still feels like it belongs to her great-aunt. The only place that hasn't been tidied and polished. It's still a mess, but it draws Mim to it. She switches on the green banker's lamp. There are teetering piles of numbered exercise books. A note on top of them all in someone else's writing: "For Miriam." She picks the note up. Esther loved her. That was something to hold on to.

She moves the note to one side and picks up one of the battered blue books. It is filled with Esther's dense scrawl, though occasionally letters, in another unfamiliar hand, seemed to have been glued in, like a scrapbook. What was she writing? Her great-aunt usually wrote plays or worked on film scripts, but this isn't formatted like either of those. It's something more personal. A diary or a memoir.

Mim feels a pang at the sight of Esther's handwriting – as familiar to her as an old friend. So much of their long-distance relationship had been lived out in letters – particularly since Mim's teen years, when she'd decided she wanted to be a writer. Esther was the only family member who greeted the idea with any kind of enthusiasm, sending her book recommendations and advice scrawled on old-fashioned aerograms.

"There's another one from Esther," her mum would say when Mim arrived home from school. And Mim came to love the sight of those slender blue rectangles waiting for her on the bed. She imagined her great-aunt's voice as she read them to herself.

"The first sentence is the hardest," she wrote. "But once you have it, things fall into place."

When she was younger, Mim was more diligent about replying to Esther's letters – and sometimes they became a place she could vent about Abi or school or her loneliness after she lost her father. Writing down her feelings – even the worst ones – was easier than saying them out loud.

But, by her twenties, her letters to Esther became less regular – something on a list in her diary that she repeatedly crossed out and moved to the next week. Her Guilty List, as Frankie called it.

Then, of course, Esther fell ill a couple of years ago and, by that time, Mim had sunk to a different place – beyond Guilty Lists and letter-writing. She'd signed a card and sent love through her mother, but she hadn't been there for Esther in her last days. Now she realises how much she'd missed and how much she wants to ask. She desperately hopes that her great-aunt wasn't alone at the end, that one of her theatre friends had been holding her hand.

As she flicks through the exercise book, a piece of paper flutters to the floor. It's a receipt for an espresso at the Heights Café – a little neighbourhood place with dark wood panelling and tiny round tables, which they moved outside in the summer. Perhaps it reminded Esther of Paris.

Mim turns the receipt over in her hand. On the other side, her great-aunt has scrawled something in her spidery handwriting. It takes Mim a moment or two to decipher it. Esther has written, "I love you, I beg you" – and then a third phrase, which Mim can't quite make out at first, because the verb is crossed out. She holds the receipt up to the light. It says, "I ~~forgive~~ you", with repeated lines striking through the word. Esther must have pressed so hard as she wrote on the delicate paper that once or twice the nib of her pen pierced the surface, leaving a tiny tear.

3

Mim wakes up hungry. When did she last eat? It must have been that meal on the plane. She pulls a pair of jeans from the top of her rucksack and gets dressed quickly. In the bathroom, she surveys herself as she brushes her teeth. Her wavy hair could do with a cut and she's still thinner than she used to be. Her mum's always reminding her to eat. She'll get a coffee and a bite at the Heights Café and then she'll have another look at Esther's desk.

She should ask her mother, next time they chat, if she knows anything about Esther's memoir – or whatever it is. She thinks of Esther crossing out the word "forgive" over and over and the thought unsettles her.

"Why me?" Mim asked, when she'd been told that Esther had named her in the will as the one responsible for sorting her great-aunt's paperwork.

"Well, she probably thought you'd have a better idea of what to do with it than the rest of us," her mother told her.

"Is it a pity project?"

"No." Abi, standing at the sink, rolled her eyes. "It's just that you were her favourite."

Mim swallowed, made a joke. "Us youngest kids need to stick together." Something like that.

Her sister, to her credit, said nothing of the legacy Esther had left Mim. A far larger sum than Abi had been given – ostensibly to cover Mim's costs for flying out and living in New York for an unspecified amount of time, while she looked through Esther's papers.

She'd known she was her great-aunt's favourite, just as she'd always been aware that Abi was her mum's. Or that's what it felt like. The pair of them had a kind of club – downtrodden family members – and they'd still be sighing to each other on the phone about her now. She knows that much. She'd been closest to her father – a warm, impetuous man, who dropped dead of a heart attack when she was just eleven. Mim missed him every day, and missed, too, the feeling of someone always being on her side, rather than tutting at her from a distance. Frankie had helped with that. But she can't think about Frankie, she tells herself. Not so early in the day. She needs to stay focused.

Outside, the morning is already heating up. A summer in New York. It isn't so bad. It's good, really, she tells herself. An escape from all the Olympics mania in London. An opportunity for a new start.

Later, energised by her breakfast, she returns to Esther's desk. Mim begins to tidy it, stacking things into neat piles.

As she lifts another of the blue exercise books that Esther seemed to have been so fond of, she spots a photograph. Mim picks it up. Two women: Esther in her usual slacks, the other in a long, glittering gown, a white gardenia tucked into her dark hair. She is holding up the dress as if she's about to give her friend a twirl – and Esther, sitting down with one leg hitched over the other, is laughing in an open-mouthed way that Mim had rarely seen.

Growing up, Mim and Abi were taught to respect Esther's sadness, and their grandmother's, their reticence on certain subjects.

"Darling, don't pester them," her mother would say, if Mim asked Grandma about the war or losing her parents. Not *losing*, she corrected herself now, it wasn't carelessness: they were murdered.

Her grandmother would sit on a deckchair on family trips to the beach, standing out in her huge Chanel sunglasses, an Hermès scarf protecting her hair. She was elegant, immaculate, supremely capable – whipping up a French onion soup or a pair of culottes for one of her granddaughters at a moment's notice, never forgetting the date of a birthday or an important exam. And yet she was always, somehow, distant. Detached. Occasionally peering at Mim through her sunglasses as if she was someone she recognised but couldn't quite place.

"*Chérie*," she would say. "You're in my sun," patting her granddaughter and her questions away when they grew too insistent.

If she cried for what she'd lost, she did so in private, or behind those huge sunglasses. One of the few times Mim could remember a rare outburst of emotion was when she and Abi had rummaged through their grandmother's old wooden sewing box, examining its treasures – a pair of antique scissors, a thimble, an old handmade pincushion – with grubby children's fingers.

"Girls, what *are* you doing?" Their grandmother swept into the living room, snatching her sewing box back. "Those aren't your things to touch."

Her fingers seemed to caress those items, carefully winding away every loose thread, as she returned them to the box and snapped its lid closed.

She apologised later, a cold drink in her hand. "My *boîte à couture* is very precious to me," she said, looking into the fire. "My father made it for my mother."

Mim wanted to ask questions about the couple she'd seen in a framed photograph: a tall handsome man, with heavy eyebrows and a gentle face, next to his petite dark-haired wife, who wore an elegant belted coat, a neat hat and gloves. And yet something about her grandmother always discouraged questions.

Esther's tack was different. "It's OK. It's good to ask," she replied when they spent time together on family trips to New York. While her mum and Abi popped into Bloomingdale's or Macy's, Esther took Mim on a tour of her favourite independent bookshops. She ruffled her great-niece's hair affectionately when she questioned her about her past, but, generally, changed the subject quickly or said something like, "What do *you* think happened?" A trick that usually worked.

Her great-aunt's plays were abstract, hard to understand. The only one Mim remembers was close to performance art: a woman sitting on her own in a room. Other people would come in – strangers and friends – and take her belongings, one by one, until she had nothing left. Mim has more of an idea of what that was about now. Esther's plays had never made much money. That had come from her work as a script consultant on a number of big Hollywood films, usually set in France during the Second World War, though the sisters escaped to New York just before its outbreak.

"The world can't get enough of that era," Esther said to Mim once, rolling her eyes. "God knows why they want to keep returning to it, but it's bought me my home, I suppose, so I mustn't complain."

Mim looks more closely at the other woman in the photo. Her face is open and friendly. And she's beautiful: slim and dark-eyed. Her hair is set in an updo. As if she's just come off stage or is about to go on. She looks fun – like someone you'd want to hang out with.

And then it comes back to her suddenly, without warning. Another ambush. Frankie bounding into the room the first time they spoke – *really* spoke – during an otherwise lacklustre lunchtime at journalism college.

Mim and one other student, a guy from their course, had been eating their homemade sandwiches in the common room. Journalism college had not lived up to Mim's expectations until that point. She'd come to it late, at twenty-eight, after trying just about everything else. It was if she had been waiting all her life for something important to happen, and then, suddenly, it did.

A girl burst into the room. A girl with her hair streaked pink, who wore her beauty lightly. The name that appeared in her by-line in the student newspaper was Francesca Khan, at the top of the best stories, the ones that made the front page, but nobody, except her Italian mother, called her Francesca, she told Mim later. It was always Frankie.

She glared at the pair of them, hands on hips. "Which of you fuckers stole my cigarettes?"

Mim finished chewing, swallowed. "He did," she said, pointing at the boy, who was pale with a yellow beanie pulled low on his head.

It wasn't true. It just slipped out. But, like everything that happened with Frankie after that, maybe she wanted to see what would happen next.

The boy spluttered and denied it, and Frankie fixed her with a look. "I'm on to you." She pointed her finger at Mim.

Later, Mim wondered if it had simply been a way to get Frankie's attention. Had she had a hunch, a premonition, that she and Frankie would later share the packet of stolen cigarettes? That they'd smoke them outside The Crown on the corner of Clerkenwell Green, swapping secrets and life stories? Had she known, too, with a fierce certainty, like falling in love, that she would always buy whatever Frankie was selling; that they would be together until the end of whatever started that day?

She blinks. Maybe she'd never get used to it – the way memories lie in wait for her in this way. She turns the photo over in her hand and sees Esther has written: "Bal Tabarin, Paris, 1942." And she nearly thinks nothing more of it, almost shoves the photograph back into one of the blue exercise books, but something has snagged in her mind, like a thread on a nail. 1942. In Paris. After it had been occupied. Esther and Rebecca had always said they'd left for the States long before, but here Esther seems to contradict that story in her own handwriting.

THE PARIS DANCER

4

Her mother's face looks weary on the laptop screen. The sound is a little crackly too, so Mim gets to her feet to move closer to the router.

"Miriam! Are you OK? Are you eating?"

"Yes, all OK. I ate some eggs." She tries to keep the impatience from her voice. "I just had a question about something I found on Esther's desk. A photo."

"A photo?" her mother repeats. "Of whom?"

"Esther and a friend." Mim crouches near the router. "A dancer, perhaps?" She thinks, for a moment, of Lucky, of his business card pushed deep into her backpack, and then shoos the idea away.

Her mother hesitates. "I always thought that perhaps..."

"The thing is," Mim interrupts, "it's taken somewhere in Paris. The Bal Tabarin. In 1942."

There's a longer pause this time. So long that Mim

wonders if the internet has dropped out. "Oh," her mother says at last. "That's strange."

"That's what I thought. They'd moved by then, hadn't they?"

Her mum pushes her hair back in a worried way. "I noticed gaps in my mother's stories over the years. Getting her dates in a muddle. Talking more about the war. But I thought, perhaps, it was just her age." She sighs. "I don't know with those two, Esther and Maman: so much going on between them. Their strange feud. Maybe it's not surprising, given everything they went through."

"Did Grandma ever talk to you about it?"

"Not much. The occasional thing later in life."

"Is it possible they were lying?"

"Lying." Her mum sighs again. "That's such a big word."

"And have you heard of the Bal Tabarin?" In the background, Mim can hear the grandfather clock chime six from the hall of her mum's Wiltshire farmhouse.

"Of course the family all worked in the theatre," her mother says. "But I'm not sure on the details. They didn't talk about it very much after everything that happened." She sighs. "Why don't you do a Google?"

"Do a Google?" Mim giggles.

"Isn't that what they say?" Her mother smiles and glances away from the screen.

"Can I ask a favour?" Mim checks. "Will you look in Grandma's boxes to see if there's anything there – about Paris in those years. Or the Bal Tabarin?"

"Of course. And will you do something for me in return?"

"I won't forget to eat," Mim reassures her.

"Or sleep. I know what you're like."

"I'll be good, I promise."

Her mother shakes her head. "You were always *ma coquine*, my naughty one, but I love you very much."

"More than Abi?" Mim teases.

But her mum doesn't seem to hear her. Her expression freezes on the screen and then she's gone.

Mim makes herself a coffee and Googles the Bal Tabarin. It was a music hall, though not as famous the Moulin Rouge or Folies Bergère. It had once stood at 36, rue Victor-Massé, not far from Pigalle Métro station, a stone's throw from Montmartre, but it was demolished in the 1960s.

She could ask Lucky, she thinks again. He's a dancer and he likes history. But no, lovely as he is, maybe his card is better where it is. It's safer for him that way.

The place largely turned up in paintings – an abstract by the futurist artist Gino Severini, which didn't tell Mim much. A naked girl astride a pair of scissors, a man with a top hat and monocle. More helpful was a piece by Pierre de Belay, showing an elegant couple watching a row of cancan dancers. The couple are in black and white but the girls are in colour – red, yellow and green. An explosion of white petticoats, black stockings and creamy thighs.

There were some Getty photos of similarly attired cancan girls with big smiles and bigger frilly knickers, and then some British Pathé footage – incredible scenes of topless girls dangling from a carousel. Elsewhere, they languished, still topless, on its horses in a way that made Mim's inner feminist tut a little.

Different times, she hears Esther's voice in her ear.

Quite liberating, I would have thought, Frankie chirps up.

Shh, Miriam tells them both. "I need to think."

She's heard before that her great-grandfather worked as a set builder in a theatre, while her great-grandmother was a *midinette* – a seamstress in the costume department.

"I was the only one in my family who couldn't sew," Esther once told her. She sounded almost proud of it.

But it wasn't impossible that Esther worked at the Tabarin too. Maybe she and her grandmother didn't leave Paris when they said they did. But why lie about it?

She knew about that period. Of course she did. She'd read Anne Frank's famous diary as a child, and *When Hitler Stole Pink Rabbit*. She'd studied the Holocaust at school and talked about it at home. It was always in the room on their occasional family trips to synagogue. There like an ever-present shadow. But there were gaps in the family history.

"Everybody wants to talk about everything these days," her grandmother would say with a slight jut of her chin. "*La parole est d'argent, mais le silence est d'or.*" She never let go of her favourite French expressions. "*Jamais deux sans trois*" was another favourite. *Never two without three.* This one was usually trotted out when Mim broke a couple of things – cups or plates. And, on this point, Grandma was usually right.

Mim has friends who researched their family's war histories, interviewed older relatives and visited the concentration camps. She hasn't done any of that. *Why?* she asks herself now. Too preoccupied with her own life, perhaps. There were always exams and goals – and then meeting Frankie and becoming a journalist. And even *then* she didn't look back, but chased stories in the present.

Maybe something happened to make the sisters lie about when they left France. It must have been a powerful secret for two such different people to keep it. Grandma, sleekly stylish and feminine, Esther in her slacks; Grandma always dieting and fussing about her looks, while Esther smoked Gitanes and drank whisky and still managed to outlive her sister by a year or so. Her grandmother never would have forgiven her for that.

Mim wanders back to Esther's desk and picks up the exercise book numbered one. Perhaps it'll contain some of the answers to her questions. Perhaps she needs to take the plunge and start reading.

5

The first sentence is the hardest, isn't that something I once said? It's a neat aphorism, but I'm not sure if it's always true. Perhaps it's like taking a car out on a journey. Easier once you've nosed it out into the road, heading in one direction, rather than the multiplicity of options that exist in your mind before you start.

As I sit here at my desk, looking out at Lady Liberty, I can see how far I've come. I both do and don't want to go back to the beginning. To the first years of my life in Paris. It is going to be difficult, but you are with me, in my head, at least. I don't have to do it alone.

As a playwright, I should be able to set the scene. But I'm not accustomed to being the protagonist – even of my own story. I grew up in the theatre, watching the spot-lit stage from the shadows, admiring the acrobats and jugglers, the comedians and cancan dancers. In fact, I was almost born in the wings of a minor Parisian music hall in 1920, the beginning of a hopeful new decade just after the Great War.

My mother, who was employed in the costume department, had a stubborn, determined streak her daughters seemed to inherit, and she insisted on working until the very last day of her pregnancy.

Labour arrived suddenly. And one of the dance captains hastily cleared her dressing room so my mother could lie on the chaise longue, gripping my father's hand, while a callboy dashed out to find a *sage-femme*. In the dressing room next door, cancan dancers jiggled my sister Rebecca on their knees, distracting her with an impromptu, child-friendly dance show.

Family folklore has it that my sister's toddler eyes widened at the shimmering feathers and silks up close. Those costumes were a cross between haute couture and swimwear. As intricately beautiful as anything you'd see on the catwalks of Paris's gilded ballrooms but strong enough to endure the high-kicking cancan routines, quick changes and general grime of theatrical life – not to mention the sweat that poured from the dancers' bodies when they spun under the spotlights.

"Couturiers might be sniffy about theatrical costumes," my mother used to say, glancing up on a break from her beloved Bernina sewing machine. "But our clothes have to be tough as well as beautiful. Like the women who wear them."

"Like *mes filles*," my father chipped in proudly. His girls. My mother, Rebecca and me. My father was the calm to her storm. Petite, elegant, vivacious, a person of ever-changing internal weather, our mother was frightening when she was angry, even to herself, I think.

When I picture her, I think of her sitting at the workbench

our father made for her in the coveted spot below the window in our tiny apartment in the Pletzl, the Jewish quarter. This imaginary version of Ima frowns as she concentrates, her small hands circling swiftly through a running stitch, a thimble glinting in the sunshine. She never stops moving. Like a hummingbird, she is diminutive, beautiful, vividly attired. Her tongue, like that tiny creature's beak, could be surprisingly sharp.

Childhood sweethearts, our parents had fled the Lwów pogrom in 1918, in what was then Poland, but is now Ukraine. I don't think they ever fully recovered from that time and what they lost there, including almost every single member of their families – or at least those who'd survived the Great War.

While our parents were keen for us to embrace the country where we were born, they didn't forget their heritage. There was always *shul* on holidays and lighting the candle for Shabbat. We called our mother Ima, the Hebrew word for mother, just as she had called hers.

Like our mother, my older sister always had a weakness for pretty things. Rebecca and my mother would coo over a shimmering silk, the cut of a collar on a satin Lanvin dress or one of Erté's fantastical designs. My mother taught my sister to sew – first by hand and later sitting at her beloved Bernina, which provided the percussive background to family life. She, in turn, had learned from her own mother and improved her skills when she arrived in Paris.

My mother drank in the city's fashion, peeping through the windows of the couturiers on its glamorous Grands Boulevards. At first, jobs came in from the Pletzl, making dresses for her neighbours, but it wasn't long before she and our father picked up regular work in the costume and set ateliers of Paris's music halls in those golden years. The *Années folles*. A time when the Fitzgeralds and Hemingway caroused around town and the world fell in love with Josephine Baker.

How to describe myself as a child? The word "ungainly" comes to mind. *Gauche*. Rebecca and I were both tall, like our father, but while my older sister glided serenely like a swan, I tripped over things and dropped them. Plates, dolls, stitches. "*Schlemiel*," my sister used to mutter under her breath. *Idiot*. She and I inherited our parents' way of talking, speaking Yiddish, Polish and French – sometimes mixed together. Ima and Papa never spoke the language of their new home with the ease of their daughters, but they brought us up to be, to all intents and purposes, Parisiennes.

Back then, I never felt comfortable in my body. Not like the dancers I grew up watching, who'd slip in and out of clothes swiftly and unself-consciously during the quick changes or wander around the house between shows in scanty *peignoirs*, which revealed more than they hid. It wasn't just their lack of self-consciousness I envied, but how at home they looked in their bodies. I tried to imitate the way they moved, unhunching my shoulders, walking with a similarly relaxed yet upright gait. But it never stuck. I always ended up shrinking back – an apology in human form. I always ended up being myself again.

My hands were all fingers and thumbs when I tried to sew. And for the same reason I was no good at carpentry – hammering or nicking my own fingers until my mother told my father to give up. Everyone else in my family had had their calling, but it hadn't come for me.

As children, Rebecca and I fought like cats. There wasn't much of a gap between us. Just eighteen months. Everything was a battle from the beginning.

After a particularly bad fight when I'd knocked over my sister's *mannequin de couture*, onto which she was pinning the makings of her first dress, Rebecca had shrieked "*Schlemiel*" loud enough for the whole neighbourhood to hear. My father took me with him to his workshop.

"Leave it for other people to quarrel amongst themselves," he told me, a pencil propped, as usual, behind his ear. "There's always a kind of peace in a workshop." He ran a hand over the *boîte à couture* he was finishing – a gift for our mother – serene pleasure on his face. "If you want to change the world," he said, "just make it a little more beautiful."

Carpentry ateliers were noisy places – all that hammering, sawing and shouted conversations taking place over the din; they all went a bit deaf in the end. And yet my father could always be found at his workbench with a look of calm satisfaction on his face like the one he'd had that day.

Temporarily at least, our family was divided into two camps. And then someone came along to join the four of us. Someone who united us. Lili. Our little sister. A surprise addition, entering stage right.

Four years younger than me, born in 1924, she was a happy accident, but I never knew Ima more cheerful than when she was expecting Lili. Her nerves seemed calmer. She sang wistful Gershwin numbers as she sewed. It was as if some spell had been cast over her. She laughed more readily, too. There were fewer spats, a bloom to her cheeks, more flesh on her bones. Being pregnant with Lili made her happy.

And then Lili was born and almost instantly she was something about which we could all agree. Everyone's favourite; everybody's baby. A child like that can bring a family closer together. Especially a third – a child that doesn't have to endure the pressure of their parents' yearning and perfectionism. A child who can just be.

Life, for me, became less lonely. For years, Lili and I would share a bed, a single mattress, and I would wake with her face close to mine on the pillow. Always a morning person, she couldn't bear to see those early hours of the day slip by. "Wake up," she used to whisper to me. "You're missing the day."

It wasn't just that Lili was beautiful, though she was, with enormous eyes and wild wavy hair. And she wasn't perfect in a sickening way, either – one of those children that's afraid to get grubby or answer back. No, she was impudent, brave, hilarious from the beginning.

"*Quel âge as-tu?*" We all asked her on her second birthday.

"*Quatorze*," she said. The age changed every time we asked. She was fourteen. Fifteen. Twenty-nine. Forty-three. Seventy-two.

Once, when Rebecca and I had a particularly vicious squabble over our mother's workbench – she wanted to sew there; I wanted to read – Lili pushed our mother's beautiful *boîte à couture* from the table to make us stop. It landed with an almighty crash. The three of us circled the carnage.

Ima swept into the room from next door, where she'd escaped to sew and gossip with one of the neighbours. "What the hell is going on here?" Her mouth tightened when she surveyed the scene. "Who did this?"

Rebecca and I exchanged a glance. Lili was in for it, we could tell. But, unaware of the rules of engagement, our sister chirped up cheerfully. "My did it, Ima."

"No, I did," I corrected her.

"It was me," Rebecca insisted.

This was not the usual way of things. Our mother's eyes flitted from one of us to the next. Suspicious. Perhaps she guessed at the truth. That Lili was the culprit. But she no more wanted to slap her youngest child than we wanted to see her punished. She sighed, a lengthy exhalation, hands on hips.

"Come on, girls," she said, in the end. "Let's tidy this up."

We helped her pick up her treasures from the dusty floor and wiped each one down – her sewing scissors, her thimble, her tape measure, darning mushroom and pincushion. I could feel her eyes on us as we worked. Perhaps she was proud of us for protecting each other. Perhaps she realised that Lili was the one who stitched us together.

6

Mim leaves the book open for a long time, staring at the pages in an unfocused way. A third sister. Lili. Her mother's middle name. Jamais deux sans trois. Did Grandma think of Lili every time she repeated those words?

She and Esther never talked much about their past. Le silence est d'or, and all that. But, even by their standards, this was a major omission. Mim pushes the book off her lap and gets to her feet. What happened to Lili? Is there a chance she is still alive? Cut off from the others by another family feud?

Mim reaches for her phone to contact her mother, but then she pauses. Esther left her books – her story – to her. Not to her mother. Or Abi. This was her project. And, for now, her secret. Once she told the others, they might become all bossy and I-know-best about it. A thought occurs to her. Her mum and Abi might even already know about Lili. They might even have kept the secret from her. She frowns, furious at the idea. That would be so like them. No, she decides, she'll keep reading on her own for now and get to

46

the bottom of this herself.

The swish of an incoming message interrupts her thoughts.

Fancy seeing if this is the dance for you? Lucky x

He's sent a link to a salsa club near Times Square and suggests going to a class there tomorrow. So, he's been thinking of her.

Mim notices her heart beating faster than usual. Her first instinct is to say no, she's fine, thanks. It would certainly be safer that way.

You always were one for self-sabotage. Frankie slips into her head without warning.

Self-protection, she corrects her. It's not the same thing.

The pair of them argued after Mim's first article was published – a piece about losing her dad. Frankie, bursting with pride, printed it out and stuck it on Mim's fridge with magnets, but Mim spotted a spelling mistake in the third sentence, and then that was all she could see. In the end, she removed it when she was alone again, folding it up into a neat square and placing it in the crisper drawer.

"Is that what you want? Just to hide away your work like a bit of wet lettuce?" Frankie held up the damp piece of paper with her thumb and forefinger when she found it there later.

"Ideally, yes." Mim poured herself a huge glass of white wine and took a gulp of it.

"True artists don't hide from the world."

"Well, luckily for us both, I'm not a true artist, just a ten-a-penny journalism student applying for jobs on local papers."

Frankie mock-shook her. "You know what I mean.

You've got to get out of the salad drawer if you want to get anywhere in life. No one else really notices your spelling mistakes. They don't notice your anything mistakes. So, just get on with it. It's not going to last forever – isn't that what your article is about?"

"Very clever," Mim laughed. "Using my own words against me."

Now, she blinks, turns her phone over in her hand. She looks at Lucky's message again. Would it be so very bad to go along? Just to see. She writes her reply quickly.

Sure, but I haven't packed my dancing shoes.

No kiss. It feels safer that way. But she's made the right decision, she tells herself. Otherwise, what will she do for the next few months? Sit on her own in Brooklyn with ghosts for company? Obsessing about her great-aunt. Or great-aunts, she corrects herself.

But, still, she feels a twitch of anxiety in her fingers at the prospect of being out in the world again. Unsure, what to do with it, she picks up Esther's battered blue exercise book again.

7

1928–1935

Our first home was our apartment in the Pletzl, but our second became the Bal Tabarin, a music hall on the border of Pigalle and Montmartre. The artistic director was Pierre Sandrini. A tall, elegant man, with slicked back dark hair, he was the son of a former prima ballerina at the Paris Opéra Ballet. The height of Sandrini belied how gentle he was. No one in the building, from the lowliest callboy to the most famous stars who crossed the stage, had a bad word to say about him.

His wife, Dédée, once showed me a photo of him at the barre as a young dancer. A tiny boy surrounded by leggy ballerinas, all towering above him. I wondered if that was the secret to his gentleness – a man who'd grown up surrounded by women. Before the Tabarin, Sandrini worked at the Moulin Rouge and revolutionised the French cancan there. He brought in classically trained dancers and smartened up the act of that famously naughty dance.

49

In 1928, he bought the Tabarin. Up until that point, my parents had been itinerant workers, shifting from music hall to music hall, filling in gaps and helping out as required on the run-up to big shows. But they hit it off with Sandrini at a gig at the Moulin Rouge – people who love what they do will often be drawn to each other. When Sandrini bought the Tabarin, he took our parents with him on a permanent basis. At their new home, my mother and father brought to life the designs of Erté – the father of Art Deco.

The Bal Tabarin was an imposing Belle Epoque building – the size of a synagogue, with a lyre at its peak, and a central arched window, flanked by a smaller one on each side, above the front entrance. Statues peered down imperiously from its grand façade. The audience entered through a narrow vestibule into the main house, where stairs on either side led to a semi-circular balcony crammed with tables covered with pristine white tablecloths.

Downstairs, the stage jutted out into the room like a runway at a fashion show. Its cutting-edge machinery – Sandrini's pride and joy – could sink it down to the basement or raise its fantastical contraptions, such as its famous merry-go-round, to the height of the balcony. On the ground floor, the audience could get up and dance to the orchestra nestled in the left corner of the room, if they could find space between the tables.

Sandrini and Erté were kindred spirits. Weavers of magic. Creators of fantasy. Born Romain de Tirtoff to a wealthy St Petersburg family, Erté always knew he wanted to be an artist and not an admiral like his father –hurling his toy soldiers out of the window in protest as a child. As soon as he could, he escaped to Paris and changed his name to Erté

– the French pronunciation of his initials.

The sight of his head bowed in deep conversation with Sandrini was a common one at the Tabarin. They favoured unusual materials for the costumes and sets, creating glimmering reflective surfaces to suit the modern age. They were keen to treat the audience to shows they wouldn't experience anywhere else – the opposite of most music halls, which rehashed the same popular ideas over and over again.

There are people who are sniffy about cabarets, but Sandrini's shows were masterpieces. It is true that they featured beautiful women, like every other music hall in Paris, but Sandrini favoured dancers who were classically trained: strong, graceful, disciplined, ambitious. It wasn't enough for him to have pretty shows with pretty girls – he wanted to create an unforgettable experience for the audience, to take them out of their humdrum world into a place of fantasy. For Château de Cristal, for example, the pair created a transparent fairytale castle, which rose, as if by magic, from the basement. Then there was Métal, for which Erté created costumes in aluminium, with one of the nudes dressed only in metallic body paint.

I was still finding my way. When it was clear to everyone I couldn't sew or do woodwork, I tried other jobs. As a dresser, I was too forgetful, so I mainly worked as an usherette, scribbling fragments of things in the notebook I always carried with me. I would have done anything to stay at the Tabarin, and not just because the rest of my family worked there. Sandrini encouraged my creativity – nudging me to help weave together the narratives for his spectacular shows.

Even Lili found her calling at the Tabarin. In 1935, Man Ray photographed our dancers hanging from a towering cylindrical frame. They balanced from its highest rung in back bends that made them look like teardrops suspended in the air.

There were some jitters in the house that day in the presence of the famous photographer: a short, bullish man with thick dark eyebrows, face scowling in concentration. But Lili, just eleven, didn't pick up on the tense atmosphere, and she pestered him with questions as he hunched over his Rolleiflex, adjusting the settings. In the end, she was told by Ima to leave the poor man alone, but she found a seat not far behind him, drinking in everything he did.

"He's taking this moment and making it live forever," she told me. "The aperture is the opening that lets light in, which then strikes the film to create an image. It's like writing on darkness with light."

There was a fierceness to the way she needed to know how it worked. In her world, things were in black and white, with sharp, defined edges. My world view was fuzzier. I didn't have the same pragmatic streak as my sisters. I felt my way through my young life, stumbled a little, without a clear sense of where I was going.

That day, I realised everyone in my family – even my little sister – had found their creative calling. Everyone, that was, except me.

I had ideas, of course – ideas of being a writer. But I hadn't written a whole thing. Just fragments. And it wasn't just a finishing problem. I hadn't, at that point, written a strong enough first sentence. I hadn't had a clear enough "I want" moment, as they call it in musical theatre, like my sisters had: Rebecca bouncing on the dancers' knees as a toddler, or Lili captivated by Man Ray's photography. But someone was about to step on to the stage and change all that for me: the one who let the light in.

8

30th June 2012

Mim is careful not to make too much of an effort for the evening. Even this late in the day, New York shimmers with heat. She dresses in an old pair of denim shorts and a white vest, no make-up. She pinches her pale cheeks before she leaves, to bring a bit of colour into them.

The subway in New York always smells the same – a distinctive mix of train oil and stale air. The Theater District is twinkly and loud after leafy Brooklyn. Bright lights and billboards and noisy tourists dressed up to the nines. Sudden gusts of hot caramelised nuts. Approaching the venue, Mim regrets her lack of effort. She watches a clutch of women in tight dresses and heeled shoes pour through an unobtrusive black door and down into the basement club.

But once they're gone, she can see Lucky is there, waiting under the burgundy awning of an Italian restaurant. He raises a hand and looks genuinely thrilled to see her, shifting almost unconsciously from foot to foot as if he's doing a little dance in her honour. She finds her gait quicken as she approaches him. He stoops to kiss her cheek and he smells fresh and clean, as if he's wearing newly laundered clothes.

"Hey," she says. "I'm wondering what I've let myself in for."

"It'll be fun," he promises.

They make their way down the sticky steps. The music gets louder as they descend, and it takes a moment for Mim's eyes to adjust to the dark.

"I thought it might remind you of Casablancas," Lucky teases, shouting over the noise. "I don't know if they'll do the 'Macarena.'"

They're surrounded by dancers – people effortlessly spinning and shimmying, all toned midriffs and swirling hair and a stunning liquid movement that Mim is sure she'll never be able to achieve in a million years. She feels a flash of panic. It was different in Casablancas, she wants to say: she was drunk, she had Frankie, everything in her life has changed since then. She doesn't know if she can do this sort of thing any more.

She feels strangely unmoored. This has been a mistake: the heat and the noise and the crowd of people around her. She feels Lucky's hand on the small of her back.

"It's OK," he says, as if she's shared the contents of her head out loud. "I'll get us some water."

By the time he's returned with a glass for each of them, someone has switched the music off, so the lesson can begin. Now it's quieter, now someone is in control, Mim's panic ebbs away.

A beaming bald man with a loud voice and rolled-up sleeves introduces himself as their teacher, Carlos. He tells them a little about the history of salsa and the rise of the mambo kings and queens in the 1940s and 1950s.

"Lots of countries lay claim to salsa – and I'm Cuban, so I'd say that's where its soul is," the man says. "But ask a Puerto Rican, or a Colombian, and they'd say exactly the same." He smiles and claps his hands together. "Vamos, let's get started."

He organises the dancers in a circle around him – "Decide whether you want to lead or follow" – and talks them through the Basic, stepping back with one foot and forward with another, and the Rumba step, which moves from side to side.

At first, it's strange to be touching Lucky in such a sober situation. To be holding hands and to feel his palm on her back. He's taller than Mim and she's glad she doesn't have to look him in the eye. At least, it's dark, she tells herself, and, anyway, after they've walked through the steps with their first partner, the followers have to move on.

Soon, the class has got the hang of the steps without music.

"Some teachers are very didactic about counting: one-two-three, five-six-seven," Carlos tells them. "But the music will tell you what to do. Listen out for the clave." He fishes out what looks like two wooden sticks from his shirt pocket and hits them together in a hypnotic rhythm. "It's the key to Latin music."

When the music starts, it's irresistible. Soon, Mim finds herself beaming for no reason, and her shoulders and hips instinctively want to move to it too. But the guy she is paired with next is profusely sweaty, stepping on her feet and dabbing his head with a handkerchief. She's relieved when it's time to change partners but the next man, lean and chiselled, wearing heaps of cologne and Cuban heels, is unsmiling and bored with the beginners' class.

After that, she dances with a woman called Juliana, who is kinder. Even though it feels strange for Mim to be led by someone so tiny, she starts to relax a little. It's sweaty as hell, but she begins to smile. It's good to be moving, to be touched by another person again.

Before she knows it, the beginners' class is over. The teacher tells everyone to be brave and ask someone to dance. Mim doesn't have the heart to turn down the sweaty man, though their pairing is a disaster. On her periphery, she catches a glimpse of Lucky dancing with a woman in a tight dress. She makes it look so easy, silkily spinning in his arms, shimmying her shoulders, wiggling her hips, enjoying the sensation of the room's eyes on her.

But Mim's not watching her, she's looking at Lucky, or trying not to. Trying not to clock the attentive way he leads his partner. Trying not to notice how he's the only man in the room whom the New York heat hasn't melted into a puddle, how he still looks as boyishly clean and immaculate as he did at the start of the class, like he's the only pure thing in the room. In all of the city. Stop it, Mim, she warns. This is how it starts.

When her dance with the sweaty man ends, Mim thinks of going – just slipping out anonymously into the night. It's OK, she's had fun, but it feels risky, somehow, to take it any further.

"You have to dance with me to this." Lucky appears by her side; he raises a finger at the song. "It's a classic. Celia Cruz."

"Is that someone important?"

He laughs. "The Queen of Salsa."

He's right about the song. It's irresistible, its refrain as urgent and compelling as an alarm, but, like in all the best tracks, there's an undercurrent of sadness. Most of the beginners move too quickly, rushing through the steps like a chore. Not Lucky. He takes his time. Chemistry on the dancefloor is like chemistry anywhere else, Mim thinks. You either have it or you don't. And they have it.

Maybe it's his training as a dancer, but his is a wonderful lead. Mim knows exactly what he's asking her, but there's no pushing or shoving or yanking. It feels like flying. Mim begins to return to her body. I've missed you, she thinks, but she doesn't know whom she's talking to.

Afterwards, her cheeks feel flushed and she finds she is grinning for no apparent reason. "I nearly ran away earlier," she tells Lucky. "I was terrified."

"I suspected as much. Are you glad you stayed?"

Mim nods. It's true – she feels like something in her has shifted.

He flushes slightly. "Do you want to grab a drink? Or an ice cream or something?"

Mim hesitates. Behind Lucky, she can see a woman with an orchid in hair loitering pointedly, waiting for a dance. It feels dangerous: these flutters, the feeling of ownership. She doesn't know where it will lead, but experience has taught her it's nowhere good. "Another time," she tells him. "I think you're in demand."

He blushes again and shrugs in an aw-shucks way, but he doesn't turn away from Mim. As the music gets a little louder, he dips his head so his mouth is close to her ear. "Do you think this is it?"

Mim laughs. By this, is he referring to the chemistry between them? Surely not. It feels too early. A thousand different answers file through her head. Most of them sarcastic. And yet there's something bright, like a hummingbird, inside her. Tiny. Hopeful. Play it cool, Mim. "I mean," she splutters. "It's too early to say."

"The dance," he specifies. "Could it be the one for you?"

She laughs, blushing furiously. "Still too early to say."

As she slips out of the club and into the street, she can still feel his hand on her waist, the defiant voice of Celia Cruz ringing in her ears. I'm thirty-three, she thinks. I thought I'd grown out of all this.

We never grow out of that, Frankie laughs, suddenly in her head again.

Frankie was a brilliant dancer – not trained, like Lucky, but uninhibited and joyful. On their first night out together, Mim remembers her friend's arms raised high above her head, her hips gyrating wildly, a sheen of sweat on her forehead.

"Who do you have your eye on?" Mim whispered, scanning the room for talent.

Frankie laughed. "I'm just dancing for myself."

Now Mim sighs. I didn't think I'd ever want to dance with anyone but you.

But Frankie has gone again, and she's alone. There are only her footsteps on the sidewalk and the sound of salsa music getting fainter in the background, as she tries to remember her way home.

9

Aside from crouching in the wings of the Tabarin, waiting for curtain-up, the place I was happiest was a bookshop. And Paris had plenty of them. Delamain. Jousseaume. Leymarie. I loved the dusty dim light inside, that musty odour of books and pages, the woody scent of them, like boarding a ship that could take you somewhere else. Staircases that curled up into galley spaces where you could sit on the floor and read all afternoon.

Perhaps, unsurprisingly for a young person who spent her spare time browsing in the city's bookshops, I became an excellent eavesdropper. So, on a warm day in May 1938, it didn't take me long to start tuning in to the conversation of three loud and rather beautiful people who had clattered into Sylvia Beach's bookshop. It was a favourite haunt of mine, with tables and shelves crammed with books and pictures of famous authors framed like the old friends they were.

The three I noticed were making each other laugh, reading naughty bits from Lady Chatterley's Lover aloud to each other.

There were two girls and a guy – I judged that they were a little older than me. Early twenties, perhaps; I was just eighteen at the time. The women – one dark, one blonde – were dancers. I knew that from being around enough of them. It wasn't so much that they were beautiful – I'd grown accustomed to beautiful people far more scantily clad than this lot. Or even that they were speaking English and I was in the middle of a committed Anglophile phase. It was that the three of them, with their lively faces and sun-kissed shoulders, seemed untouched by the woes of the city at the time. They were an open window, breathing fresh air into the dark, dusty bookshop.

Earlier in the year, Germany's annexation of Austria hadn't led to the international condemnation you might expect. But, as the Nazis turned their attention to Czechoslovakia, my parents and their friends in the Pletzl, who were mostly also immigrants from eastern and central Europe, grew nervous. Their nagging fear of a return to the horrors of their early years never quietened, like a child banging from inside a locked cupboard, refusing to be forgotten.

As long as I knew them, my parents remained rake-thin, taut and sinewy, as if some part of them remembered they might have to run again. My mother, never a huge eater, had lost weight with the worry, while my father was quieter than usual, reaching for an additional glass of gros rouge – the cheap red wine he drank – when he thought my mother wasn't looking.

It was the dark-haired dancer I couldn't stop looking at.

Her name was Annie Mayer, as I came to learn. She had a lively face – the kind that looked as if it were on the cusp of sharing an indiscreet revelation. One that it might be worth leaning in closer to hear. Her expression, in that moment, was wistful.

"I've been in Paris almost a month and not so much as a sniff of the Ballet Russe," she sighed. "Can you believe it?"

I couldn't quite place her accent. American, perhaps, but I wasn't sure. I peeked at her from my place in the corner, where I was reading Colette's La Vagabonde for the millionth time.

"Look on the bright side," said her blonde friend, Dot Monroe, who reminded me of those sassy dames that Ginger Rogers played. "At least we have a day off from those blasted fouettés with Madame Egorova."

Egorova was one of the most famous ballet mistresses in Paris, who made a memorable appearance in Zelda Fitzgerald's Save Me the Waltz.

She was a former dancer with the Ballets Russes. And all the wannabe dancers in Paris were still swoony about that company – famous for the riot it caused at the Théâtre des Champs-Elysées with the premiere of The Rite of Spring in 1913.

The company had disbanded with the death of its founder, the impresario Sergei Diaghilev, in 1929. But others tried to pick up the mantle. Companies emerged with similar names, such as the Ballet Russe de Monte Carlo or the Original Ballet Russe, offering a home to the former star dancers and choreographers of the disbanded troupe. And it was these itinerant companies Annie and her friends were eyeing up now.

"I know what you both need to do," suggested Luc, the dancers' friend, a handsome dark-haired man carrying a sketchbook under his arm. "Until one of the Russian companies comes knocking, at least: you should audition for the Bal Tabarin."

I found it harder to hide my interest at that point. In fact, I almost dropped Colette.

"The music hall?" Dot asked sniffily.

"No," Luc insisted. "Much more than a music hall. The director Pierre Sandrini is an artiste – the son of a prima ballerina."

"Yes!" I chipped in, rising from behind a bookshelf like an apparition. "I work there," I explained hastily, when the three of them looked my way. "Just backstage," I added, as if that needed to be said.

I was in my slacks, as usual. Would you believe it wasn't actually legal for women to wear pants back then in France? But if Colette could wear trousers, I always thought, then so could I.

"His choreographer, Marcel Bergé, used to dance with Anna Pavlova," I said. Dropping that particular name always worked a treat. The prima ballerina was responsible for countless little girls – and boys – of our generation falling in love with dance. "And Erté himself designs for them."

"Le tout-Paris goes to a new Tabarin show," agreed Luc. "It's an unmissable event. And they pay well."

"Now you're talking," said Dot.

Annie was still quiet.

"My pal here is saving herself for the Ballet Russe." Dot slung her arm around Annie's shoulders. "Which is all very well, but winter is coming." She glanced at her friend's skimpy shorts. "You should be better prepared, as a Canadian."

Canadian, I corrected my earlier thought. Not American.

"We can audition, I suppose," she agreed reluctantly. And perhaps it was my imagination, perhaps I was seeking a reflection of my own feelings about her, but it seemed to me that her answer was aimed at me.

The rest of us grinned and, in that moment, I felt I had found people who, in some important way, might become mine. But my triumph didn't last long. Before I knew it, they were cheerily clattering out of the shop, with grins, goodbyes and all the glittering confidence with which they'd arrived.

After they left, I did something unusual: I bought the book I was reading, for once. Sylvia ran a library service, but I knew I wanted to keep this one as a memento of that day. On the way out of the shop, I spotted a piece of a paper that must have fallen from Luc's sketchbook lying on the dusty floor. I recognised the face immediately – it was a pencil sketch of Annie, which caught perfectly her vivacity, her keen alertness. The hint that she might be about to do something naughty. Something unexpected.

I could still hear the three of them as they made their way noisily down rue de l'Odéon towards the river. It wasn't too late to run after them, but, instead, the urge arose, unbidden, to push the piece of paper in my mouth and swallow it down whole as if some of Annie's energy might be transmitted to me. I took neither course of action in the end, but folded the sketch up neatly and hid it on my person like a talisman.

10

She hoped the dancing might help her sleep through, but Mim is woken again at four in the morning by the usual dream. She thinks of Lucky, of what it felt like to dance with him, how her limbs, which have felt so heavy and stiff for the last couple of years, felt they were softening, thawing. But she doesn't want to lie awake thinking about a man. Or for her thoughts to turn to Frankie, as they usually do at this hour. She needs to find a task to tire herself out. On impulse, she decides to take on Esther's desk.

There's plenty of rubbish piled on it – more old receipts and napkins with illegible scribbling on them, which Mim collects to look at later. She piles the numbered blue exercise books in the correct order and, when she gets to the fourth one, she notices a careful pencil sketch folded tightly within its pages.

It's a drawing of a woman – lively, alert, with large eyes, dark hair worn loose to her shoulders. She's relaxed and smiling – and it's the smile Mim recognises from the Bal Tabarin photograph. She finds it again and holds the two images next to each other. Annie. It must be.

On a mission, Mim searches the desk for more photographs. She doesn't find many – a couple of tiny ones of Rebecca and Esther, which look like they've been cropped. Mim wonders if one of the sisters cut their parents out of the photographs after their death. Or, perhaps, she thinks now, holding one of the tiny squares in her hands, Esther cut Lili out? But why would she do that?

Mim keeps looking for more, but there's mainly tat – dead batteries, lone playing cards and, mystifyingly, in the bottom left drawer, a pair of strappy silver heels, not at all the kind of thing Esther would have worn. She returns to the photograph of Annie – and there they are: what seems to be the same pair of shoes strapped to her narrow feet. Why on earth would she have given them to Esther?

The next morning, she wakes thinking of Frankie. That's not unusual. It's been the same almost every day for two years. Too long, according to the world's judgement. Or at least, perhaps, her family's. She thinks of the passage she read yesterday. That's what it feels like when you meet someone you want to be friends with. No, she corrects herself. More than that. When you meet a person whose magic you think might rub off on you. It wasn't about sex. It was about hope; it was about escape from the bars of being yourself.

She'd never known anyone as bold as Frankie – the youngest of four, the only girl after three older brothers, she was totally fearless, and totally adored. She'd never known anything different.

Which of you fuckers has stolen my cigarettes?

Stop, Mim, stop, she warns herself, picking up her phone as a distraction.

A text from Lucky.

Hope you got home OK? Did you like salsa? x

Yes. At least with you.

But...

He's waiting for a reply. She types quickly, without overthinking it.

It's all about sex, isn't it? And I don't know if that's for me at the moment.

She hadn't quite known that was the case until she wrote it down. Sex – even the idea of it – still feels dangerous to her. Something that could destabilise her, like alcohol. Anything that made her too happy or too sad was dangerous. She just wants a neutral life. Calm, steady, bubble-wrapped.

Her mind flickers back, without warning, to the first time Robbie spoke to her voluntarily. He'd complimented one of her pieces – an interview she'd done with a dying man. It was her first year in her first staff job on a daily paper in Brighton. She and Frankie had moved to the seaside city together after journalism college – a new start for them both. Frankie had started a job at an arty magazine in town – a role she loved, albeit under a tyrannical editor.

On the drive home, the article began in Mim's head. Esther was right: once you had the first line, it was going to be OK. She knew it was something special even as she filed it, but thought perhaps it would be a secret thing – a tiny glittering treasure that the weary world wouldn't notice, but it didn't turn out that way.

Robbie, the features editor, walked past her desk in the

newsroom and murmured, "Great piece, Mim," without hanging around for a reaction.

Marion, a lifer on the features desk who sat next to Mim, did an exaggerated jaw-drop. "Well, fuck me, I think that's the first time I've heard him say anything nice."

Mim shuffled through some papers, trying to hide how pleased she felt.

Of course, she doesn't share any of this with Lucky. And there's no taking the sex line back now, either, she thinks as she tosses her phone to one side and gets out of bed. Some men – people, to be fair – can't cope with too much early on, and that's OK, but she needs to be truthful. It's the least she can do. But after she's brushed her teeth and made herself a cup of coffee, she sees he's replied.

That's OK – I get it. Not the dance for you. What shall we try next?

Mim thinks as she sips her coffee. When her father was still alive, her mum and dad would dance together in the kitchen if the right track came on: some rock 'n' roll by Ray Charles or one of Benny Goodman's big band quicksteps. Her parents knew how to move to these songs: their feet tapped the ground in exactly the right rhythm and her mother seemed to understand instinctively what her father wanted her to do, spinning away from him or rolling back in.

Sometimes, Mim and Abi would beg to dance with their father too, standing on his feet as he stepped through the pattern of a waltz, though they never picked up their mother's following skills, honed from years of courtship.

Mim might be safe with the waltz, she thinks. Surely there's no chance of that getting too heated. She makes the suggestion to Lucky and adds:

It's not that I didn't like dancing with you.

The three dots bounce across her screen, but after a few minutes there's no reply. Sod it, Mim decides: she's not going to wait around for an answer. She needs some fresh air. It's almost lunchtime. She decides to take a break from her phone and leaves it charging on the kitchen counter.

Outside the day is heating up already. Mim notices, once she's out, how hungry she is from the late night, but it's only as she's about to order at the Heights Café that she remembers her debit card is still tucked into her phone cover, where she put it last night so she could travel light.

Then, back at the apartment block, Mim realises she's also forgotten her key and that the lovely doorman from the other day is off duty. In his place is a stern, matronly woman who is unwilling to part with Esther's spare.

"But I live here – I'm her great-niece."

She shrugs. "I've never seen you before."

"Please."

"I'm going to need some kind of proof."

"I have an email somewhere."

Mim tries to remember the to-and-fro between her mum and Esther's lawyers. There'll be something in her inbox, but her phone and laptop are, of course, both upstairs. She glances at the computer in the back room behind reception.

"There's an internet café a couple of blocks away." The doorwoman smiles to herself, as if she's just recalled something privately hilarious. "Actually, it might have closed."

Mim is not sure which is nearer to the surface now – tears or fury. "Please," she almost begs. "Just let me have the spare."

"I have one," a voice behind her chirps up.

Mim turns to face a tiny octogenarian with tightly curled red hair. She has one of those silly little dogs, which looks almost as powdered and scented as its owner. The silly thing – as red and fluffy as a fox cub – jumps up to greet her like an old friend and she finds can't resist stooping to pat it.

"A spare?" she repeats.

"Yes." The woman's accent is hard to place – some New York and then something more European. "Esther and I were friends."

The woman has a smear of pink lipstick on her teeth. Mim fights the urge to lean forward and wipe it off.

Esther's friend turns to address the doorwoman. "If it's OK with you, Deborah, I'll take this young lady up to my apartment and give her my spare key."

The receptionist, who seems cowed by this latest development, nods. There's an almost imperceptible change in her body language. She's unfolded her arms and that smirk has been wiped off her face.

Mim offers to take the woman's shopping bags, which, she realises immediately, are filled with clinking bottles.

"You're just in time for a drink." Her new friend tells her in the elevator. "I'm Bibi, by the way. And this is FeeFee."

"Bibi and FeeFee." Mim tries not to giggle.

"FeeFee La Rouge, to give her her full title. Esther thought it was ridiculous too," she said, adding. "You are so like her. Same sense of style." She seemed to be taking in Mim's jeans and T-shirt.

"Or lack of it?"

"Darling, I'm not saying a thing." Her new friend presses

her painted lips together in amusement.

Bibi's apartment looks as if it's been decorated by Barbara Cartland. A kitsch explosion of pink, with lace tablecloths, figurines and an odd abundance of clocks of all shapes and sizes, each telling a different time. Mim glances around, trying to disguise her blatant interest.

"I think we're just about in time for a martini." Bibi makes a show of consulting a cuckoo clock on the mantelpiece that seems to be on Swiss time. "Certainly in Europe, we'd be well into cocktail hour."

"I don't drink, actually." Mim feels a pang of guilt for being a party-pooper.

"That's fine, my dear." She grins cheekily. "How about a cup of tea instead?" She adopts a passable British accent as she makes the offer.

"Are you sure?" Mim frowns, uncertain about this sparrowlike octogenarian waiting on her.

"Absolutely, take a seat by the window."

Although the layout of this flat is very similar to Esther's, Bibi has kept the room with the view of the river for visitors. Her bedroom, Mim guesses, must be at the back of the apartment, facing inland, where Esther has a small guestroom. How like Esther to keep the best room in her flat for writing and this woman, whom Mim barely knows, but is starting to get a measure of, for entertaining.

There are two enormous pink armchairs arranged by the window. Mim sinks into one of them and FeeFee La Rouge, taking this as an invitation, leaps on to her lap, circles a couple of times and flops with a sigh that suggests she has had a day too exhausting for Mim to even guess at.

"She likes you," Bibi gives her a small smile. "Perhaps

you remind her of Esther too."

"Esther was more of a cat person, wasn't she?" Mim puts a hand on FeeFee's warm coat: the dog has found the sunniest spot in the flat.

"Well," says Bibi, tottering off to the kitchen, with a chuckle. "I'm not claiming she had taste."

When Bibi's unsteady step returns, Mim blinks awake, realising she's been snoozing in the sun for a couple of minutes. Bibi arranges her tea in a bone china cup and saucer next to a plate with a couple of chocolate biscuits on it.

"You look like you don't eat enough."

"You can talk," smiles Mim, sinking her teeth into a biscuit. FeeFee raises her head hopefully. "Have you been chatting to my mum?"

"It's a nice thing to have people who worry about you," Bibi tells her. "It's something you miss after they're gone."

"I bet you have plenty of friends." Mim lets her gaze roam again around the flat. There are framed photos everywhere, crammed between the figurines, dog ornaments and tiny clocks.

"Oh, yes," Bibi says. "Plenty."

Mim catches a glimpse of sadness in Bibi's face, but the old woman seems to blink it away.

"Here's to new ones," she raises her martini glass.

Mim lifts her cup to Bibi in return. "What happened to Esther's cats?" The question just slips out.

"Oh, we found them good homes," Bibi says. "They all went to friends – I would have had them, but FeeFee is an only child."

FeeFee, on hearing her name, cocks her head to one side

and jumps off Mim's lap, hurling herself on to Bibi's instead, sending her martini flying.

"FeeFee La Rouge!" Bibi exclaims, half-pleased, half-cross. There's a kerfuffle as her host gets to her feet and scurries to the kitchen to find a cloth.

"Can I help?" Mim stands up too, trying to look useful.

"No, no, it's all in hand," Bibi replies.

Mim stays on her feet and glances around at the apartment. One of the photographs catches her eye: Bibi, done up to the nines, in a coat with a fur collar, next to a grinning familiar face.

"Were you friends with Marlene Dietrich?"

"Yes, dear," Bibi calls back from the kitchen. "We did a couple of projects together."

Mim carries on looking. There was Sinatra, Ava Gardner. "Were you famous?" she asks stupidly when Bibi is back in the room, wearing a fresh, dry pink top, but still, Mim notices, in her heels.

"I had my moment," Bibi grins.

Then a familiar face jumps out of one photograph: Esther sandwiched between a younger Bibi and Edith Piaf in a New York café. Mim stops to look at it.

"That was just before she lost her big love, Marcel Cerdan." Bibi stands next to Mim, looking at the photograph.

"Esther?" Mim checks. She realises what's familiar about Bibi: it's the scent of Chanel No 5. A popular enough perfume, after all.

"No," laughs Bibi, but not unkindly. "Edith." She says the word the French way, Ay-deet. "He was a famous boxer, the world champion. He was married but he and Edith adored each other. They say she was never the same after he died in that plane crash. We lost touch with her."

"How did you know her?"

"Marlene introduced us," Bibi says matter-of-factly. She takes the photograph from the wall and brings it with her as she returns to her armchair. "She and Esther knew the same people back at the Tabarin."

Mim swallows. It was strange to hear someone say the name of this mysterious place out loud. "Did Esther talk about her time there?" She keeps her eyes on the photograph, as if it's no big deal. She has the sudden urge to ask about Lili, but reminds herself to keep that secret for now.

Bibi nods. "She'd often tell stories about the Tabarin – she loved that place. Terrible to think it's gone now. I went with her once to the spot where it stood."

"You went with her?" Mim asks, incredulous. Almost angry. Esther kept so much of her life from her. Secret family members. Secret trips. "But Esther hated Europe."

"Did she tell you that?" Bibi lifts her topped up martini to her lips and Mim longs, for a moment, for such a drink in her hand. Her own edges are feeling far too sharp. "I don't think it was as simple as that."

"She wouldn't even come to my bat mitzvah." Mim's voice sounds petulant even to her own ears. Childish.

"My dear." Bibi leans forward and pats her knee. "Esther left you her most precious possessions – her books – so you can't be in any doubt about whether she loved you or not."

Mim still has the feeling of a being a child, stuck outside of an adult matter that is somehow beyond her understanding, cut out of the photo, like Lili. "I know she loved me," she says, hearing the crack in her voice. "But it feels like she kept so much from me. Why did she never talk about her life in Paris? At the Tabarin? Why did she lie about being in France when it was occupied?"

Bibi is quiet, running her finger back and forth around the rim of her glass. "You have to remember," she says, not looking at Mim as she speaks, "that terrible things happened at that time – things people still don't want to talk about. Things people don't even want to remember. In an occupied country it's not always as straightforward as the history books make out: good or bad, black or white. Almost everyone feels compromised in some way. That's the wickedness of it."

Her voice, Mim thinks, a mixture of New York and other places – France, maybe Germany too. She must be younger than Esther – in her eighties, rather than her nineties. Mim finds herself wondering about Bibi's war. Was she in Europe too or did her family get away in time? But she hesitates at asking such a personal question, and anyway, before she has the chance, Bibi is on her feet again, offering her another cup of tea, and the moment passes.

II

May 1938

The first time I saw Annie dance, she was dying.

On the day of her audition, I found an excuse to bump into Pierre Sandrini and mentioned, as casually as I could, that I had friends trying out for the Tabarin.

"Where are they from?" asked the director.

But I realised I had only the vaguest of information about the pair: the truth was I hadn't seen the lively Canadian dancer and her pretty American friend since that day in the bookshop.

"They dance with Madame Egorova." I remembered just in time. "Mastering their fouettés. They want to join the Ballet Russe."

"Well," said Sandrini in his usual genial manner, "we must put them through their paces."

He was as good as his word when Annie and Dot arrived that day. I crouched in the wings, watching everything, crossing my fingers for their success. Lili was next to me, just fourteen, a favourite bow still pinned in her hair. She stared at Annie. "Is that the girl from your drawing?"

"Lili," I sighed. "You shouldn't snoop through other people's belongings."

"It's investigative work." She giggled. "Practice for my career as a photojournalist." She looked at Annie. "She's pretty, isn't she?"

I maintained a dignified silence.

First, Dot danced The Fairy Doll, a piece about a toy coming to life, made famous by Anna Pavlova. It suited her sweet, nimble style. Afterwards, Annie took on a more sombre solo, The Dying Swan, Pavlova's most famous dance.

The house fell silent as her feet pattered through those tiny bourrée steps, but it was her slender arms that did most of the work, fluttering as lightly as feathers, even as the Swan battled death. An aerial creature rebelling against the laws of Earth. How could something so delicate contain so much fight in it?

After that, the dance captain Belle, a haughty blonde, taught the girls a little cancan choreography, which also went smoothly. I could read Sandrini well enough to guess they'd probably be accepted, but he couldn't resist a little tease.

"We hear you've been practising your fouettés for Swan Lake."

Annie and Dot exchanged a nervous glance. The thirty-two fouettés – the whiplike spins that Odile performs in Swan Lake – are one of ballet's most famous challenges.

"How are they going?" the choreographer Bergé asked.

"Comme ci, comme ça," said Dot, who'd gone a bit green.

"Pas mal," Annie said, more defiantly.

"Great." Sandrini grinned. "How about we see them now, Annie? How about..." He paused. "Thirty-two?"

"Here?" She swallowed. "Now?"

"Why not?" Sandrini asked.

Why not? Because it could take a lifetime to master thirty-two fouettés en tournant – a challenge some of the greatest ballerinas in the world have struggled with.

Maybe Annie thought about how she had come all this way, boarded a ship and put an ocean between herself and all the people she loved to follow her dream. Maybe she focused on the ultimate goal – touring the world with the Ballet Russe. Maybe she simply thought of the Tabarin pay cheque. I don't know, but, in that moment, she said, "D'accord," nodded at the pianist, found a steadying spot on which to fix her gaze, and off she went.

Shaking in the wings on her behalf, I began to count, as I knew Sandrini and Bergé would. One, two, three, four. Everyone in the theatre seemed to stop breathing, as Annie held her balance steady, whipping her right leg out and in again. A human spinning top.

She must have known what some of her audience were thinking: that little Canadian dancer who wants to join the Ballet Russe, become the next Pavlova, who does she think she is? I caught a glimpse of Belle's face in the wings opposite me. She looked as if she were sucking a lemon. Always insecure about her own lack of classical training, she'd worked her way up the ranks in Montmartre's music halls with blood, sweat "and other bodily fluids", as gossip had it. I don't know about that. But now Belle was almost at the top of the tree at the Tabarin – and careful to protect her perch.

While I was counting, captivated in the wings, Dédée, Sandrini's wife, crept up next to Lili and me, with her fox terrier, Cancan, straining at the lead.

A striking, dark-haired woman with a wide laughing mouth and a fondness for hats, Dédée was as warm and charming as her husband. For years she'd worked as a dance captain at the Tabarin, and at the Folies Bergère before, but, newly pregnant, she'd recently retired from the stage.

"No one wants to see Maman dance the cancan," she laughed. But we all knew that wouldn't stop her at the Tabarin's legendary parties.

"What have we here?" she whispered to me. She was still in her fur and turban.

"An audition," Lili whispered back. "Thirty-two fouettés."

Dédée knew what that meant. "Where is she?"

"Sixteen." I hadn't taken my eyes off Annie. Cancan leaned into me and I could feel his heart beating pitter-patter like my own.

At twenty-six, we started to count out loud: "Twenty-seven, twenty-eight, twenty-nine." There was a tremor in Annie's supporting leg. I could only imagine at the burning sensation in her calf.

One by one, everyone in the theatre began to join in, from the musicians in the orchestra to a stagehand in the flies. "Thirty, thirty-one, thirty-two." She'd made it.

Sandrini jumped to his feet to applaud. Lili and I hugged each other. Cancan broke lose to lollop on stage and jump on Annie. Even haughty Belle clapped a little, though I heard her say, "We'll give her the idea she's too good for this place."

"Who's that?" drawled an intrigued voice from the darkness behind me. The speaker stepped forward, eyes still fixed on the stage. It was Antoine, a friend of Dédée's from her Folies Bergère days. He was always hanging around the Tabarin, having already dated all the dancers in his own theatre.

"Our newest dancer," she told him.

Antoine smiled. "Très jolie."

Dédée gave him a teasing prod in the ribs. "More important, she can really dance."

She left us then to join her husband, while I gazed at Annie, sitting crumpled on the floor, her face, still flushed, being blessed by Cancan's celebratory licks.

"Annie and Dot, welcome to the Tabarin," Sandrini called up, his arm slung around Dédée.

Annie squealed with joy, kissed Cancan on the nose and leapt to her feet to cartwheel across the stage to where Dot was waiting for her in the wings. Antoine and I exchanged a look – I don't know which of us was more pleased she'd be there permanently.

*

The cramped dressing rooms of the Tabarin were on the ground floor. They were the hub of backstage life, where the dancers gossiped, darned their stockings and heated their curling irons on small alcohol stoves.

In the winter, the dressing rooms smelled of melted glue when the dancers' toe shoes got too close to the stoves, and the whole place always reeked of hard work and the ointments the girls slathered on to their aching limbs after a performance.

It didn't take me long to find Annie and Dot that first week. They spoke in English when it was just the two of them, and I was keen to practise whenever I could. That wasn't the only reason, though. After Annie's audition, I'd gone home and started writing a piece about a dancer who comes to Paris determined to join the Ballet Russe.

"This is how I imagine it," I wrote. "A young girl of six or seven, sitting in a theatre. Her thick dark hair is bobbed in the fashion of the day, her lively face is enraptured. On the stage is Anna Pavlova on a trip to Toronto. It's not Camille Saint-Saëns's music – although it's enough to make you weep – or the dancer's elaborate feathered tutu, usually cited as the reason for little girls falling in love with ballet. It's the dancing itself.

"The small girl sits up. As the music soars, she leans forward. Everything else drops away. She wants to tell such a story. She wants to move like this…"

The piece came as quickly and easily as rain dropping from the sky in the way writing rarely does. I had a feeling that had something to do with Annie.

That day, I loitered at the door, as Annie and Dot chatted about how they'd spend their first pay cheque.

"Can you believe this girl has come to Europe without enough clothes for winter?" Dot told me when she saw me loitering. "And she doesn't even know how to sew?"

"I never learned," Annie told me proudly, fingering the pages of Dot's pattern magazine as if it was written in hieroglyphs. "Too busy dancing."

"Me neither." I leaned against the doorframe, grateful for the entry into the conversation. "My mother can, though. And my sister. They work in the costume department. I'm terrible at it – I get told off for daydreaming and scribbling things in my notepad." I had it tucked under my arm, as usual.

"You're a writer?" Annie asked.

"Trying to be." The standard answer of new writers too nervous to use the word. "Sandrini lets me help to plot out the stories of some of the shows. And it was my suggestion to do the piece this year to poetry instead of music."

"Oh, we've got you to thank for that then," Dot teased, rubbing her feet. "It's harder than you'd think."

"Would your mother – or sister – be able to make me some clothes?" Annie looked up from the magazine. "Once I've bought the fabric."

I nodded. "Of course, I could get you a good price."

"Would you?" Annie jumped up to fling her arms around me in gratitude. "I'm so glad we bumped into you at the bookshop – we might not be here otherwise." She paused. "I think that was the day I must have lost the little sketch of me. I never saw it since."

"What sketch?" I asked, pulling away from her embrace. But I knew exactly which one she meant.

12

May 1938

The dance captain, Belle, never forgave Annie for the impression she'd made at her audition. Word of her feat quickly swept through the theatre: the Canadian dancer who could do thirty-two fouettés.

If Belle's beauty had a coolness to it, like one of Hitchcock's heroines, Annie's was all life and warmth. It was a clash of opposites from the beginning.

Their first public disagreement was in rehearsal over the rhythm of a phrase in the poetry they were dancing to in that year's show. The situation escalated quickly – Belle became furious, Annie increasingly stubborn; even Dot murmured to her friend in English, "Let's do it her way – she's the captain."

But to my horror, Annie called me over as I hovered in the shadows, pretending to polish a seat.

"You're asking Esther?" said Belle, incredulous. "The usherette?"

"She's a writer," Annie insisted. It was the first time I'd heard anyone call me that out loud. "She understands poetry – and it was her idea."

I blushed at hearing my boast repeated in public.

"Go on then. What do you think?" Belle fixed me with a glare that said: "I've been working here for years and could lose you your job."

In truth, this was a dancing matter and none of my business, but a choice between the two women in front of me was no choice at all.

"Annie's way is right," I said quietly. "It works better with the poetry."

Perhaps I imagined it, but a hush seemed to fall on the house. Everyone looked at Belle. Not just the dancers, but the pianist, a couple of stagehands and old Bernadette who swept the floors increasingly slowly but whom Sandrini didn't have the heart to sack.

Belle glanced from me to Annie and said, "Of course, you would say that. You always help your own, don't you?" And then she murmured to herself, though loud enough for people to hear, "Les Juives."

Something ugly from the outside world crept into the Tabarin that afternoon. I glanced over at Annie and saw that her eyes had searched for mine across the room full of people. Something unspoken passed between us in that instant. Maybe that was the moment we truly became friends.

There was another person who noticed Annie that day: Antoine, the dancer who'd admired her at her audition.

He sidled up to me as I was unboxing programmes. "You're friends with the Canadian dancer, aren't you?"

He had a handsome face – haughty, almost – as though he were secretly amused at something he was keeping to himself.

"Perhaps." I fished out a programme from the top of the pile and my eyes searched automatically for Annie's name. Someone had misspelled it with one N. I tutted to myself and frowned at Antoine. I wasn't sure about him, either: everyone knew he had an eye for the ladies.

"I didn't like that scene with Belle," he told me.

I glanced at him, reassessing. "Me neither."

"Are you all right?" he checked. "Your family?"

I was quiet. I was surprised he knew much about my parents but I suppose he was at the Tabarin often enough. I thought about Ima and Papa, how they stayed up late into the night, whispering to each other in Yiddish when they thought we'd gone to bed.

My mother had taken on Annie's dresses without a murmur. "We need the extra money at the moment."

"I don't know," I said truthfully. "I'm all right, but my parents are worried."

He brushed a little dust from his sleeve. "Will you tell them, if they ever need a friend…"

I nodded, though I wasn't sure what a besuited dancer could do for my family.

"And will you tell Annie I'm on her side too?" he added.

"Better to tell her yourself."

I'd read enough to know what happened to messengers in stories. Plus, I wasn't sure I wanted to share Annie with anyone. I hung around her dressing room whenever I had a spare moment, lapping up her stories.

She grew up in a poor Jewish neighbourhood in Toronto

called the Ward; she was the youngest of five children. In photographs, they had the same similar striking looks as Annie: the boys with slick side-partings and the girls with 1920s bobs. Their parents worked in Kensington Market, selling fish.

Annie's mother had been a schoolteacher back in Poland, before they had to move, for the same reason as mine had. She took what books she could with her as she moved from Poland to London and then over to Canada. They were packed and re-packed, just like her life.

She never lost her love of reading, always kept a book on her, which she'd return to in rare quiet moments, stirring a pot, sitting behind the fish stand. They kept a bottle behind the stand too – a makeshift weapon when anti-Semitic gangs came to attack the market. It was on such a raid that Annie's older sister, helping her mother, collapsed from an asthma attack. She lost consciousness and never woke up. Afterwards, her mother's mind unravelled.

"I was at school the day she died," Annie said. "But I'll never forget what home was like when I returned. My three other siblings hiding in our bedroom, while our mother howled."

They thought the shrieking would stop. But it didn't. Even when two men and a woman dressed in starched white came to take her to an asylum.

"Always keep a packed bag by the door," she told her children in a rare moment of clarity, before she left. "You never know when you might need it. You never know when they might come again."

It was perhaps because of her mother that Giselle became Annie's favourite ballet. "You remember the story," she told me once. "Giselle is a simple peasant girl who loves to dance. She falls in love with Albrecht but he's engaged to someone else and he breaks her heart. And, you know, it's the usual scenario." Annie drew a line across her neck with her finger. "Actually," she said, suddenly serious, "Giselle goes mad." She fell quiet for a moment. "She collapses," Annie continued, "and just as she is dying of a broken heart she starts to mime to Albrecht, 'I… you…' But she dies mid-breath and so you never know, if she is going to say, 'I love you.' Or 'I beg you.' Or maybe, even, 'I forgive you.' The question is never answered. Isn't that the cruellest thing for Albrecht? Not to know if he has been forgiven or not?"

I love you. I beg you. I forgive you. I couldn't know how those words would haunt me.

If Annie learned from her mother that too much sadness could be a dangerous thing, she learned from her first ballet teacher that the same was true of anger. Annie's family never had much money, but she worked at a local dance school – cleaning floors and assisting with the younger students – in exchange for lessons. It was hard for her, just as school was, where she was teased for the odour of fish that lingered around her, and her obsession with ballet, practising her pliés or port de bras in the playground.

But when the teacher struck her with a cane, something in Annie snapped at this final humiliation. She broke it in two and stormed out of the class. Before she left the room, the teacher told her, in icily polite tones, that she wouldn't be allowed back unless she replaced it. Which, despite her rage, Annie did. Dance was the only thing in life that never let her down.

She never stopped experiencing the shimmering fury that

led her to break her teacher's cane – certainly not in the years I knew her in Paris. But she learned to hide it better, and that stood her in good stead.

Her first meeting with Antoine didn't go well. I happened to be sitting in the corner of her dressing room with a book, shielded from his view by a costume rail. Annie was at her dressing table, removing greasepaint from her face with cold cream after a show.

"Mademoiselle Annie?"

She glanced up at him.

"My name's Antoine."

"I know who you are."

He nodded as if to say fair enough. He'd had a thing going with one of our dancers, which had ended in tears. Hers not his.

"I like the way you dance," he said. "You're very athletic. Those fouettés." He gave a low whistle. "And you're musical, too."

"It sounds as if there's a 'but' coming." Annie's gaze returned to the mirror. Years of dance training had taught her there usually was a "but" coming.

"No, you're a good dancer."

"But..." She persisted, one neatly plucked eyebrow raised.

"You move too much," he began. "You're not so good at stillness. At holding a moment. A great performance needs shade as well as light."

It occurred to me, as I eavesdropped on this conversation, that Antoine was right: Annie was athletic – acrobatic even – but I rarely saw her, in life or on stage, capture the kind of stillness, or emotion, a truly great dancer is capable of.

She always needed to be spinning, cartwheeling, jumping through the air. She could never sit still with things; she was always on the move.

"You've got what it takes to be one of the best dancers here…"

"What it takes?" Her gaze became steely.

Why, I thought, can't some men resist the temptation to give advice instead of praise?

"Remind me," she added. "Where did you train?"

Antoine's background didn't have the classical credentials that Annie's did. There had been no ballet classes, no Egorova. Like Belle he'd worked his way up from the streets, taking whatever odd jobs he could before breaking through at the Folies Bergère.

"I've been in the business a long time," he said calmly. "I've done every kind of work. And dancing is the toughest of them all."

"I know about tough." Annie wiped the last smear of greasepaint from her face. "Believe me." She got to her feet: I wondered if she was actually going to push him out of the room.

They stood glaring at each other, this dark-haired pair, both tall, elegant and ambitious. Annie and Antoine. Even their names sat well together. I'd never felt so invisible.

And yet I guessed at Antoine's influence when, the next day, Belle came to Annie's dressing room to apologise. Someone had spoken to Sandrini, who wouldn't put up with anti-Semitism in his theatre. Nevertheless, it was an apology through gritted teeth.

"I'm sorry for what I said," Belle said, her contrition undercut by the feathered headdress she was still wearing.

"Apologise to Esther too," Annie said, glancing in my direction.

This was unbearable for Belle – that a dance captain should apologise to a lowly usherette – but she somehow managed it.

"I won't be here much longer, in any case," Annie said airily when she was done. "I'm heading for the Ballet Russe. And Esther is going to be a famous writer."

Belle's gaze shifted from Annie to me and back again. She didn't say the words again, but maybe she was thinking them: Les Juives.

"Well" – she gave a delicate shrug – "we'll see." She said it in the manner of someone who's had the final word on a matter.

13

Annie settled into life at the Tabarin: she and Dot made friends easily and I was happy to stay on the edges of things with my notebook. And there was always something of interest happening at the Tabarin: a duke or an earl or a world-famous artist out there in the audience. One night, my writing hero Colette was in, and Annie made me speak to her.

"I can't," I muttered, as my friend steered me towards Colette, her cool hand in the small of my back.

"You can," Annie hissed. "Just keep putting one foot after another – you'll regret it if you don't."

She was right about that, but, as we reached Colette, my words abandoned me. My hero was in her sixties by then, but still sleekly stylish in one of her androgynous tailored jackets. Her hair, a mass of greying curls, framed her regal face.

When I stood mute, Annie spoke for me: "My friend here

is a writer. Do you have any advice?"

Colette smiled wryly at us, a cigarette burning between her fingers. "It's probably not a good idea to place too much importance on money," she said. "Or on comfort. But as theatre people you'll be used to that. What you'll always need is the capacity to be astounded. And write under your own name," she added. "Don't hide behind anyone else's."

Everyone knew what had happened to Colette – how her first four novels had appeared under the name of her first husband, Willy, who'd retained their copyright. She'd run away and become a music-hall mime, found her freedom in the theatre like the rest of us.

"Do you think artists should always keep their own names?" Annie asked. She mentioned how dancers joining the Russian companies were often renamed: Alicia Markova, who joined the Ballets Russes as a teenager, had been born plain old Lilian Marks. "Who would pay to see Marks dance?" Diaghilev was said to have scoffed.

"It depends on the circumstances," Colette said thoughtfully. "Markova blended in with the other names around her. Sometimes that's better."

Maybe she was thinking of her current and – as it would turn out – final husband, Maurice Goudeket, who was Jewish and likely as frightened as the rest of us, despite his powerful wife. But who can guess at the minds of others? My hero Colette went on to write for the collaborationist press in the years of Occupation that followed, and in 1941 published a book, Julie de Carneilhan, full of anti-Semitic slurs. Nothing is as neat and tidy as we would like it to be.

*

One morning in November that year, I woke to find my

parents huddled at the kitchen table, listening to the radio. My mother hadn't prepared anything for breakfast. She cradled a cold cup of coffee in her hands.

"What's happened?" Rebecca moved the kettle on to the stove.

Our parents exchanged a glance. "Mass violence against the Jews in Germany," my mother said.

"Thirty thousand arrested." Our father got to his feet. He always had a head for numbers – it was one of the things that made him such a good carpenter. "Ninety-one dead. Two hundred and sixty-seven synagogues destroyed. Seven and a half thousand shop windows smashed."

I pictured it then: streets littered with shattered fragments, the crunch of it underfoot, shopkeepers out there sweeping it up as we spoke. It was easier to think about glass than the fear of those who saw it being smashed, of bodies in the streets, of people taken away in the middle of the night. Up until that moment, I think our parents had been trying to protect us, but their resolve seemed to fracture that morning. Or maybe the problem just got too big.

"They're saying it's thugs." Annie clutched one of the British papers, when I made it into the Tabarin that afternoon. She was sitting on the floor of the dressing room, still in her day clothes, even though I could hear the music for rehearsals had started.

"No it's worse than that – organised violence, I think." I took a seat on the floor next to her.

She was quiet for a moment then. "Always keep a bag packed by the door," she murmured, more to herself than to me.

"I mean it's terrible," I said. "But it's…"

Far away, I meant. Far enough away.

We sat quietly together, while the usual business of the theatre seemed to rattle on – the shout of a callboy on an errand, Belle's tense voice asking one of the midinettes to mend a petticoat for her, the pianist warming up for rehearsal.

"In his last letter, my father said he wants me to come home," Annie said eventually. "He thinks I'm still training with Egorova. He doesn't know about all of this." She gestured at the feathered costume waiting for her, as skimpy as a bathing suit.

I didn't know what to say to that, so we sat in silence on the floor of the dressing room for a while, our backs against the wall.

Later that day, Annie was called for a chat with Sandrini.

"Chérie," he said. "You're my most promising dancer and I don't want to lose you, but have you thought any more about auditioning for one of the Russian ballet companies?"

Annie said, rather breathlessly, that she had been thinking of just that. De Basil's Ballet Russe was due to return to Covent Garden in May 1939, the following year. Maybe she could try then.

Sandrini agreed to give Annie and Dot a week's leave when the time came. "And he even offered to pay for my fare," Annie told me triumphantly.

"Could I come?" The words fell out of my mouth without any planning.

I didn't want to be away from her: she was the reason I'd started to write. Somehow, a ballet dancer from Canada seemed to have offered me the key to something. My work. Myself.

Of course, Annie was delighted with the idea, but the challenge was to persuade my parents. Naïve as I was, I didn't anticipate their response.

After days of conferring between themselves and, I suspected, Sandrini, they called a family meeting around the kitchen table. They would send my sisters and me with the dancers to London. But there was a condition: they wanted us to stay there.

"You'll be safer." Our mother's voice was steely when she told the three of us, sitting at the kitchen table, but she reached out to take Lili's hand.

Rebecca was silent, leaving the rest of us to guess at what she was thinking.

"I only meant it as a trip," I said, suddenly panicked. I couldn't help feeling responsible for this decision. How would we live without our parents? Lili and I were teenagers – barely out of childhood.

"Can't you see what's happening out there?" Ima got sharply to her feet, waved at the front door. "We have an opportunity: we must take it. I don't want you to experience what we did when we were young."

"But what about you?" Lili ran over to our mother and wrapped her arms around her.

Ima buried her face in Lili's hair. When she looked up, her wet eyes met our father's. "Maybe we could join you later – when this season at the Tabarin is over."

It was clearly something they'd discussed, but I was eighteen years old and naïve, back then. Our parents had lived through something like this before: they had an idea of what might happen next.

14

Mim takes the A train to Harlem, like the Duke Ellington song. The city feels jaded and sleepy after the Fourth of July celebrations. Lucky had mentioned a party, but, in the end, Mim had stayed in with Esther's books, watching the fireworks from her window. It's not as long a journey to Harlem as she imagined – just over half an hour from Brooklyn all the way up to 125th Street station. There were places they could learn the waltz that were closer to them both, but, with the Bal Tabarin on her mind, she'd been determined to find an old vaudeville venue – and the Harlem Alhambra was one of the few places where you could still dance. In their messages, Lucky told her how its biggest rival, the Savoy Ballroom on Lenox Avenue, a famous Lindy hop, venue was demolished in the 1950s.

Her mind drifts to Lucky. She's definitely drawn to him. (Drawn to him, ha! Frankie mocks. Just admit you fancy him.) But she wonders if perhaps he's too sweet, too young, too undamaged by life. She's always been attracted to older men before – people with secrets and hidden pain. (And how did that work out? Frankie checks.)

The day Robbie complimented her article might have been the first time he'd singled out Mim for praise, but it wasn't the first time she'd noticed him. Newsroom gossip informed her that he was going through a divorce. He came into work looking crumpled: a touch of stubble on his cheeks, his white shirt unironed. He was slim to the point of gauntness. His salt-and-pepper hair looked as if it hadn't seen a brush in weeks. Sometimes Mim wondered what it would feel like to run her hands through it.

She started smoking again, despite the fact it had been hell to give up – something she and Frankie had done together – just so she could stand in the bus shelter next to him on his smoking breaks. But he didn't seem to notice her. Not really. There was the odd quip. A rare smile. Crumbs dropped her way.

The next time she received any kind of attention from him was in an editorial meeting, discussing upcoming anniversaries. It was January 2010 – the sixty-fifth anniversary of the liberation of Auschwitz-Birkenau.

"My great-grandparents died in the Holocaust," she said to the room.

It was as if Robbie looked at her for the first time then. And she knew from his gaze that he hadn't realised she was Jewish until that moment. "You should write about it for the magazine," he told her.

She shook her head. "I don't know."

"Think about it," he pressed. "You could find your own way into the story – like you did with the other one. The dying man who made his own coffin."

Mim tried her best not to smile. He'd remembered her piece.

No one on the paper had spoken to her about writing in that way before: as if it was something to be taken seriously. Not just ad sales and page clicks. She wanted to step up to the moment and say something unforgettable – something that Robbie would lie awake thinking of, in the way she thought about him. But she knew she wasn't ready to write about her great-grandparents or, more accurately, that her grandmother and Esther – her best sources – would probably never feel like talking.

In the end, she just repeated, "I don't know." And the flicker of interest he'd shown seemed to gutter like a candle.

She discussed the problem with Frankie that night, while her friend cooked pasta. She'd learned from her Neapolitan mother: an intimidatingly glamorous woman, who always wore red lipstick and with whom Frankie had enormous rows and emotional reunions. Her parents were both actors – they'd met on a film set. It was all very different from how Mim's family did things.

"I'm not sure I like the sound of it," Frankie continued. "Older, your boss, divorced. Not great on paper."

"I don't even know about the divorced bit."

"Oh, that's OK, then." Frankie drained the pasta and mixed in the sauce. "Why can't you like someone normal?"

"Like your tattoo artist?"

Frankie had recently started obsessing about a big bearded man at their local tattoo parlour. She'd already talked Mim into getting matching quill tattoos. "Ink sisters," Frankie joked, holding her left wrist close to Mim's right.

"At least he knows when he's inflicting pain." She handed Mim her bowl of pasta.

"I'm not in pain," Mim argued.

"Not yet."

Frankie walked through to the living room and switched on the television. But later she agreed to go shopping with Mim in the Lanes and persuaded her to buy a black dress with a bold white collar and a nipped in waist. A little bit Audrey Hepburn. Even as she tried it on, Mim imagined how she'd wear it to the office on Monday for Robbie.

On the train, she wishes, more than anything, that she could go back to that conversation with Frankie and listen to her friend. That she could do it all again. She spent her life – her youth, as she thinks of it now – rushing into decisions and parties and bedrooms. Charging into everything until the one thing she couldn't rush away from.

Why don't you just go for it with Lucky? Frankie asks her, after being quiet for a couple of minutes.

Mim doesn't haven't an easy answer for this. She likes Lucky, is definitely interested, but she's frightened too. Of those flutters in her belly. Of where it could all lead. I just don't deserve him, she replies in the end.

Frankie seems to have nothing to say to that.

She knows she's talking to herself really – that the Frankie in her head is only her own version of her friend. Not the Frankie she knew, who loved glossy magazines and vintage clothes. Not the Frankie who had a quill inked on her left wrist and knew Breakfast at Tiffany's almost by heart. Not the Frankie who could tell you the best tomatoes to buy, who danced purely for herself and was the only person in Mim's life who would always tell her the truth.

Mainly she talks to Frankie in her head, she suspects, because the idea of not being able to talk to Frankie, on top of everything else, would be unbearable.

Lucky is waiting for her outside the Alhambra – a huge red-brick cube of a building. He's on the phone and raises a hand, smiling warmly, miming the ballroom hold at her. As she approaches, she can hear his tone on the phone is tender, affectionate. Her antennae quiver. She needs to be careful; she can't get involved with someone who's taken. Not again.

"OK," he says gently. "I've got to go. My friend's here."

Friend, Mim, thinks. She can definitely hear a female voice at the other end.

"Yes, yes, I will," Lucky says. "Love you too. No, I won't forget." He rolls his eyes at Mim as he hangs up. "My mum," he says, shoving his phone into his pocket and giving her a quick hug. "She's worried they're not feeding me in New York."

"A city famously short on food." Mim smiles, pushing her own worry to one side. "Mine's the same. She still reminds me to cross roads safely."

"They're unstoppable, aren't they?" He glances up at the building's ornate façade, its name written in cursive. "What a place."

"It was built in 1905," Mim recalls from her internet research. "Billie Holiday played there. And Duke Ellington and Bessie Smith."

"You could join History Club any day." Lucky grins. "In fact, I think you'd be our first female member."

They make their way into the building and get into the lift to the ballroom on the top floor.

"Did you find out more about the place you mentioned in your message?" he checks.

"The Tabarin?" Mim asks. "Not much. It was a music hall in Paris, but it's been demolished now."

"I'm sorry to hear that."

"Yes," she agrees. "It's something I'm reading about in my great-aunt's papers. She never talked to me about it." She hesitates. "But maybe it just made her too sad. Imagine a place with all those memories being knocked down. Somewhere you worked and made friends and maybe fell in love."

She realises, as she says the words out loud, that she really has no idea at all about Esther's love life.

The Grand Ballroom at the Alhambra is an enormous space with an arched ceiling and glittering chandelier. A balcony overlooks the dancefloor, which is surrounded by small round tables. It makes Mim think, again, of the Tabarin.

She and Lucky find a seat at one of the tables and he pops to the loo, leaving his phone behind. Glancing around her, Mim picks it up quickly and checks his recent calls. Sure enough, the name at the top is Mamita Bailarina, which she imagines must mean something like Mummy Dancer. The sweetness of the nickname makes her flush with shame as she returns the phone to its place on the table. Glancing up, she briefly locks eyes with a fierce-looking woman with dyed black hair, who struts on to the dancefloor and claps her hands.

People begin to gather around her and the teacher introduces herself as Katya. She wears peach satin shoes and a slinky black dress that clings to her hips. Her severe expression only softens when she says the name of her younger assistant, Sergei – a lean man with a neatly combed side parting, who's also dressed smartly in a shirt and tie.

"Do you think they're lovers?" Mim murmurs to Lucky, as they gather around the teachers with other awkward-looking students.

"Almost certainly. Dancers are always at it," he tells her. "Not me," he adds hastily. He takes his glasses off and cleans them furiously, blushing so fiercely that she believes him.

The classroom is divided into leaders and followers: Lucky joins Sergei and the other leaders, while Mim stands behind Katya. The basic box step is fairly simple in the one-two-three count that everyone knows, but Katya insists on the followers straining their heads to the left in a way that doesn't feel at all natural.

Once the leaders and followers have mastered their steps separately, they're allowed to dance together. Mim, standing opposite Lucky, stares hard at a shirt button on her eye level to prevent her gaze from roaming to the hollow of his neck. This place isn't like the salsa club, which was hot and dark. It's too well-lit for this kind of intimacy.

"Gentlemen," Katya instructs, "make the ballroom frame like Sergei's and invite your partner in." Her handsome young partner creates a perfect frame, left arm outstretched, right arm slightly crooked. "Ladies – or followers," Katya corrects herself, "when you feel ready, step in."

Mim hesitates and steps in to Lucky's arms. She is aware, in this brightly lit room, of every single point their bodies are in contact – his left palm on her right, his fingers closed around hers, his right hand on her shoulder blade, his right wrist resting just under her left arm.

She can smell his freshly washed skin, his clean minty breath, but, even then, it's still not enough proximity for Katya when she comes round to check their position.

"No, no, no." She adjusts Mim's head and pushes her hips closer to Lucky's.

Mim fidgets. "Isn't that a bit…"

"What?" Katya glares at her.

"Intimate?"

"You've seen it on TV, haven't you?"

Mim doesn't answer out loud but she's always dismissed ballroom dancing on the television as a bit silly. A pastime for people who like to dress up in glitter and feathers and paint themselves orange. She knows better, though, than to voice such opinions to someone as terrifying as Katya.

"You need to trust your partner," the teacher says pointedly. "Trust is key."

Mim can feel herself flush, remembering Lucky's phone. It's not snooping, she tells herself, stealing a line from Lili. It's investigative.

But she doesn't convince herself. She thinks of Lili as they begin to dance again. What happened to her? Why was she cut out of the photographs? Out of their lives? Her minds drifts and she feels herself edging away from Lucky, millimetre by millimetre, until their hips are no longer touching.

He stops her for a moment. "We've lost contact. It's probably my fault." He rubs his forehead. "The leader is usually to blame."

"No, it's mine," Mim admits. "It's all so uncomfortable. 'Hold your head here, keep your hips there.' Everything hurts."

"Well," Lucky smiles apologetically, "that's dancing."

"It doesn't bother you? Being poked and prodded and rearranged all the time?"

"It's just part of learning." There's a flicker of a smile at her impatience. "I know it's not easy," he adds, "but you can't avoid the body when you're dancing."

"Avoid the body," she repeats the words more to herself than to him. They sound familiar, like something Frankie might have said. She wants to deny it, but isn't that just what she was doing – her mind drifting away instead of being here with Lucky. She hoped that the waltz would be easier than the salsa. Or, at least, that it wouldn't stir up those bad old fluttery feelings – and the familiar panic when it came to desire. And intimacy. And yes, the reality of having a body.

"Shall we try again?" He opens his arms in invitation and Mim steps in, promising herself she'll do better.

There's a dreamy romanticism to the music. This time, as "Moon River" begins to play, Mim doesn't edge away from him and they start to move around the room like a single creature with four legs. For a few short minutes, she lets the rest of it float away – Katya's nagging and poking and prodding – and other things too: all the other things she has carried with her to New York that weigh heavy on her mind and limbs. For just the length of a song, she lets them all go, feels them float from her like the weight of ice melting away, and it's just her and Lucky: two drifters, flying around the room.

15

Spring 1939

While we made plans for the trip to London, everyone else at the Tabarin was deep in preparations for the next spring show. Un Vrai Paradis was not an apt title, in retrospect, for 1939, though the narrative was about the loss of paradise as well as its return.

Sandrini always wanted to outdo what had been done before, and that year was no exception. My mother whispered that Erté's designs were as glorious as any she'd seen, her worried face lightening briefly at the thought of them. I'd catch her occasionally scurrying between workrooms with armfuls of sumptuous silks. She was different with the three of us in those months – more tender and attentive, reminding us how to cook borscht, make challah or keep household accounts, her eyes lingering on our faces a moment or two longer than usual.

Rumour had it that Sandrini was sleeping in his office, surviving on the ham sandwiches and coffee Dédée brought him and napping in his chair. Occasionally, he or Bergé darted out of meetings and grabbed one of the dancers to try out a piece of choreography. "Chérie, can I borrow you for a second?"

The girl might roll her eyes and stub out her Gitanes to go with the men, but secretly we all knew she was pleased to have been chosen.

The first two parts of the show came easily to Sandrini – in the first section, the tableau of dancers would represent the Garden of Eden and its earthly paradise, with Eve – one of the nude dancers – taking centre stage. For the second, Paradise Lost, there was an industrial section choreographed to a futurist score by Alexander Mosolov.

But Sandrini wasn't sure how to conclude the narrative with a third segment. There would be nudes, of course, and some sort of grand tableau, but what would it all mean?

"What does our budding writer think?" Sandrini asked. "I imagine you're the only one of us who's read Milton. It needs to end happily, doesn't it?"

I'm sure he was just making conversation, but I blushed furiously at the honour of being asked and told him I'd think about it. Meanwhile, Annie set her heart on being picked for the French cancan troupe that year. No show at the Tabarin was complete without the cancan, and only the eight best dancers performed it.

The more sophisticated audience members might have come to admire the designs by Erté or Sandrini's ground-breaking concepts for the revues, but plenty of our bread-and-butter customers simply wanted to see the famous French cancan danced at its best. One of the Tabarin's innovations was to place a mirror at the back of the stage so the view could be admired, from both sides, of the girls' scissoring legs, frothy white petticoats and peachy derrières.

What did I make of all this? And of the nudes at the Tabarin? Was it right for us all to make our living from them taking off their clothes? It's something I've given a lot of thought to in the years that have passed and I'm still not sure. I don't know if there's an easy answer. In dance, you can't separate yourself from your flesh. In my art form, as a writer, no one much cares what you look like, but if you dance, your body is the instrument.

Sandrini and Bergé used to laugh at the men who gathered at the stage door in anticipation of meeting the nudes and other dancers; they usually didn't have the success they hoped for with the goddesses they'd admired on stage. The women at the Tabarin were as strong as any I've known before or since – they were there for the love of dance, and revealing their bodies was part of that. Most of them were classically trained – they'd gone through years and years of dance lessons to get there. Of course, their bodies were beautiful, powerful and athletic, and the intimacy of the Tabarin – the fact that the audience could sit so close to the stage that they could smell the sweat, even feel it splash, at times, on to them – no doubt increased the potency of the situation for some.

So, yes, they made their living from the male gaze – we all did, directly or indirectly. Yet all of the dancers I knew who performed on that Tabarin stage – and particularly those who took on the cancan – found in it a kind of freedom. I will never be able to hear the opening bars of Offenbach's "Galop Infernal" and not instantly be yanked back to those nights when the whole house shook – physically quaked

– with the rhythmic scissoring kicks and joyous squeals of the Tabarin dancers. Determination, elation, pride and power writ large on their faces.

For ages, I fretted on the question of how to close the show until one night, as I drifted off to sleep, I had an idea that came to me, perhaps, through thinking of Annie and the freedom she found in dancing. What if paradise was restored in the final segment through the sweat and effort in the second section? What could be a better conclusion for a Tabarin show? Through the dancers' effort and art, Freedom, Hope and Desire could return, represented by the dancers in the tableau.

"Why are you grinning to yourself?" Rebecca asked at breakfast the next day.

"I had an idea for the third part of the revue – it's a good one, I think."

"You really think Sandrini is going to listen to you?" Rebecca smirked.

"He does," I insisted. "He did before."

Her words needled at me in the way only a sister's can. Perhaps Sandrini was just humouring me, perhaps my input didn't really count for much at all. But what else could I do? I couldn't sew like my mother and Rebecca – and the idea of being on show like Annie made me want to hide in a box in the basement.

My father had his carpentry atelier, and even Lili was given a tiny space in the basement. A place she could use as a darkroom, where she learned to develop the first pictures she took with her precious Leica – a gift from Sandrini. But thinking of stories, of scenes; that was how I could contribute. And being close to Annie inspired me. I had even found the confidence to start sending my first story about her to a magazine or two to see if they'd like to publish it, though I'd heard nothing back yet.

Our father frowned. He was always on my side in family rows. "Rebecca," he told her curtly, "if your sister says she's helping Sandrini with his show, then she is." He paused, looking at the three of us. "I hope you will all support each other in London when we're not there to guide you?"

A familiar tension crackled between Rebecca and me. She blamed me for this move to London – I could feel fury radiating from her. My sister popped a piece of challah in her mouth and glared at me. So much left unsaid between us.

16

When I told Sandrini my idea later, I knew I'd got it right. His gaze shifted into the distance as if he was picturing the scene: his dancers symbolising Freedom and Hope, even as shadows darkened over Europe. He squeezed my shoulder, "That's it! You've done it again."

I couldn't wait to tell Annie. In her determination to make the cancan troupe, she'd worked hard on a move known as le grand écart – the jump splits, which always made the audience catch its breath. Many a cancan girl had come unstuck with this move over the years. It wasn't just its physicality, but the chutzpah it required, as my mother would have put it. An immodest brashness that classically trained dancers often struggled to embrace. Nice girls didn't take on le grand écart. Dédée told us a story of how, after leaping into the splits in the schoolyard as a dare, her headteacher had called her to his office and told her she'd be forbidden from taking first communion.

"I thought I'd never recover from the shame," she told us, before glancing naughtily around her at a typical scene at the Tabarin: cancan girls, someone trying on a leotard, Gisy, a statuesque nude, wandering around in a barely tied up peignoir. "Funny how wrong I was."

I found Annie stretching in her dressing room, using her chair as a makeshift barre, dropping slowly into the splits. "Do you think I'll ever be a great artiste?" she asked.

"You already are." I picked up one of her stockings to make myself useful and began to darn it very badly. "Don't listen to what Antoine said – he doesn't know what he's talking about."

"He does, I think," she said thoughtfully. "But I won't tell him that."

It struck me then that she was a more mature artist than I was. She was already sharing her work with the world, and handling criticism too.

"Once you've mastered le grand écart you'll be in the cancan troupe in no time," I promised. And I was right about that.

The ease with which she mastered the move was another thing that marked her card with Belle, who'd taken years to join the troupe and work her way up to the top. In fact, Belle had been increasingly snappish with us all in the run-up to the show. Looking paler and drawn, she seemed to be struggling with routines that never gave her any bother before.

"Jealous," Dot mouthed to Annie after our friend had been the victim of a particularly vicious verbal attack from the dance captain. Belle had not said anything overtly anti-Semitic this time, but she still had it in for Annie, never missing an opportunity to put my friend in her place.

Afterwards, in a rare moment of boldness, I followed Belle to the bathroom, meaning to say something in Annie's defence. Something about how much my friend was missing her family. The city was filling with refugees from Germany and Spain and the right-wing press wrote about them as if they were vermin or criminals. Despite her bravado, Annie was anxious. After all, she was a foreigner too. And a Jewish foreigner at that.

Those thoughts ran through my head as I stood outside the toilet, planning what I'd say to Belle, but as I waited they were interrupted by the distinct sound of her vomiting. It went on for ages and, in the end, I crept away, unwilling to face her after such a vulnerable act.

I expected her to mention it at the next rehearsal – she was a hypochondriac, particularly protective of her precious legs. "The Mistinguett of the Bal Tabarin," someone joked. "Except Belle's aren't insured for half a million francs."

But after her bout of sickness, she didn't say anything at all.

"I think she's got food poisoning," I whispered to Dédée when she mentioned how poorly Belle looked. "I heard her being sick."

"Did you now?" Dédée gave me a meaningful look, but back then I knew so little about the ways of the world I couldn't for the life of me work out what she meant by it.

17

Spring 1939

I heard second-hand that Dédée had had a discreet word, but Belle denied her condition outright. Maybe she was hoping it would just go away; maybe she'd already visited a certain sage-femme, who, she'd been told, could solve her problem. Either way, the next time she turned up to work she was plainly very ill indeed, dripping with sweat, her skin taking on the unnatural hue of a carmine-dyed carnation.

The dancers were practising a number from Un Vrai Paradis, dressed in white togas, surrounding Gisy as Eve, naked but for a cache-sexe, a pearlescent shell held precariously in place by glue. The other dancers circled her, leaning into each other in deep back bends, a dizzying position at the best of times, but they had to hold it for longer than usual that day, as the mechanism stuttered, bringing Gisy up from the basement.

"Belle, you're sweating on me," murmured the girl behind her.

"How do you know it's not your own sweat?" she snapped. "I suggest you…"

But we never learned what she suggested because her legs gave way beneath her and she collapsed in a faint. Everyone gathered around her in shock as blood began to seep through her white tunic.

The Tabarin, like the tiny town it was, had its own doctor, Gilbert Doukan. The old joke everyone repeated was that he was the only medic in the world who didn't need to ask his patients to undress. He arrived swiftly on the scene. Short and bespectacled, he wasn't a traditionally handsome man, but he was so gentle with Belle, so kind, that we all fell a little in love with him.

"She's got herself pregnant," one of the acrobats muttered.

"I doubt she did it alone," the doctor pointed out sympathetically.

"That's what I want," Gisy told us later, perched on a chair with her peignoir barely hiding her breasts. "The gentle touch of a man like that. Not these stage-door Johnnies with their ham hands. I bet he would know his way around a woman's body."

Annie and I exchanged glances. We were still virgins, but didn't want to say that in front of Gisy, who would wander into our clique from time to time, dispensing worldly advice. Not for the first time I wondered what it would be like to live in London, outside this world of easy camaraderie.

Annie was never short on admirers. She was cheerfully polite to the men who bought her carnations at the stage door and complimented her dancing, but none of them seemed to interest her. The only one who got under her skin was Antoine, and that, in my opinion, was because he'd said something uncomplimentary. A critical word always lingers in the mind, like a drop of ink on snow, in the way that light, bright words never do.

"If you're thinking about Antoine again, he was wrong," I told her, after Gisy had left us alone. "It's like a boy pulling a girl's pigtails in school. It's because he is attracted to you."

"No," Annie replied. "He's right – I can portray light but I can't do shade. I don't want to dwell in darkness. It's because…"

I waited, as she reached out for the right words.

"I think it's because of what happened to my mother. When she gave in to sorrow for my sister, she was taken away."

I had the opposite problem, I confessed: too much shade, not enough light. Just then we heard the skittering of Cancan's toenails on the boards. A sure sign that Dédée was nearby.

She knocked on the dressing room door, wearing a hat with a bright orange poppy on it. "Annie," she smiled. "Sandrini wants to see you."

"Am I in trouble?" She jumped to her feet, dusting herself down.

"Not this time." Dédée laughed. "Between you and me, he's looking for someone to replace Belle in the cancan. She's indisposed for a while."

Annie glanced back at me and I grinned at her. All her hard work was about to pay off.

That evening, in the cancan she performed le grand écart with such ease that it brought the entire house to its feet.

Belle never forgave her. She returned a few weeks later, thinner, quieter, adding brandy to her coffee when she thought no one was watching, hissing with discontent to anyone who'd listen. A serpent in our paradise.

By then Annie had captured the hearts of the Tabarin regulars, and Belle, because of her fragile health, was kept out of the troupe for the foreseeable future.

"It's her fault," I overheard Belle say, watching from the wings. "I could have kept it a secret, if she hadn't gone running to Dédée. I could have worked it out somehow." She blinked away brandy-induced tears.

Of course, it was me who spoke to Dédée, but to my shame I never corrected her. Annie was so strong, so popular, she could brush off such a slight. And, anyway, I told myself, we'd both be gone soon.

I wasn't the star of the Tabarin. I was the person who showed people to their seats, who helped with the cleaning. I hid in Annie's shadow when I should have forged my own path. The secret endured like an invisible spore in our friendship: a tiny speck of cowardice in me that might bloom like a fungus in the darkness.

18

May 1939

When the call to London came, it came quite quickly. Colonel de Basil's Ballet Russe was about to start its six-week season at the Royal Opera House in Covent Garden. Could Annie and Dot make the trip then to audition? "Could we ever?" Dot laughed.

But when the time came, it was a wrench to leave.

"To think this could be the end of us and the Tabarin." Annie placed a sentimental palm on the filthy floor of the stage – the dirt and dust from all of those dance shoes, dried sweat and skin particles, the odd feather and sequin that had dropped there yet to be swept up by Bernadette.

"Don't be a twit," Dot said cheerfully. "We'll be back – they're not going to take us straight away."

Annie was quiet. Maybe she was thinking about Antoine – I don't know if she'd said goodbye to him or not, though he passed a phone number on to her. Somewhere he said she could always find him. Dot's comment caused me to fall quiet too. I'd promised my parents that I'd remain in London but it had never occurred to me that Annie wouldn't stay too.

Meanwhile, my mother buzzed around us as we packed, tucking little bits of money and food in among my books.

Lili's packing, my mother did for her; it was Lili she hugged the closest; Lili's whose hair she wept into. My little sister shook her off like a pony tossing back its mane, cantering from room to room, saying goodbye to each cheerfully.

Just before we left for the station, my mother remembered a letter that had arrived for me while I was out doing last-minute errands. In the bathroom, when I had a moment alone, I tore it open. It was a reply from a reasonably well-known literary magazine, one of the many to whom I'd sent my story about Annie. The editor said they would be delighted to print my story and offered me what seemed like a princely sum on publication.

I couldn't believe it, hugging my secret to my chest all the way to the train station. Our parents came to see us off at the Gare du Nord. Our father strangely silent, our mother a ball of nervous energy, saying repeatedly, "I know this is the right thing to do."

Rebecca was quiet during the journey, while Annie, Dot and Lili chatted away. Lili, meanwhile, held her precious Leica on her lap as carefully as if it were a baby. Sandrini, who'd always adored his youngest employee, asked her to catalogue the adventures of his dancers abroad.

If some of London was a little grey and disappointing for a young person who had grown up in Paris, Hampstead Heath made up for it. I made Lili tramp with me around that vast expanse, while I told her stories of Keats, Shelley, Byron and Coleridge, who'd all lived in that part of London. One energetic day, we walked all the way across the Heath to visit George Eliot and Christina Rossetti in Highgate Cemetery, while Lili spoke to every single dog and baby we met on the way. She was always soft like that. People sometimes think softness and courage can't exist equally in a person, but they're wrong. I was glad of her cheerful company, while Annie and Dot fretted about their audition.

It was hard to ignore the signs of the city preparing for war – posters about evacuation procedures and air raid shelters; instructions for blackout; and an ominous number of soldiers in uniform, and policemen too, when we went into the city centre.

Before long, Rebecca was nagging us to look for work. Spotting the only other grown-up in the vicinity, she swiftly made friends with Mrs Cleverly, the owner of the boarding house where we were staying in Golders Green. She'd offered to darn something for her and before she knew it, she was up in our landlady's flat in charge of laundry and mending clothes for the entire building. Rebecca always knew how to get what she wanted with minimal fuss.

"There are enough drama queens around," she used to say in a pointed manner.

Annie and Dot, meanwhile, were obsessing about their audition, rehearsing in any space they could find, taking turns to use the sink in our cramped rooms as a barre.

"Could you two take it outside?" Rebecca snapped, one particularly hot afternoon.

The mood was tetchy. The dancers had their audition the next day and nowhere sensible to practise. Rebecca, meanwhile, had a large pile of stitching to get through.

"We should go to the Heath," Lili suggested. "Leap into one of the ponds to cool down."

"Good idea," Rebecca said firmly, wanting some space. "Off you go." She practically pushed the four of us out of the room. Dot and Lili skipped ahead of us, while Annie and I hung behind. I could tell something was on her mind.

"I'm scared," she told me, as we passed Kenwood House. "About tomorrow."

"You'll be fine," I said. "I have a good feeling about it."

She was silent for a couple of seconds. "That's what I'm afraid of," she said at last. "What if I finally get what I want? And what if it's not as I hoped? What then?"

"Then you'll return to the Tabarin," I told her. "Sandrini would always take you back – you know that."

There was a moment of silence between us. We passed a group of schoolchildren carrying gas masks. In front of us, Lili stooped to pet a fox terrier that looked like Cancan.

"I have something to tell you." The words came out in a rush. "Someone wants to publish one of my stories. Can you believe it?"

"Oh, Esther." Annie flung her arms around my neck. "I'm so pleased." She grinned. "It's all just beginning for us, isn't it?"

She took my arm and gave it a squeeze and we caught up with the others a little further down the hill from us. Lili said goodbye to her new friend and we made our way to the pond together, changing swiftly and hurrying to the water.

"Strike a pose, girls." Lili raised her camera to Annie before she leapt in.

She paused and lifted a leg in a perfect arabesque. When I

think of her today, I still remember her as she was standing at the edge of that icy water, before flashing us a grin and diving in. Perhaps she was capable of stillness, after all. She certainly never lost her capacity to astound me. I loved her – not, I think, like that. But in the same way that falling in love with another makes us fall in love, a little, with ourselves, or at least with their view of us, my friendship with Annie made me believe that anything was possible. I had a superstitious belief that she was the key to my own creative success, and not only because my first published story had been about her: things seemed to happen when Annie was around.

In the end, despite their nerves, the audition went well.

"It actually wasn't as bad as the Tabarin," laughed Annie. "I didn't have to do thirty-two fouettés."

They still hadn't told us whether they'd been accepted or not. "Was it a yes?" I asked impatiently. "Are they going to take you?"

"They are!" Annie threw her hat into the air. "You are looking at two future dancers of De Basil's Ballet Russe. They're going to pick us up in Paris in December."

Well, I squealed and hugged them and made all the right noises about how happy I was, but, even then, I could hear a voice in my head, asking, What about me? What would it mean for my own work? And what was I going to do without Annie?

19

Mim sighs, pacing around Esther's desk. Questions buzz through her head. What had gone on? How had the sisters ended up back in Paris? And whatever happened to Lili? On impulse, she reaches for her laptop and before she can overthink it Skype's bubbly ringtone is playing.

The face of her mum comes into focus. She's with Abi and there's a racket in the background, the sound of one of the children screaming. Mim almost thinks of finding some excuse to go – it's so hard to chat to her mum when the grandchildren are over.

"Mim." Her mother's face on the screen looks worried as usual. "Are you calling for Evie?"

"Evie?" Mim repeats.

"Yes," her mother says. "For her birthday?"

Mim swallows. Her niece is two today – she'd completely forgotten. Her mum must be hosting a family tea party. She probably thought that's why Mim called. The expression on

Abi's face flattens for a second and she slides out of view. Mim can hear a deeper voice in the background – Boring Ben's, no doubt.

"They're in the playroom," her mother explains, sharing a view of the kitchen tiles as she carries her laptop through. "She'll be thrilled you called."

I doubt that, thinks Mim, but she is in this now. The faces of the gathered children – none of whom Mim recognises except Evie – are completely blank. The entrance of the adults has clearly brought some kind of game to a halt.

"Hello," she bellows like an idiot. A small boy with wild curls eyes her with suspicion. Her mother turns the camera to Evie. "Happy birthday!" Mim shouts. The two-year-old, lollipop in mouth, stares at the screen and, by way of response, slowly and deliberately drops into the splits.

"Did you want to speak to anyone else?" Mim's mum checks afterwards.

"Yes, you, actually. Did you find anything in Grandma 's papers about the Bal Tabarin? Or her life in Paris?"

"No." Her mother glances around her. "Nothing. She'd thrown everything away. You know what she was like about the past."

Mim sighs. A dead end. "And did you ever hear of Esther talk about anyone called Annie?"

"I don't think so."

"How about Lili?" Mim goes in for the kill.

Something tightens in her mother's face. A little tell. "No, I don't think so." The lightness of her tone is unconvincing.

Mim uncrosses her legs and then crosses them again. "You're not keeping anything from me?"

"Keeping? No." Her mother sounds a little breathless

as she climbs up the stairs, in search of somewhere quieter to chat. "What are you doing there? What has Esther left you?"

"Just some books." Two can play at the evasion game, Mim tells herself. "A memoir, I guess."

Her mother's face suddenly appears very close and quiet on the screen. She has shut herself in the airing cupboard. "I don't want you to go upsetting yourself."

"I'm not upset," Mim insists, sounding as though she might be. "I just don't know why no one wants to talk about it."

"Surely you can guess," her mother says quietly. And this is a harder thing to argue against – the weight of their family's history, scars too deep to pick at. "My mum never really wanted to discuss any of it, not until the end, and by then she was quite confused, as you know." She sighs. "And neither did Esther, for a long time."

"Well," Mim says, "she obviously changed her mind."

Her mum is silent. "Look," she says, in the end, "Esther adored you – I'm not denying that, and it's a privilege she left you her papers, but you don't have to look at them now. Not all at once – and not on your own. Not after everything."

Not after everything. A perfect piece of family code. Unpleasant business. Mim picks at a small scab on her knee.

"Maybe it's not good for you to be spending so much time alone."

"I'm fine." A speck of bloods wells up beneath the excavation. "You don't have to worry about me any more."

"I'm your mother. That's my job." Her mum opens the door of the airing cupboard and the noises of the house seep through – one of the children wailing, Buster the chocolate Labrador joining in the cacophony. "I'll tell Abi that your present for Evie is on its way," her mother concludes pointedly, before hanging up.

Mim gets to her feet and stretches, trying not to replay the conversation. She forgot Evie's birthday, it's true, and she hasn't really been there for Abi over the last couple of years, even though she knows her sister has been weighed down, juggling childcare and work, with a husband too busy and important to help in any real way.

Abi's are normal problems, she tells herself. Not like what she has been through. But what did Rebecca say to Esther? "There are enough drama queens."

Maybe it is tiring to be the sensible one in the family. Like Rebecca. Like Abi. Always holding things together, while other people fell apart. She should have been there more for Abi. And for her grandmother and great-aunt, in their old age.

Had it been difficult for Esther? Being the less dazzling one in her relationship with Annie? Mim knows what that is like.

Robbie hadn't noticed her in her Audrey Hepburn dress. It struck her that Monday that he hadn't noticed her, full stop. Not really. There'd been that compliment on her article. The occasional interest in her writing. It wasn't a lot to go on. Perhaps, it really was a waste of time, like Frankie said. She texted her friend.

Shitty day at work. Fancy a drink afterwards?

But then, oddly, when she arrived at the Fortune of War, one of their favourite seafront pubs, she was confronted with the confusing sight of Frankie and Robbie chatting like old friends. And Frankie was soaking wet.

"What's up?" Mim said, but really she meant, What the fuck is going on here?

"Miriam," Robbie smiled. "Your flatmate's been getting into trouble."

"Some drunk idiots." Frankie couldn't meet her gaze.

"A passerby threw a beer can on to the beach," Robbie said. "And this one said, 'Aren't you going to pick that up?'"

"So he threw his next can all over me," Frankie finished.

This one. There was a familiarity to the way Robbie was speaking, a lightness to him that Mim hadn't noticed before. And they were completing each other's sentences.

"Anyway, we got talking and realised we had a friend in common," Robbie explained.

A friend, Mim thought. Well, that was better than colleague. She tried looking at Frankie through his eyes – beautiful, bold, even with pink hair and drenched in beer. Not sidling up to him and thinking of impressive things to say, but just completely herself. Fearless. Truthful. Wearing her beauty lightly.

And then without even checking with Mim first, without so much as a knowing glance, Frankie said, "We were just going for a drink, if you fancy joining us?"

It was one of those oddly warm March days, the sea glittering in front of them, after-work drinkers clutching pints or large glasses of Sauvignon Blanc.

"Why not?" Robbie smiled again in a way Mim hadn't seen before.

It struck her hard in the stomach: he was drawn to Frankie's dazzle, just like she was. Even standing there, drenched in beer, looking dishevelled and flustered, Frankie still drew Robbie's eyes to her like a magnet. That was the first time Mim felt jealous of Frankie. It was the first time she'd wished her away.

20

8th July 2012

Guilt gnaws at Mim – not, for once, related to Frankie, but about Abi. How quickly her sister's expression shifted to cover her disappointment when she realised that Mim had forgotten Evie's birthday.

Was her sister ever jealous of Mim's closeness to Frankie? Has Mim ever wished she'd lost Abi instead? No, of course not. And yet she can't help remembering the time Abi stayed with them in Brighton that spring. Mim had scoured the flat before her arrival, relocated the Hoover, bought some bleach.

"I don't know what's going on," Frankie said from the sofa as Mim aggressively vacuumed around her.

"You don't understand my sister – she'll notice if it's not spit-spot."

"Why have you turned into Mary Poppins?"

Mim switched off the machine and glared at her. "Mary Poppins could do all of this with magic."

"OK, OK," Frankie held her hands up in defeat. "It's just: it's your sister – not your mum. I think you're being weird about this."

Frankie didn't understand. She only had brothers and they all spoiled her rotten. No wonder she wasn't scared of anything. "You must promise not to leave us alone," Mim said. "She'll want to talk about how my life is going."

"And I'll just say you're in love with your married boss. It's fine."

Mim shot her a look.

"Divorced, I know. Like he kept saying the other night."

Robbie had mentioned his wife that night when they'd all gone for drinks. In fact, he'd opened up more than he'd ever done before.

"She's even taken the dog," he told them glumly, a few drinks in. "Can you believe it? Here," he said. "What do you think?" He showed them a picture of a baby-faced pug. "We thought we'd start with a dog, and if that turned out well, move to having a kid instead."

"Great plan," Frankie agreed, shooting a worried glance at Mim.

"Hmm," said Mim. She'd already done some snooping on social media and was well acquainted with Otis the pug, as well as the glowingly athletic beauty of Robbie's wife. Frida was strong and capable; she liked cold-water swimming and hiking. The dog would probably be happier with her.

"It's been so good to talk," Robbie said, at the end of the night, addressing Frankie.

It hadn't been an unmitigated disaster, Mim kept telling herself. Not if you ran it through a certain filter. They'd been drinking together outside of work, after all. After Robbie went home, she initiated a post-mortem over a bottle of tequila.

"So, what do you think?"

"I think he's still in love with his wife," Frankie said. "I think you don't know why she threw him out."

Mim knocked back a shot. "Thanks for the vote of confidence."

"For the honesty," Frankie said. "Thanks for the honesty."

She'd been candid, too, after Abi's stay. "Gosh, maybe you were right. She's a little…"

"Uptight?" offered Mim.

"Actually," Frankie said, "I was going to say she seems a little sad."

Mim was silent for a moment. She'd never seen it that way, but maybe Frankie was right. Her sister had been quiet, barely touching her wine over dinner. She'd put on a little weight, too, though, of course, Mim didn't mention that, putting it down to work pressures. True to her promise, Frankie hadn't left the sisters alone for a minute, filling every awkward silence with her bright chatter. It hadn't been until an hour or so before Abi's train was due to leave that she'd taken the opportunity for a quiet word with Mim, while Frankie was making tea.

"Ben proposed." She said it quickly, like ripping off a plaster.

"Oh." Mim stared at the floor and wished Frankie would come back. Had this been the thing she was dreading? She didn't hate Ben, whom Abi had been with forever – a lawyer, like her sister was. It wasn't that. But she thought, in that moment, of a holiday in Mexico years ago – long before Abi met Ben; long before adulthood – jumping off a pier hand-in-hand with her sister into the deep blue sea.

"I know you're not sure about him," Abi filled the silence between them.

"I never said that."

"You didn't have to." Her sister brushed some imaginary dust off her skirt. "But he's very reliable and kind. And he'll probably make partner in the next few years."

"Sexy," Mim said. It just slipped out. She knew it was the kind of thing that would have made Frankie laugh.

"Maybe I should be going." Abi got to her feet, looked around for her bag.

"I'm sorry," Mim said. "That was stupid." She'd ruined everything, as usual, and rushed to hug her sister but Abi remained as stiff as a board. "I just don't want you to be trapped."

"I love you," Abi said. "But you have a lot to learn."

Her sister wriggled out of the embrace and Mim experienced the same feeling she had when her grandmother gave her a little shove and said, "Darling, you're in my sun."

Was it any wonder she'd sunk into Frankie's warmth like a cold swimmer into a hot bath?

"Anyway," added Abi, shrugging on her coat, "we're all trapped by something."

After they said goodbye, Mim reached for the tequila bottle. "I need a shot."

"That bad?"

"She's getting married to Boring Ben."

"Shit." Frankie said. "I might need a shot too."

Mim poured both of them a generous measure. "To Boring Ben," said Frankie.   "To Boring Ben," Mim echoed cheerfully.

There was a rap at the door then. The front door of the flat led straight into the kitchen and as soon as Mim saw her sister's face she knew instinctively that Abi had heard her toast.

"I forgot my phone," she said, not looking at either of them.

She had been pregnant with Evie, of course, her bump clearly visible by the time of her wedding in May that year.

It's funny, Mim thinks now, the way Abi replied: We're all trapped by something. She has the urge to pick up the phone to her sister and tell her she was right, but of course now it's far too late.

21

May 1939

We needed to celebrate, and Mrs Cleverly at the boarding house was full of warnings about dens of iniquity and vice in Soho.

"So Soho it is," Annie told us cheerfully, as she and Dot squabbled for space in front of the mirror, painting their lips pillar-box red with a swift and enviable accuracy. ("Just down to practice," said Annie. "I'm expecting the knock of the callboy any minute.")

"Are you sure?" Rebecca said. "The Hammersmith Palais is meant to be nice."

"No, no," Dot said bossily. "We don't want nice tonight. We want fun. We want outrageous."

There was one place the landlady particularly warned us against. The Rainbow Roof. "It used to be called the Shim Sham Club," she told us. "They say it's London's miniature Harlem. They play American music all night – and boys dress as girls and girls dress as boys." She shivered dramatically.

"We need to go there," Annie had whispered at the time.

"I don't know," murmured Rebecca later, when the suggestion came up.

"Come on, it'll be swell, Becky," Dot insisted. No one ever called her Becky. "Look at us, togged to the bricks and free to do whatever we choose."

"What about the Café de Paris?" Rebecca said. "Didn't the Duke of Windsor used to dance there?"

"You know he's taken now, right?" Dot said. "An American, of course. A man of taste."

Rebecca shot her a look. "I promised our mother I'd look out for you all."

"She doesn't need to know." I found I couldn't bear to think of my parents.

"We shouldn't be spending our money on fripperies." Rebecca pointedly picked up a piece of darning, as if she was considering staying back at the boarding house, after all.

"Tonight," Annie said, scooping up Rebecca in a tango hold, causing her to drop her darning, "is all about fripperies."

In the end, Rebecca relented and we kissed Lili goodbye and set off into the night.

"I won't be able to sleep a wink until you're back," my little sister said crossly. "Esther, you must tell me everything tomorrow. It's not too late for you to change your mind, Rebecca."

"It is," she said firmly. "You're only fifteen. What would Ima say?"

"Fifteen. Twenty-nine. Forty-three. Seventy-two," I teased

Lili, double-kissing her goodbye. It was the old family joke. Something we always said on her birthday.

"When I'm twenty-nine, try and stop me coming with you," she retorted. "I want to know everything, Esther, remember."

We reached Piccadilly Circus just as the neon lights came on: huge letters advertising Wrigley's, Bovril and Guinness. Annie and Dot strutted ahead, past the theatres on Shaftesbury Avenue, their nipped in jackets showing off their slender dancers' figures.

Then we turned right into Wardour Street, where the sound of jazz music seeped up from Soho's basement clubs and every other building was a cinema. Men in trilbies pulled low on their heads ogled at my friends, while the hammy face of Charles Laughton in a top hat leered down at us from billboards advertising Hitchcock's Jamaica Inn. I hung back, still in my usual slacks. I tried to imagine my future here in London, but I found I couldn't picture it without my friends leading the way.

On the door at the Rainbow Roof, they claimed to be holding a bottle party for private guests – a way around the London licensing laws – but Annie and Dot swiftly talked our way on to the "guest list". Inside, it was sticky and crowded. There was a small elevated bandstand, lots of space for dancing and a bar that curved around the room.

"Fresh meat," enthused one of the patrons. She was wearing a gentleman's hat and monocle. Rebecca's grip on my arm tightened. "Don't worry, little girls," the woman laughed. "I don't bite."

Dot ordered a Sidecar and a Rusty Nail for us all to share, but then the band started to play "Jeepers Creepers" and she, Annie and, shortly after, Rebecca were whisked onto the dancefloor.

"Can I tell you something?" asked a mournful-looking older man. He wore a woman's hairwrap and, up close I realised, deep pink nail varnish.

"OK." I took a sip of the group-owned Sidecar and wondered what it was about my face that always made people want to tell me things.

"There's going to be a war."

I shrugged. Everyone knew that: there were a couple of soldiers dancing among us, even in this bohemian place.

"I mean any day now," he insisted. "And all of this will be gone."

I looked at him. "They'll shut the Rainbow Roof if there's a war?" Maybe I'd had more than my fair share of the communal drinks.

"No," he sighed. "I mean this world – this kind of freedom. It's what they want to destroy. Not just in Germany. Here too." He looked dewy-eyed. "I feel safe here, you see," he said. "I don't have to pretend."

Something shifted in me; something I couldn't give words to. His face wasn't so much mournful as kind, I reassessed. Knowing. He introduced himself as Ambrose and offered to buy me a drink. He worked in the costume department at the Phoenix, so we had plenty to chat about.

"I like your nail varnish," I told him.

"Dusky Rose." He twinkled his fingers at me.

"How did you know that you liked men?" I asked, emboldened by liquor. I knew gay men at the Tabarin but I'd never had the opportunity to talk frankly.

"I just always did." He patted my arm in an avuncular

way, dismissing me kindly as he was joined by a younger friend. "Don't worry," he said. "You'll find her one day."

"Who?" I blushed, peering into my Sidecar.

"You'll know," he said.

I spent too much of that night drinking, watching the slip of Annie's silvery dress moving through the crowded dancefloor: I never quite knew if I wanted to be her or the person she was dancing with.

"Esther," she said, catching her breath on a break between tunes, "why aren't you dancing?"

The problem was I'd never really learned how – I'd been around it all my life, of course. But at the Tabarin parties, when everyone took to the floor, I stayed in the shadows as much as I could, just watching. I told myself I was happy there.

"Dance with me," Annie got to her feet, proffered her arms.

I gazed at her, frozen.

"I can lead, no problem," she reassured me. "And everyone's dancing with everyone in here."

I glanced over at Rebecca on the other side of the dancefloor. She wouldn't like it, but did that matter here in London? Who was there to tell?

The few times I had danced before it had been with my father, or one of the more chivalrous men at the Tabarin who took pity on wallflowers. I was used to being steered by someone bigger and hairier than me, but when I stepped into Annie's arms it was strange, at first, to be guided by someone so light. Yet her lead was better than any of the men I'd danced with.

"Regardez publique." She grinned, tapping me briefly on

the chin. "Look up – not at your feet. And hold yourself together." She placed a light hand on my belly. "Then you'll be able to feel my lead better." After a few more bars, she praised me. "See, you can dance. You just haven't had the right teacher."

I laughed at the immodesty, but I realised, as I danced with Annie, that perhaps I hadn't been the only problem in those dances at the Tabarin. Maybe it had been my partners.

For the duration of that song, I felt as dazzling as the bright young things I'd read about in books – the shimmying silver of Annie's dress, our legs kicking up beneath us, a feeling of weightlessness, of flight. I felt visible for the first time in my life. That everyone in the room might be looking at us. Wanting to be us. There was power in this – the feeling that you could almost get away with anything. But the sensation, for me at least, was fleeting. The song was barely over before Annie was whipped away by her next partner.

I returned, breathless, to our table, where Rebecca was drinking a glass of water.

"I saw you dancing with Annie." My sister's tone of voice reminded me of the way she used to talk when she'd caught me doing something naughty. A little drizzle on my parade.

"Everyone's dancing with everyone here." I cast my eyes around the table for a napkin, or receipt. Something to jot down my thoughts. An idea had come to me while we were dancing, and I didn't want to let it go.

Rebecca shrugged, as if it didn't matter so very much to her, after all. Her cheeks looked flushed and happy. It hadn't escaped my notice that one partner, more than any other, had been hogging her attention. A handsome man in a naval uniform, a little older than us.

"If you squint, he looks like Jimmy Stewart," Rebecca told me as he made his way back from the bathroom to our table to reclaim her.

"Sure," I said, squinting hard.

She squeezed my hand. A rare show of affection before she got up to dance again. "I think we could have a good life here."

Left on my own, I started scribbling on any scraps of paper I could find. Not far from me, a couple of men, who were more traditionally dressed than the rest of us, stood stiffly with their drinks. Off-duty military men, I suspected, finding it hard to unwind.

I didn't pay them much attention until another pair of men, who were dancing very closely together, began to run their hands over each other's bodies: the older of them, slight and handsome, in a smoking jacket, the younger, tall and muscular, dressed in ballet tights like Nijinsky.

"Police!" one of the stiffs shouted, grabbing the older man by the lapels of his smoking jacket and yanking him away from his partner, who made a very Nijinsky-like dive for the door.

In the ensuing scuffle, with people diving under tables or towards exits, and more plain-clothed policemen scuttling like spiders out of the club's dark corners, Annie appeared by my side.

"Come on," she said. "I've heard there's a way out through the kitchen."

"What about the others?" My eyes scanned the room but I couldn't see my sister anywhere.

"They'll meet us at home."

"I don't want to leave without Rebecca," I insisted.

"Esther, come on." Annie's grip was tight on my hand.

Near us, a cop wrestled Ambrose to the floor. Another stamped down hard on his delicate varnished fingers.

"Pervert," the policeman spat.

He whimpered with pain, and I felt the violence as if it had been done to my own body. I wanted to scream at the men who were dismantling our night of harmless pleasures so cruelly. But, coward that I am, I didn't fight or shriek. I simply let Annie take my hand and pull me out of there. In the middle of that storm, she managed to keep her head. Her grip never faltered – she was so much stronger than she looked.

22

May 1939

The crunch of the policeman's boot on Ambrose's Dusky Rose fingers changed everything for me. I couldn't get it out of my head.

It was a long, winding journey on the number twenty-four bus back to Hampstead Heath, and I could feel the ache of the Rusty Nails at my temples. Annie dropped off on my shoulder almost as soon as the bus started moving. I sat staring out at the London night, watching revellers spilling out on to the streets, swaying with inebriation or clutching each other to stay steady.

I played the scene we'd just witnessed in my mind. I feel safe here, he'd said. But he hadn't been safe. In fact, London didn't feel much better than Paris, with violent policemen and soldiers congregating in the streets.

"I'm going to come back with you," I told Annie's dozing frame. "I don't think I belong here – I don't know if I belong anywhere, to be honest, but at least Paris is home. And you'd be there. For a bit longer."

She gave my hand a squeeze in response and I drifted off myself and only woke to find the conductor standing over us at the last stop. Outside, dawn was pinkening the sky. Annie stretched like a cat and hopped off the bus, kicking off her heels for the walk across the Heath.

"My feet are killing me," she sighed.

"Are you sure it's safe?" I glanced around. There were a few early-morning dog walkers and the odd solitary gentleman.

"Of course I'm not," she said cheerfully.

I followed her anyway; we began to climb. In Hampstead you're always either walking uphill or down. As dawn grew peachy in the sky, I stopped worrying so much. The vast expanse of wildness, where livestock grazed in those days, felt like miles away from the city.

It was only as we started to climb again that I realised we were going the wrong way – up Parliament Hill instead of heading west towards Golders Green. It wasn't something we discussed, but it felt, in that moment, the right thing to be doing: watching the sun rise over London for our last day in the city. At the top of the hill, we threw down our coats and sat on them, watching the skyline in silence.

"So, you're coming back to Paris?" Annie said.

"I thought you were asleep?"

"I do that with my ears open like a dog," she laughed. "Force of habit being the youngest – I don't want to miss out on anything good. Are you sure?" she checked, serious and still in a way she rarely was. "It might be dangerous. Particularly for us."

"It's dangerous here too. We saw that tonight. And you're

going back."

"It's different for me; I'll be travelling with the company."
She looked away from me then.

"The thing is" – I let my gaze wander too – "if there's
a war, if terrible things happen, they'll need writers to
document them. To remember." I thought of Ambrose again.
Perhaps, in truth, it was cowardice rather than bravery that
was driving me.

Annie squeezed my hand.

"I don't want a safe life," I insisted.

If I could go back now, I would shake that silly young girl
sitting on the damp grass of Parliament Hill and tell her to
stay in London, to get all of her family out of France. But I
had no idea of what was to come.

By the time we reached the boarding house, Mrs Cleverly
had packed up our things and left them for us to collect
in the front garden. We found Lili sitting among them
forlornly, clutching her camera.

I was too dazed to understand fully what was going on,
but I got the gist of it from Mrs Cleverly's reappearance for
an encore of her refrain about "dens of iniquity" and "nice
girls sticking to the curfew".

"I expected more from you," she told Rebecca, who was
the last of us to make it back, arriving just in time for the
scene in the front garden.

"Never mind," my sister said, a dreamy look on her face
I'd never seen before. "Everybody does."

"What've you been up to, Becky?" asked Dot over
breakfast, in a local café, carefully wrapping a scarf around
her own neck to cover a hickey or two.

"Just walking and talking," my sister said primly, adding

an extra sugar to her coffee.

"Et cetera, et cetera," teased Dot.

"There was no et cetera." Rebecca allowed herself a smile. "But we're going to meet again when he's next in London."

Annie shot me a look. I needed to talk to Rebecca about my change of heart.

"Shall we cover up the evidence?" she suggested to Dot, glancing at her neck. "You too, Lili," she added. "Let's leave them to it." The three of them disappeared to the bathroom.

"What's the matter?" asked Rebecca, her gaze finding mine.

"I want to go back to Paris," I said simply.

Rebecca stirred her coffee again, though the sugar must have long since dissolved. "We promised we'd stay," she said eventually. "They only gave us the money because they thought we would."

"I can't," I said. "I won't."

"Why?"

I hesitated. I didn't know how to explain about Ambrose and his broken fingers and the contents of my conversation with him. "Our parents," I said instead. "The Tabarin. My career. I have a story that's about to be published." The news sounded flat, even to me.

"Is it because of Annie? Because she'll be moving on soon." She sounded weary then. "And you know there's going to be a war?"

"That's what everyone keeps saying."

"Do you understand what it will mean for us?" I could feel her gaze boring into my face. "You've seen the Jewish families coming over from Germany."

"Surely we should be together? All of us."

There was a long silence. "The thing is, Esther," she said, "we're here because you wanted to make this trip. And now you're saying we should all go back again, because you want to." Her voice was so low and controlled I had a sense of the fury she was keeping in check. "If you go back, Lili will," she said slowly. "And if Lili does, I will."

That was just the way of it. It always was: Lili stitching us together.

"You could stay," I suggested. I spooned sugar into my empty cup and ground down the granules under the teaspoon. I couldn't look at her. "What about your new friend, Jimmy Stewart?"

"Don't." The warmth between us last night had iced over again.

"Rebecca," I said, seeing the others re-emerge from the loos. "Will you forgive me?" I was the kid sister, always, begging her to play with me, to overlook my faults.

"Forgiveness takes time," she said. "And he was more than a friend. Or he could have been."

In the Tabarin and in our family, Rebecca was the fixer, the mender, the reliable stalwart, the person who darned the petticoats of the dancing girls. But last night she'd had the chance to step out of the wings, to be the leading lady. The one under the spotlight.

"What's between us – that's more than friendship too." She glanced over at Annie and Dot tiptoeing self-consciously towards us. "Friends come and go – remember that, Esther – but I'll always be your sister. And you'll always be mine."

23

May – September 1939

There were a lot of emotions at the Tabarin, on our return.

"Oh, you're back." – Belle, with a tight smile on her lips.

"How did it go?" – Dédée, a wide grin on hers.

"How was De Basil?" – Sandrini, smiling like his wife.

"Did you get in?" – Antoine, pretending he wanted to hear they had.

"Tant de questions!" – Annie, covering her blushing face with her hands.

"We did it!" – Dot. "We're joining De Basil's Ballet Russe!"

And then a resulting melee of emotions, largely sadness dressed up as celebration, like a down-at-heel flapper with a mink coat around her shoulders and an expectant coupe in her hand.

Sandrini opened a magnum of champagne and everyone raised a glass to our star dancers – to the bright future they had ahead of them, to the places they'd go, the stages they'd dance on.

The noise drew my mother from the atelier, her arms full of costumes, her mouth full of needles. Her face was white: "What are you doing back? My girls."

"Ask Esther!" – Rebecca, also needles, as Annie tapped lightly on her glass.

"We could never forget you all," Annie raised her glass to the room, her eyes lingering on Antoine's handsome face.

But before De Basil's company reached Paris to pick up Annie and Dot, Germany invaded Poland, and France and Britain declared war.

Not long after that, a telegram arrived from the ballet director: his company would not be coming to Paris for the winter, after all. Annie and Dot would not be able to join them.

I heard most of this from Dédée, in an unusually sombre mood. "Annie has been very quiet since receiving the news," she told me. "She doesn't want to talk to anyone." She paused. "Though she might speak to you. Take this one." She stooped to pick up Cancan and passed her dog over to me.

The pup's warm body wriggling in my arms was a comfort. The door of Annie's dressing room, which was usually propped open, was closed. I knocked, softly at first.

"Please go away," Annie snapped. "I want to be toute seule."

"It's only me."

She opened the door just a crack, her lively face empty of expression in a way I'd never seen before.

"I brought Cancan." I held him out to her, and she took the dog into her arms and buried her face in his fur, thinking perhaps of her triumphant audition all those months before.

She had the telegram from De Basil laid out on her dressing table, and beside it another piece of paper. A ticket, I realised.

"My father sent me this." She touched it briefly. "I've no idea how my father got the money. He wants me to go back to Canada."

"And will you?" I tried not to hide my thrumming panic.

"I don't know. What do you think?"

"Don't ask me that." The thoughts in my head then were loud and insistent – what my return to Paris had cost me: my family's trust, Rebecca's warmth, my parents' approval.

There was a knock at the door. One of the callboys said: "Annie, you're on in ten."

Standing up, she stared at herself in the mirror. "What happens now?"

"You get dressed and go out and dance," I told her.

At the Tabarin, the show always went on.

"Le grand écart." She began to stretch, warming up her limbs. "The great gap. Between what I have and what I want." She picked up the ticket and ripped it into tiny pieces. "I don't want a safe life," she told me. "Isn't that what you said?"

Annie's dancing that night was extraordinary. Something seemed to shimmer through her – something you felt lucky to be in the room with. I watched Antoine's face from the wings and it seemed to lighten with approval.

As for me, the repetition of my own words back to me didn't feel good. It felt like an incantation. Or a curse. I don't want a safe life. Maybe Annie was the reason I didn't get out in time. Maybe I was the reason she didn't.

THE PARIS DANCER

24

Closing the first of Esther's exercise books, Mim's heart is still thrumming. She still has so many questions. And her mother hasn't helped her answer them. Maybe she needs to try someone else. On impulse, she pops up to Bibi's apartment and knocks on the door. She hasn't been there since the last visit, though she occasionally bumps into her and FeeFee in the hallway.

"Did Esther ever mention a dancer called Annie?" she blurts out when Bibi opens the door.

It feels safer to start with Annie, rather than Lili.

"By all means," Bibi grins, "come in."

"Did she?"

"What are you talking about?" Bibi holds on to FeeFee as Mim slips into the flat.

"I'm making my way through Esther's papers." Mim stoops to greet the dog, perhaps to avoid Bibi's piercing gaze. "A memoir, I think. She's writing about someone called

Annie? A dancer? I thought you might know something about it?" Everything is coming out as a question.

Bibi is silent for an uncomfortably long time. "Would you like a drink?" she asks in the end.

Mim shakes her head.

"Well, I would. Sit down, take a deep breath. You seem jangly today. You're making me nervous."

Mim obediently takes a seat. Bibi's right. She needs to calm down. It's not good for her to get excited. Any wild mood – even a good one – can lead to a crash. She sits cross-legged on one of Bibi's enormous pink armchairs, looking out at the sprawling river, the New York skyline, the speck that is the Statue of Liberty. She is feeling calmer when Bibi returns with a cup of tea for her and a martini for herself.

Bibi takes a sip of her drink. "The honest answer is: I don't know exactly what Esther was writing," she begins, "and, even if I was clearer on the details of it, I wouldn't want to share them. It was her story and she wanted you to read it. In fact, I think she specifically had you in mind as she wrote it."

"Why me?"

Bibi pauses, lowers a hand to FeeFee who is sitting at the foot of her chair. "She saw something of herself in you – and not just because you were both writers. I think she knew that you were finding things hard. Maybe it was her misguided attempt at helping."

"Misguided?" Mim takes a sip of tea but it is still too hot to drink. Esther's words, scribbled on a receipt, return to her: I love you, I beg you, I forgive you. What or who couldn't Esther forgive? And how much did she know of Mim's own experience?

151

"In my opinion, yes. And if you want my opinion – and maybe you don't – I'd take a break. I would close that book for a while." She sighs. "It's summer in New York. Go for picnics, go on dates, go dancing. Leave all this behind. It's hers – not yours. I agreed with Esther about many things. But not this particular project. All that looking back." She shivers, as if the idea appals her. "I know it was her way of working things out, but she's not here anymore – she lived her life her way. And you have to work things out in yours."

"I don't know." Mim hesitates. "It feels like it's been helping."

"How far into it are you?" Bibi checks.

"It's 1939, and she, Rebecca and" – Mim catches herself in time before saying Lili's name – "have just returned to Paris from London."

"1939." Bibi repeats back to her. She cocks her head to one side like a bird. "If you keep reading, you might learn something you can't unknow. Do you want that burden? With everything you're going through?"

Mim sighs. Maybe Bibi's right. Maybe she needs a break.

"I'd suggest closing the book. Putting it away," continues Bibi. "If you want to, you can take it with you when you go home and finish it with your family around you." She pauses. "Or you can build a bonfire in the garden and burn it. After all," she adds more lightly, "do you want to read about the war when New York is out there, waiting for you?" She gestures to the skyline through the window.

"Well," Mim says, blushing, "there is a guy."

Bibi claps her hands together. "Of course, there is. Cherchez le homme." She smiles. "Tell me all about him."

And so Mim begins to share the little she knows about

Lucky – how sweet he is, how keen, what a wonderful dancer. It's as easy as chatting to one of her friends. As easy, almost, as talking to Frankie.

"If he's suggested the first couple of dates, it's your turn to make the move," Bibi decides. "Why don't you ask him out? Take him to the ballet, then you can dress up, have a glass of champagne – or soda," she corrects herself. "And then..." The old woman winks theatrically.

Mim feels herself blushing to the roots of her hair. "I don't think we're at that stage yet."

"But you've thought about it?"

God, Mim thinks, she is like Frankie.

"What's the worst that could happen?"

She pauses. "It could all go wrong again."

A different type of person might tell her not to be so dramatic or self-indulgent but Bibi whips back. "Well, that's the risk we take, isn't it?"

Mim blinks.

"Why not send him a message now?"

"Like now now?"

"Yes, now. Don't wait – if you leave it too long, you'll talk yourself out of it."

"What should I say?" Mim can hear the panic in her voice.

"Well, you say, 'Hi...'" Bibi waits for his name.

"Lucky," Mim offers.

"Hi Lucky. Would you like to go to the ballet with me?"

"And that's it?"

"You can jazz it up if you insist, but I think that works." Bibi sips her drink. "Now send it."

Mim touches the screen. The message flies off.

"Shall we have another drink to celebrate?" Bibi gets unsteadily to her feet.

It's only later – much later, when she's alone again – that Mim realises that Bibi never answered her original question.

25

It's good to be out. Mim sits by the fountain at Lincoln Center, enjoying the cool spray of water on her back. She watches a couple nearby snuggle into each other as they're photographed. Bibi was right – she buried herself so deeply in Esther's story she forgot about the city outside her apartment.

On seeing Lucky across the square, Mim gets to her feet and takes a few steps towards him. He's dressed smartly for their date – white shirt, braces, wide grey trousers. His gait has a lilting bounce to it. Excitement, perhaps, at seeing her. Or maybe she's flattering herself.

Shyness overtakes her, as she reaches him. "Aren't you hot?" she asks, touching the sleeve of his shirt.

"I just wanted you to see I'd made an effort," he says bashfully. "You look nice too." He casts an eye over the black and white dress she'd bought with Frankie. "Very Audrey Hepburn."

"Thanks." Mim raises a hand to her hair, self-conscious. There was a time when she'd thought of giving the dress away. Now she's glad she still has it.

"Look," Lucky pulls a clean, white handkerchief from his pocket. "I even have a clean handkerchief this time. Not a ratty old tissue. My mum would be so proud."

Mim takes his arm. Mamita Bailarina, she nearly says, but stops herself in time. "I'm not going to cry tonight," she promises.

But the surge of music at the beginning of Giselle does something funny to the back of her throat. To be sitting in the David H. Koch Theater – a glorious place, with five rings of balconies, a gold-panelled ceiling – with a kind man by her side, feels like being lifted out of her ordinary life and dropped into a film. She's pleased to have found a Paris Opéra Ballet performance, with Aurélie Dupont dancing Giselle.

She hasn't seen any ballet since a family trip to The Nutcracker when she and Abi were just girls in party dresses. As Lucky predicted, the music moves her almost to tears. Just an itch at the back of her throat, a prickle behind her eyes, but he puts his warm hand over hers, and it stays there for most of the performance.

"I mean, Dupont was good," says Lucky afterwards, over tiramisu at Cafe Fiorello. "But do you reckon she can do the 'Macarena'?"

"Not as well as you, I'm sure," Mim tells him. The restaurant is a soothingly old-fashioned place with wood panelling, soft lighting and Italian waiters who pay precisely the right amount of attention to you. "I imagine ballet is incredibly painful," she adds, digging her spoon into the pudding and pausing to take a bite. "But they make it look so light and effortless."

"Why were you so keen to see Giselle?" Lucky's gaze lingers on Mim's for a moment.

"I read something about the mad scene that interested me." She swallows. "That just before she dies, Giselle mimes to Albrecht, 'I,' 'you,' but she doesn't finish, so you never know what the third word is. Does she mean 'I love you' or 'I beg you,' or even 'I forgive you'? That's the hardest thing, isn't it? Forgiveness. Letting go."

"I suppose she forgives him in the second act, at least." Lucky picks up a spoon. "But are we talking about Giselle, or something else?"

Mim's mouth is dry all of a sudden. She pushes the bowl over to Lucky. "I forgot my niece's birthday," she says at last. "She's only two, but it just fell from my mind." She thinks, then, of Lili, the family joke that had originated on her second birthday. "I've just been preoccupied," she adds. "For so long."

"Don't be so hard on yourself," he says. "You could send her a present from New York – I'll help you pick something, if you'd like?"

"Do you have siblings?" Mim asks.

He shakes his head. "It was always just my mum and me – I think that's why we're so close."

"What about your dad? Are they still together?"

"They were never together, exactly. Both dancers. Ships that passed in the night. I barely see him."

"What kind of dance does your mum do?"

"The Argentine tango – she grew up there, but she moved to the UK before I came along." He pushes the bowl back to Mim.

"Did you she want you to teach tango too?"

"No. She was happy for me to go my own way. Find my own dance."

Mim thinks of her childhood, how Abi is plaited into almost every memory. Even the difficult ones. She takes another spoonful. "Was it lonely?"

He shrugs. "Not really. There were always other worlds. Black and white movies. Fred and Ginger. Dancing." "History Club?"

"Of course." He grins. "But maybe dance has always been how I've connected with people. Copying routines from the telly. Though trying to run up a wall is something you only do once." He rubs his elbows, as if remembering the bruises. "Or attempting the splits as you jump down a staircase."

"Ouch," laughs Mim. "Maybe you're right," she agrees, looping back. "Maybe I can be too hard on myself."

"Perhaps there are just times when you have to allow yourself to be between things," Lucky says. "Make a den and watch old movies. Or explore New York with an incredibly witty Lindy hop dancer who thinks you're pretty swell." "Swell," she laughs. "The bee's knees."

"The cat's pyjamas."

"The dog's bollocks," Mim giggles. "Thanks for cheering me up," she adds. "I was feeling shit about it." She sighs. "I haven't always appreciated my sister."

A memory bubbles up suddenly. Abi's white face at her flat that night –arriving before her mother, before anyone. Leaving her newborn to be by Mim's side. Speeding from London to Brighton. And Abi hated speeding. Her sister, with her pyjamas on under her trenchcoat, her hair plaited for bed, taking Mim into her arms, even though she was dry and Mim's hair was still dripping wet; her sister, saying over and over, "Darling girl, you poor darling girl." Forgiving her instantly, even as Mim could never forgive herself.

"Can I tell you something?" Lucky stops for a moment, the last spoon of tiramisu still hovering in the air. "It's not too late to change."

"Change what?" Mim returns to the bustling restaurant, smells the coffee-sweetness of the pudding.

"The steps, I suppose." He offers the spoon to her and she takes it. "The choreography."

And it's not a planned move. It's not even something she thinks about before doing it, but, with the spoon still in her hand, Mim leans forward and kisses Lucky.

26

14th July 2012

Mim wakes the next morning to her phone ringing. It's Lucky. She can tell he's smiling as she answers. "Sorry, I couldn't wait," he laughs.

In the event, it had been quite a 1940s night. All Casablancan restraint and good behaviour. Not the kiss so much, but their conduct afterwards. He walked her to the 66th Street subway and they kissed again. A lovely, swooning summer-in-the-city kiss, until they had to peel their sticky limbs from each other.

She has never been involved with someone so straightforward. She's used to the push and pull of love, of wondering where they were and the fluttering fear of losing something that hadn't been given to her properly yet. She catches a glimpse of herself in the mirror as she gets out of bed. She's beaming.

"What are you up to today?" she asks.

"Not much. I wondered if you wanted to do not much

with me?"

Mim glances over at Esther's desk, quietly resentful. The book is still shut away in the drawer. "Sounds good." She grins again at her reflection and dances a couple of gleeful steps at herself.

He offers to meet her on Brooklyn Bridge, and because he's being so sweet, she agrees, doesn't mention her problem with bridges – one of the things she used to avoid: the proximity to all that water, that vertiginous emergency-exit feeling. But today the sensation is quieter, the loud, rattling thoughts in her head are gentler too. She's come to recognise them: there's the voice that resembles Frankie's; then the one that always sounds worried, which must derive from her mother's; and another she calls The Teacher, who's always trying to organise her; and the small frightened child who longs for things she can't have.

How do other people manage it, she wonders, watching as New Yorkers stride over the East River towards Manhattan? How do they cope with the pain of being alive? Or is it like dancing – is it just a matter of hiding the effort of it?

She keeps her eye fixed on the metallic gleam of the skyscrapers in the sun and not the water below her. When she catches sight of Lucky, there's the usual flutter when she first sees him, but something else – a kind of peace she's not used to.

They walk towards Manhattan, their arms around each other. And there's only a moment, when her eyes drop to the river for a second, that she shivers, unsure if it's because of the proximity of the water or a cyclist, casting a shadow over them, like a ghost on the move.

Drifting through the day, they slowly make their way

up through Manhattan, stopping to admire vintage knickknacks in the East Village and kissing in the shade in Central Park.

"We mustn't forget our table at Swing 46 tonight," Lucky checks his phone. "It's only seven, so we've got a couple of hours."

"I don't think I can leave this bench – let alone dance." Mim stretches out her tired legs. They've tanned a little in the sun.

"I'm guessing, from what you said last night, that ballet isn't the dance for you," Lucky checks.

"It looks too much like hard work," she laughs, correcting herself. "No, I mean it's beautiful – you can't help but admire it, but I can't see myself in a tutu." She glances over to a bronze statue of Shakespeare, around which a few people have started to drop their belongings – their coats and bags. Others perch on nearby benches to change their shoes.

Music begins to play through loudspeakers and a woman in a flowery dress and a short man in a fedora approach each other wordlessly and start to dance. It's a mournful song that sounds familiar to Mim, though she's not sure where she's heard it before. She watches as a woman in a strappy black dress traces a pattern with her feet through a sprinkling of talcum powder on the hexagonal paving stones.

Her shoes, Mim realises, are just like the pair in Esther's drawer – silver and strappy. Maybe they were tango shoes, she thinks. But Annie was a ballet dancer – and Esther herself had never worn heels, as far as Mim could remember.

She watches the tango dancers, mesmerised. At one point, Lucky asks her if she wants to have a go, but she shakes her head, happy to linger as a spectator. They're almost late for their booking at Swing 46 – a dark jazz club in the Theater District with tables arranged around a central dancefloor.

"Do you fancy joining the class?" Lucky asks once they're at their table.

She nods and follows him to where a tall, jolly man in a Zoot suit, hat and brogues is leading diners through some simple moves. It's much more relaxed than the waltz, more goofy than the salsa. She can see why it's Lucky's dance – it has a boyish bounce to it, an endearing playfulness. But she finds herself thinking of the tango.

"The music really moved me," she tells Lucky over supper.

"It was written by immigrants to Argentina," he says. "They came from Europe to build the railways. Young men mainly – they were missing their families."

"Dancing in bordellos?" Mim teases.

"Not just that," he says, suddenly serious. "It's about longing. They say it's the only dance in the world that doesn't express joy."

"Maybe that's why it speaks to me," she says, only half-joking.

"We could take a trip tomorrow." Lucky reaches out to take her hand. "Brighton Beach or Coney Island, perhaps?"

"I don't know." Mim glances away from him to the dancefloor. "I'd like to try the tango – could we do that instead?"

He takes her hand and lifts it to his lips. "Of course, Mimacita Bailarina,"

Maybe it's the mention of Brighton Beach that's responsible, causing something to sour in her mood. "I'm not your mum," she says. The words just slip out.

"Did I mention I call her that?" He releases her hand, blushing. "That's not very cool."

It's Mim's turn to pinken now, remembering how she knows the nickname.

She is saved by a woman in a canary yellow dress, appearing at their table to ask Lucky to dance.

He turns her down, with his lovely dimpled smile. "I'm here with my friend."

"It's OK," Mim says. "Go on – I'd like to watch you."

And so Lucky follows the woman onto the dancefloor. Observing him with a more experienced dancer, Mim can see how good he is. There's a gorgeous fluidity to the way he moves. A playfulness that's not flirty or sleazy, just joyful. It looks like she's got away with the phone thing. But she promises herself, while she watches him, there will be no more snooping. No more creepy behaviour. Not this time.

When Lucky returns, he smiles apologetically. "I'm sorry," he says, after taking a sip of water. "I can't get it out of my head. I don't remember telling you about my mum's nickname."

Mim takes a breath. Maybe she can put this right. "I saw it on your phone," she begins.

"Saw it?" he checks.

She feels her face getting hotter. "I'm sorry. I picked it up, at the waltz lesson. I just wanted to check you didn't have a wife."

"Why would I have a wife?"

"Well, it's not impossible," she snaps, on the back foot. "I had a thing – with someone who was... taken, before. I just wanted to make sure."

She could tell him, she thinks. Now might be the right time. I had a friend... she tries the words out in her head. He's waiting. His face sweet face looks hurt, let down.

"I'm sorry," Mim says instead. "I'm not really a snoop – that's not who I am."

I beg you, she thinks. But she can't beg. She's too proud.

He takes his glasses off, cleans them and puts them on again.

"I'm sorry," Mim tries again. "I really am. I have trust issues."

Lucky nods. "Maybe we should call it a night."

"I said I'm sorry," Mim repeats petulantly, once they're out of the club, saying goodbye in the street.

"I know," he says. "Just give me a little time. Forgiveness–"

"Don't talk to me about forgiveness." Mim glares at him, aware of a couple getting out of a cab nearby. She's in a beautiful blue frock with layers of petticoats; their night is just beginning. "I don't expect you to understand what I've been through," she adds furiously. "I don't expect anyone to." Her pain is an ocean, threatening to spill out of her, to drown everything good.

He looks hurt now. Properly hurt. "Will you let me know when you get home?" He kisses her brusquely on the cheek and walks away; all the bounce is gone from his step.

What surprises Mim, she thinks on the subway, is how familiar it feels – the knowledge that she's disappointed Lucky. It is what she does; it's the one thing she's good at. The tears start on the subway and the voices return – all of them, clamouring for her attention. They chat in her head all the way back on the walk from the subway. Her mother's voice fretting, the frightened child whimpering,

Frankie disappointed – telling her how nice Lucky was.

I know he was nice, she points out. That's why I went out with him.

You don't have history of going out with nice guys, her friend says primly. That's all I'm saying.

Had Robbie been awful? Mim wonders now. A bit, but he never misled her – his lack of interest was always pretty clear, in retrospect. Just as his attraction to Frankie was never hidden.

She remembers that walk along the beach so clearly – a daily ritual after work, when they weren't out drinking, for venting the day's frustrations to each other. Frankie, usually full of complaints about her bitchy editor, was quiet that day, picking up pebbles and holding them in her palm like worry beads – occasionally plopping one into the water as they headed towards the pier.

"What's up?" Mim checked.

Frankie dropped another stone into the sea. "I'm going to tell you something and you have to promise not to get mad?"

"OK." Mim felt her heart flutter in anticipation.

"Your boss got in touch with me today, through Facebook, and asked me out." Frankie's glance landed on Mim's face and then shifted away again.

"Greg?" Mim asked, stupidly. "That's weird."

Greg was the editor of the paper – a quiet, serious man, whose desk was decorated with framed photographs of his beloved granddaughter.

"Not Greg, no." Frankie paused. "Robbie-I-said-no-of-course." The words came out like that, crammed into each other.

Robbie. Of course. The features editor. The boss Frankie had met: that made far more of sense. Her brain was scrambling everything.

"Oh. Robbie," Mim says, her mind spooling back to standing next to him on her smoking break earlier that day, prattling away as usual, about how fun it had been going for drinks with him and Frankie. Even though it hadn't been fun at all; even though she had spent the evening feeling like someone trying to hold a goldfish in her hand; that the harder she tried to grasp it, the more it was guaranteed to slip away. Had he sent the Facebook message to Frankie by then? Had he been thinking about her?

"I wouldn't go there," Frankie said. "And I don't like him in that way – you know I've got something going on with Paul at the tattoo parlour. I just thought you should know."

"Oh," said Mim. "Thank you for telling me." Her voice sounded overly formal. She found she couldn't look at Frankie. Her gaze turned out to sea instead, landing on the burned-out skeleton of the West Pier. The feeling was as if someone had inserted a hand inside her, grabbed a handful of her guts and twisted them.

"It's a shitter," Frankie kept talking, even though Mim wished she wouldn't. Even though Mim wished, for only the second time in her life, that Frankie would just go away. "But I've never thought he was right for you."

"I'm absolutely fine." It was still that funny, formal voice answering for her. "It's really not a big deal." But it felt like a part of her was splitting off from herself. "It's fine to be mad."

"I'm not mad." What she really, really wanted to do was to howl into a pillow, or hit something. Or someone. "I just need to get drunk."

"OK, whatever you want." Frankie took her arm and they made their way to the Northern Lights and Mim did indeed get very drunk and went home with one of the regulars there – a skater guy with peroxide blonde hair – but she didn't know, thinking about it the next day, whether she was trying to escape from thoughts of Robbie. Or to have a break from Frankie.

Back in Esther's apartment, she sinks to the floor. It's been a while since she's been here, but the despair is always waiting for her like an armchair she can crawl into. She doesn't deserve to be happy, doesn't deserve anything good. The feeling is back, clogging up in her: the need to cry and cry. It's so easy to give in to it.

She's making such a noise that she doesn't hear the knock at first. Then there's Bibi's voice coming through the other side of the door. "Miriam, are you OK?"

Mim pulls herself reluctantly to her feet and opens the door. "I'm fine." She's sure she doesn't look it, but maybe Bibi will take the hint and leave her alone.

"Do you want to talk about it?" Bibi is in her slippers. She has FeeFee in her arms. "You could just come and sit with us?" she checks. "Maybe a cup of tea?"

In her flat, FeeFee lies across Mim like a tiny blanket, occasionally glancing up at her mournfully.

"Dogs always know," Bibi says.

Mim knots her hand in the animal's fur. She can feel her heart rate easing back to normal, the panicky sensation ebbing away.

"I know about your friend," Bibi says, after a few moments of silence. "The one who died. Esther told me.

How awful to lose someone so important."

Mim finds she doesn't know what to say, so she doesn't say anything. She misses Esther in that moment, misses the feeling of being seen and loved by someone who knew her as a child.

"I'm sure it's hard to start again," Bibi continues, "to make new friends."

"I went on a date with Lucky," Mim says at last. "And I was horrible to him."

"Well, he might forgive you." Bibi pauses. "But perhaps it's harder to forgive yourself."

"You don't know what I've done." Mim pushes FeeFee's fur the wrong way and then smooths it back again. She knows, even though she doesn't say it aloud, that she'll return to Esther's story that night. It might upset her, but she is upset already.

"Maybe it's not as bad as you think?"

"But what if it is?" That's what it always comes back to. Mim had hoped to leave herself behind. To start again. But perhaps that just isn't possible. She sighs, exhausted with herself. "What if I don't deserve to be forgiven?"

27

May 1939 – June 1940

I don't think Ima ever forgave me for bringing my sisters back into France. Her punishment was brutal. She stormed into our bedroom and rained slaps down on me. Sudden, stinging, relentless. I fell to the floor, too shocked to fight her off. In the end, Lili and Rebecca pulled her away, Lili crying on my behalf. The spell of her fury broken, our mother began to weep too – hot, angry tears.

"You have put your sisters in danger," she said. "Bringing them back here. For your own vanity."

She never actually said the words, "I can never forgive you," but something between us broke that day and I don't think it ever fully repaired.

"Why did you tell her?" I turned on Rebecca furiously, after she'd left, my face still flushed from where Ima had struck it. "How could you?"

"It was me," Lili said quietly. "I told her about your story – I was proud of you."

"Oh," I said.

Rebecca turned away wordlessly. There was everything in that silence between the three of us: the ancient scar tissue between Rebecca and me. Lili's honesty. Her courage. My did it, Ima. I couldn't be angry with her the way I could at Rebecca. Even if I knew that wasn't fair.

If this is my final confession – and maybe it is – this was the first of my major crimes. My mother was right: I put my sisters in danger. If we'd stayed in London, everything might have been different. Perhaps that's why it hurts to return to the UK – the memory of our brief time there never fades. My other minor thefts and betrayals pale in comparison. Far worse than a dropped plate or stitch, it is a mistake I can never undo.

Papa wasn't in the apartment to witness my beating, but he spoke to me later as we walked through Luxembourg Garden. The city around us had become a shifting, panicking place – the start of what they called the Drôle de guerre – the phoney war. Refugees arrived, clutching suitcases to their sides, holding the hands of their children tightly. Their faces were pale, unsmiling, but, sometimes, on seeing a woman with immaculately painted lips, a man with slender pianist's fingers, you'd be reminded of how thin the line was between their fate and ours. But still I thought – like they did – that Paris would be a place of safety. It was impossible to imagine the worst as I walked with my father, watching children pushing their little sailboats on the Grand Bassin duckpond. We didn't know then that it was simply a matter of time.

"You have to be patient with your mother," he said. "She had a difficult time, in the pogrom." He always spoke slowly and softly, but I could tell that whatever he was talking about that day caused him some pain.

"So did you." I picked up a pebble and threw it into the water.

"But I'm a man." He joined me, looking out over the pond. "There is a certain difficulty in being a beautiful woman. Or any woman," he corrected himself hastily.

It was true, life was hard for women. Even in France, my family's adopted home, we couldn't vote or open our own bank accounts. The state did its best to limit our lives, our choices. Still, I didn't know what my father meant.

"There was a group of men around her," he said quietly. "I think I got there in time. Before there was any real harm done." His voice faded away. "But I don't know."

A surge of nausea passed through me. I was old enough by then to have a sense of what he was talking about. But I couldn't bear to ask more. Something shifted, though: it was like looking at my mother from a new angle: her violent rages, her inability to sit still, her fiercely protective streak. She suddenly made more sense to me.

"That's why it's so important to her to try and keep her daughters safe," my father continued after a few moments of silence. "I just wanted you to understand."

Not long after that, our dreamy pacifist father joined the French Foreign Legion. Determined to protect those he loved and to serve the country that had offered his family a safe place to start again. He touched our cheeks with his callused carpenter's hands as he said goodbye, as if trying to commit our faces to memory.

He was far too old to be fighting, I was sure of it, but mine was a child's perspective. He was only in his early forties and there he remained in aspic. Strange to think that as I write this I am decades older than him. That he is just as he was that day. Handsome in his belted greatcoat, which was rough against our cheeks as we hugged him. A stubby carpenter's pencil, no doubt, somewhere on his person. He never reprimanded me for my return to Paris. He only asked once why I'd come back.

"I need to be in Paris to write," I'd said simply.

He nodded, didn't question me further. He never asked me, not even wordlessly, as my mother sometimes did, why I wasn't more like Rebecca or Lili. He just accepted me as I was. I am grateful to him for that and so much more.

When my story was published, he was the only family member I shared it with. Lili was still feeling so guilty – and I didn't dare show Ima or Rebecca. He squeezed my hand. "Well done," he said. "I'm glad you've found your boîte à couture."

I asked what he meant.

"Somewhere beautiful to store your feelings," he replied.

It was a strange thing to see my name in print. Strange, too, when I showed Annie, who had repeatedly asked if the story was out yet. I left it on her dressing table with a note.

"It's about me," she said, when I felt brave enough to return.

I nodded, joining her by the dressing table. "Do you mind?"

She gave me a quick smile in the mirror. "Of course not. You know how I feel about the limelight." She turned the page back to the story's opening, ran a finger under my name. "But, of course, it's not about me, really," she added. "The ambition, the journey, everything about her mother

– it's about you."

She was right. Exploring her mother's madness was a way of looking at something much closer to home. I don't know what Annie's mother was like. The woman in the story. The woman in the asylum, whom the dancer will never escape, no matter how far she travels, whose memory will return every time she dances Giselle: that woman was my mother, whose quick step and ready slaps, furious glances and wistful singing voice will be with me forever. Buried deep in my boîte à couture, as soft and as sharp as a pincushion.

She and my father said their goodbyes in private, leaving my mother red-eyed and distracted.

"You'll look after her, won't you?" Papa said to Rebecca and me before he left.

"Of course, Papa," my sister promised dutifully, but I felt his meaningful gaze on my face, sensed that I was the only one he'd trusted with the story of what had happened in the pogrom.

Lili crawled into Ima's bed that night, knowing our mother would benefit from a warm body next to her. I longed for the same physical closeness but I didn't know how to offer it. My body was a stranger to me then.

With wartime, the neon lights of Pigalle and the rest of Paris were turned off. We stumbled around in the dark – the city's mellow amber streetlights were dimmed, with white paint splashed on trees and kerbstones to make it easier for us to navigate, for all the good it did. Private cars were requisitioned and the few remaining in the city had to mask their headlights. The City of Light went dark.

Sandrini panicked at first, like the rest of Paris, and closed the Tabarin, and for a time our beloved theatre became an artists' canteen. The male performers were drafted out. The female artists dispersed like the sycamore leaves fluttering down from the trees on the Champs-Élysées that autumn. Some joined Sandrini, who was commissioned by Léon Volterra to stage a show at the Lido, known at that time for the nautical spectacles in its large indoor pool.

Others found their way however they could. I caught sight of Belle one day outside Maxim's, a new fox fur slung around her neck. She was on the arm of an older, whiskery gentleman – a familiar face from one of the seats near the orchestra at the Tabarin. She smiled wanly, but I looked away: to make conversation would have felt like disloyalty to Annie.

On a happier occasion, while catching up with Annie and Dot over a vin rouge, we spotted Gisy snuggled up in the corner of the bistro next to Gilbert Doukan, the Jewish doctor at the Tabarin, whom she'd admired from afar when he helped Belle.

"It looks like he's making her better," I joked.

Annie was quiet. No one had seen Antoine for a while. We assumed he'd signed up like the other boys we knew. Annie carried his number around with her in her pocket, but she was too proud to dial it.

"It might be easier to leave," I told her when she remained silent. "Without complications."

No one knew whether to stay or go. Families were criss-crossing the country in a panic. Dot's family begged her to return to the States. As far as I know Annie hadn't told her father about the fate of the ticket he'd sent.

Meanwhile, my family and I huddled at home, sheltering under the sturdy kitchen table our father had made, when the Germans rained down bombs on the suburbs, hitting the Citroën factory and killing hundreds.

My mother and Rebecca helped out at the Lido, where Sandrini was working, but the theatre had its own workrooms and midinettes. They took on private customers, sewing and darning until their fingers were sore and their eyes ached. I did what I could to support them but I felt my uselessness weigh heavily on me. I looked for work on magazines, but some publications were closing and others became circumspect about employing Jewish writers. The France of my youth was changing.

We were all in limbo, waiting for something to happen. And then, of course, after a long, cold winter, something did. In May 1940, the Battle of France proved the Maginot Line less impenetrable than we all imagined.

Everyone had assured each other that the fortifications built along the French border with Germany would hold. I pictured the Maginot Line like a monster baring its incisors at the enemy, but, when it came down to it, its teeth and claws weren't sharp enough for the German Panzers. The French army began to retreat, and in Paris, too, everyone's mind turned to flight.

People began to flee, grabbing whatever they could – shoving belongings or elderly relatives into cars or wheelbarrrows, strapping mattresses to the roofs of vehicles. Whole families crammed in, and pets too. Others killed their animals or let them run wild in the streets. The iron shutters of shops clattered down; the city was protecting itself. My mother blacked out our windows. It had been weeks since we'd heard from my father.

"If we go, he won't know where to find us," she said.

"We could leave a letter," I said. "A message with our neighbours."

She shook her head. "We stay," she said simply. "We stay and we wait for him."

To her credit, she didn't remind me, once again, of how my sisters could be safely in London, but I could feel her bitterness – and Rebecca's – curdling beneath everything. Lili, who had that photographer's knack for living in the present, for working with whatever was in front of her, was the only one who didn't hold a grudge.

Maybe Rebecca had more reason to. One evening, while searching for a book I'd lost in our shared bedroom, I opened a drawer to find a piece of embroidery – something she'd kept hidden from my eyes. A tiny sampler stitched with delicate blue flowers, the words "forget-me-not". I thought of a handsome man who looked like Jimmy Stewart. If you squinted. I tried to remember the last time I'd heard my sister laugh.

Rebecca caught me with her precious item in my hands and snatched it back.

"Was it worth it?" she snapped. "Just to see your name in print?"

"Rebecca," I began, but I didn't know what would come next. "I don't think I'll have children," I said in the end, surprising myself as much as her.

"What does that have to do with anything?" She placed her treasure back in the drawer and shut it firmly.

I couldn't explain, but even then it was something I knew about myself. There would be no handsome naval officers for me, no marriage, no offspring. Writing was the only way I had to ensure anything of me lived on.

Annie and Dot came to say goodbye – they'd decided to leave the city on foot before the Germans arrived. They had a vague contact – a friend of a friend with a house in the countryside. It was impossible to get out by train – the gates of the stations had been closed, the military called in to deal with the desperate hordes.

"Come," Annie said.

But I couldn't let my family down. Not again. I tried to commit everything to memory as I looked at her face for the last time.

28

Mim reaches for her phone. It's been a few days since that bad night out with Lucky and she's heard nothing from him since. She's spent some time with Esther's books, but also catching up with other things in her life. She found a musical jewellery box for Evie, with a ballerina that popped up and twirled to the sound of "La vie en rose". She also wrote Abi a note, apologising for the lateness of the gift. It wasn't going to put everything right, but it was a start.

Sometimes she turns her phone over in her hands. She misses Lucky. When she replays the worst moments of the evening – which she does, often – she feels a hot flush of shame. In the end, she taps out the message quickly, without giving herself too much time to think.

I'm really sorry – do you think we could talk things through? I loved the tango music in the park. Can we try that next? X

She paces around the apartment waiting for his response.

At one point, the three dots begin to dance across the screen, but then they stop again and no answer comes through.

Has she always been so crap with men? She didn't know how to behave around Robbie after she learned that he'd asked Frankie out. At work, she sensed a new eagerness in him; like a dog being ignored, he kept coming over to her desk for no real reason. Finally, on a smoking break, he blurted, "Did Frankie mention me?"

Mim couldn't look at him. "She said you asked her out."

"I don't think she likes me," he said, petulant like a schoolboy. "Is it because of you?"

"Me?" she asked, too shrilly.

"Because I'm your boss."

She wanted to take his cold hand and place it under her shirt, to say, "Do you feel my heart? It is beating for you."

"Maybe it's not appropriate." He said the words quickly, guiltily. He glanced towards the newsroom. "You won't say anything, will you?"

"It's because I like you."

Telling the truth, in the end, was remarkably straightforward. Freeing. She dropped the cigarette and ground it out with her heel.

"And Frankie's my best friend. She wouldn't do that to me."

In films, people make a kind of sputtering noise at such news, but Robbie's exhalation was quieter.

"Just so you know, I wouldn't say anything to anyone. Ever."

They were standing very close together by that point, with Mim's back to the building. It was the first time she felt any kind of power over him. And it was delicious to watch him shift and stir, running a hand down his forearm as he considered her proposal.

Mim wraps her arms around herself. She should have stopped there, but she didn't. She ignored all the warning signs and ploughed ahead.

She checks her phone. A text from Lucky.

Sure, we can try the tango.

No kiss. She is still on probation. That's fair enough. Maybe this time she can get it right. Maybe she's been given another chance.

A couple of days later, Mim arrives at the brownstone in Brooklyn where the tango class is taking place. Lucky isn't there yet. She waits for a few minutes out in the quiet street. The heat has made everyone sluggish. New Yorkers, usually so brisk and purposeful, amble by with their weekend lattes, dogs panting heavily at the end of their leads. There's the gentle reek of rubbish rotting somewhere nearby – a ubiquitous stench on hot days. Sweat begins to prickle at the back of Mim's neck.

She waits until music, similar to the mournful tune she heard in the park, drifts down the stairs from the first floor. The song is in Spanish, so Mim doesn't know what the lyrics are saying but she imagines them to be laments about lost jobs, cars, houses, people.

Still no Lucky. Maybe it's the music calling her, but Mim finds herself making her way upstairs to the class. Just to see. She can always wait for him up there.

It takes her a moment to adjust to the low light after the searing sunshine outside. Most people are sitting on chairs at the edges of the room, changing into their dance shoes. Mim peers into her bag to check her own – or Esther's, or

Annie's. They're still there. Maybe it wouldn't hurt to try them on. She's pleased at the sight of her tanned feet under the glimmering silver straps.

"Nice shoes," says the woman sitting next to her. Mim's age, perhaps, or a little older – petite, Latina, her hair swept neatly into low chignon. "Are they vintage?"

Mim nods. "It's the first time I've worn them."

"They fit you perfectly."

"All the gear and no idea." Mim smiles. "Is that something you say here?"

"I get the sentiment." The woman smiles warmly. "And don't worry, Eduardo and Felipe are lovely. I've only done a few classes myself. I'm Chita, by the way. Like Chita Rivera. I have my parents to blame for that." She rolls her eyes as if it's a line she's used many times before.

Almost on cue, the teachers call their students to form a circle around them. Eduardo is taller than his partner, with a moustache and beard and a long, mournful face. Felipe is short and assertive, alert like a bull, with the kind of charisma that demands the room's attention.

"I know what newcomers might be thinking," he smiles. "Two guys! In fact, tango began its life with men dancing together, but we'll tell you a little more about that in a bit. They say it takes two to tango, but actually you need three things: a leader, a follower and the music. Now who here has seen the Argentine tango performed on television?"

Every one of the eleven students puts their hand up.

"Forget that," Felipe laughs. "Forget everything you know about tango. That image you see on the screen with people kicking up their legs, roses in their teeth – it's just for the movies. It takes a long time to learn how to perform like that and it's not what the dance is about." He pauses. "Tango isn't so much about passion as it is about sorrow."

At his words, Mim feels a small crackle of recognition.

"It's thought that the word 'tango' comes from the Bantu African word for drum, 'tambor'. Enslaved people were among the first to dance candombe, one of the forebears of tango, in South America. From what we know about the movement then, it was sensuous and trancelike, which you'll find is still true of tango today. Dancers moved on their own at first, and later in couples and groups. But there was a lot of European influence on tango's development, too – a large number of young men had arrived from Spain, Italy and Germany to build Argentina's railways. And they were homesick, congregating in bars, gambling houses and brothels, where they listened and danced to the mournful bandoneón – a type of concertina that arrived with the German immigrants. Tango legend always has it that they danced while they waited for their time with the sex workers, missing the touch of women, their families and homes. The tango embrace, the abrazo, is the same word in Spanish for what?"

"A hug," says Chita.

"Right." Eduardo smiles. "Tango is about touch, it's about connection and it's about listening and responding to another human being. It's an improvised dance – much more so than the ballroom dances. It's a continuous conversation between two people. So think of it that way: today you'll be starting a new conversation. But first, we need to start with the tango walk."

They practise walking in circles on their own – calmly, gracefully and in time to the music, which Mim finds is harder than it sounds.

When it's time to pair up, Chita grins at Mim. "Would you like to lead or follow?"

"I'll be the man," Mim says gallantly.

It quickly becomes apparent that it's easier for Chita, who's more experienced, to lead. At first, they walk around in a practice hold, with their arms out as if they're holding a huge beach ball between them.

Mim begins to understand what the teachers mean when they say tango is about deep communication. It's about working out what someone's body is doing, what theirs wants yours to do. It is strangely intimate, without being sexual, though in such close contact it's impossible not to notice things about Chita: a slight tension in her shoulders, a silver pendant glinting at her sternum. Mim remembers Esther dancing with Annie. She wonders if it had been more than friendship for Esther. If Annie had been her first love. Had Frankie been hers? She doesn't think so – she never wanted to sleep with Frankie, but maybe she wanted to be her.

They swap partners. Mim finds it different every time – not just because of different levels of experience, but because of how individual each body is: some dancers are heavier than others, some stiffer or more relaxed, sometimes the lead is light and sometimes it is more controlling. The styles are as varied as the people are.

The next exercise involves the follower closing their eyes to feel the lead, and Mim is so absorbed in what she's doing that she doesn't notice Lucky coming into the room and taking a seat. When she opens her eyes, she sees him sitting there, watching her, and she realises with a jolt how relieved she is that he's there.

"I'm sorry," he says, when she comes to sit next to him. "I got stuck on the subway."

"I'm sorry too," she says. "I really am."

"That's OK," he replies. "We can talk about it later."

"Please can I say it now?" Mim's words come out in a panicked rush. "I'm truly, properly sorry. I should never have looked at your phone. I should never even have touched it. I should have trusted you." She sighs. "I hoped that I might be able to start again – not to bring all of this old shit with me to New York. But I would be so grateful if you could give me another chance. If you could let me change the choreography."

There's a moment or two of silence between them, while they watch the other dancers circle around the room. Mim wants to take Lucky's hand in hers, is struck again by how strongly she feels about him.

"OK," he says at last. "You can trust me, though: I want you to know that, so…"

"No more snooping," Mim cuts in, relieved. "I promise." She leans into him, feels the heat of the streets, the subway, still shimmering off him. "Do you want to dance?"

A new seriousness seems to have come over them both, but maybe it's the effect of the tango's music. As they move to the slow, sad tune, Mim feels sorrow running through her like a current – something that's been there all her life that she's tried to ignore, or diminish, or starve, or block out. Sorrow for Frankie. For Robbie. For her beloved father, lost to her so early in life. For Abi. For her mother. For Esther and Annie and for the terrible things people did to each other then. And for the terrible things people were still doing to each other now. She sees it all, like a bird hovering above, held by the energy of it, and, for once, she doesn't try to fight it or suffocate it or numb it out; for once, she just accepts her sorrow and the world's sorrow too, and briefly she finds a kind of bliss in that acceptance, closing her eyes as she glides across the room.

29

14th June 1940

We woke early to a sharp knock on the door. It was a neighbour, a thin woman with a baby wrapped around her.

"They're coming," she hissed. "We should have left with the others. But it's too late now."

Our mother tried to comfort the hysterical woman, but she was soon in the grip of a terrible headache of her own and retired to her room, where Rebecca sat sentinel with her stitching. Lili and I were given strict instructions to stay inside.

In our bedroom, we were restless in the June heat. Outside in the Pletzl, it was eerily silent, though we could sense others crouching behind their own poorly blacked out windows. The morning crept on slowly, the occasional drone of an aeroplane overhead, the echo of footsteps in the distance.

Lili sat on the bed, fiddling with her Leica; I lay down and tried to read, but the words swam in front of my eyes.

My mind turned to London. We would have been safe there. "I think Rebecca's in love," I whispered to my sister. "I found some stitching she'd been doing..."

"Snooping?" Lili shot me a cheeky glance.

I smiled. "Investigative work."

My sister paused, looked down at her camera. "Should we do some investigative work today? Go and see them?"

"Too dangerous." I shook my head. "And Ima would kill us."

She began to put a film in the camera. I could see she'd already made up her mind.

"I'll say it was my fault." She got to her feet and crept to the door. "And I'll tell Ima you only came along to protect me."

We weren't the only ones pulled from our home that day. Our neighbourhood was quiet. But, as we passed closed shops and restaurants, abandoned cars with "for sale" signs on them and the occasional frightened passerby, with shoulders hunched, eyes lowered, the thrumming of marching feet and the rumble of wheels grew louder.

At the Champs-Elysées, we elbowed our way through the crowds to stand next to a pair of veterans, medals from the Great War pinned to their chests. All of us watched as the Germans marched in, lines and lines of them. More than we could ever have imagined. When the swastika was unfurled from the Arc de Triomphe, a horrified hush fell upon the crowd. Next to me, I heard the telltale wind and click of Lili's camera.

Meandering back home, we passed a group of students singing "La Marseillaise". I tried to creep by – sure that they would attract trouble – but something about the way a dark-haired woman was swaying to the music struck me as familiar. It took me a moment to register who it was. Annie. I pushed through the crowd to get to her.

She told us her story over a glass of vin rouge in one of the few places open that day. Like many others, she and Dot had walked for hours, carrying nothing with them but water and a little to eat. When they finally reached the countryside – she couldn't remember the name of the village – their feet were bleeding. All the rooms were taken by others who'd got there first. Exhausted, they curled up to sleep in a field, in the shelter of a hedge.

They woke to find themselves encircled by a cluster of sullen villagers, men and women clutching makeshift weapons – a broom, a shovel. "They started shouting," she sighed. "One of them threw a rock." She rubbed her bruised arms at the memory. "'Crasseuses immigrées.' They spat at us. 'Filthy immigrants, get out! It is your fault – what's happening to France.'"

How quickly Annie and Dot, the glittering stars of the Bal Tabarin were reduced to outsiders. Something other.

The pair of them returned to Paris on foot, and Dot had finally given in to the emotional pleas of her family and returned to America. "She said to say, 'So long,'" Annie said. A silence fell between us then. We listened to the murmur of other drinkers.

"I'm so angry with myself." She scratched at a spot on the table. "I haven't thought about anything except dancing, and look where we are now. We have to do something – don't you feel that?"

Lili nodded vigorously. "What can we do?"

I shot her a look. "Our mother won't leave."

"I'm not talking about running away again," Annie said. "I'm talking about fighting. I feel like I've been asleep," she continued. "Like Aurora in The Sleeping Beauty. But there's no handsome Prince to rescue me."

"But what can we do?"

"I tell you what we mustn't do." She glanced around her and fixed Lili and me with a steely look. "We mustn't register, if it comes to it. I saw Sandrini the other day and he told me never to let them know that I'm Jewish – not to declare it – and you mustn't either."

"But everyone knows," I said helplessly. "We grew up in Paris."

"Don't tell them," she said. "You mustn't."

I nodded, but I had no idea of what was ahead of us. "Could Sandrini help you get work at the Lido?" I suggested. "I've never seen you dance as well as you did the day you ripped up your ticket."

It was true: the memory of that night hadn't left me. Her dancing then was proof to me that pain can be spun into something beautiful.

She shook her head. "I'm not dancing anymore."

I stared at her. "Not dancing?" I repeated.

"I'm going to think of something else to do," she said. "Something helpful. There are people I know," she added. "Communists. They're discussing ways we can come together. I want to be useful." She took a final sip of wine. "Dancing would be a waste of my time."

30

December 1940

One afternoon in December 1940, I was queuing to buy vegetables, grumbling, like everyone else, about how long we'd been waiting. Ration cards had been introduced that September and, without employment, I was the one who spent most of her days waiting in queues.

It was a miserable time. We'd received confirmation that our father had been taken, held prisoner in a stalag. A postcard had arrived written in French, with a very long word in German printed on it. Kriegsgefangenenlager.

"What does it mean?" Lili asked my mother.

"It means he's a prisoner of war."

Our father's handwriting was as neat as ever. I'm safe. Please don't worry. All my love to my girls.

He wrote in French. There was nothing he could write that wouldn't be seen by other people.

"Will they know he's Jewish?" Lili kept asking us.

We couldn't answer.

"It's happening again," Ima said. "Worse this time – and we can't stop it."

Slowly, at first, and then more quickly, our mother began to unravel like thread unwinding from a spool. That winter, the first of the Occupation, was bitingly cold. Paris was adjusting to life under its new masters; the clocks were brought forward by an hour, so that the city ran on German time.

New signs labelled the city – black writing on white arrows pointing towards army institutions and the city's hospitals. The country was carved like a joint of meat into the Occupied Zone in the north-west and the Unoccupied in the south-east, with border posts and customs separating the two. At the spa town of Vichy in central France, Marshal Felipe Pétain, a former hero of the First World War, formed an authoritarian government that collaborated with the Axis.

Life had settled a little since the chaotic days of l'Exode, as it became known: the Exodus earlier that year. But there was a curfew, permits required to do almost anything and daily displays of power by the Wehrmacht, marching down the Champs-Elysées.

The German soldiers had taken over some of the city's most famous buildings – but, in some ways, they acted almost as if they were on holiday. They went shopping; they frequented the cafés and theatres. They were attentive to us women. They settled their bills, they clicked their heels as polite punctuation to conversations. Up close, you could see they were just people.

I always carried my notebook in the pocket of an overcoat my father had left behind, but the words wouldn't come. I'd quarrelled with Annie who'd made new friends with connections to the Communist party. She'd come to me not so very long before that day in the queue, her eyes bright and hopeful.

"I have a proposal for you, for your writing." She linked arms with me as we walked alongside the river. "How would you like to be a proper writer?"

I pulled my arm from hers, but she didn't seem to notice the slight. "I am a proper writer," I said. "Or I thought I was."

"Yes, yes." She didn't seem to notice how hurt I was. "But how would you like to write for a cause?"

"The Communists?" I couldn't keep the doubt from my voice.

She glanced around her as if someone might be listening and gave me a quick nod. "Look what I did," she said proudly. She pulled from her pocket the shards of one of the posters that had started to appear around Paris. A German soldier feeding a hungry French child. She could have got into serious trouble for that.

"People don't know what's going on," she said. "Not really. At our meetings, we listen to international programmes on the radio – speeches by Charles de Gaulle. You could help us to inform people."

"I don't know," I said. But I did know: I wanted no part of it. I'd absorbed the belief from my parents that the Communists were the kind of people who made trouble for trouble's sake. A quiet life, that's what my parents wanted since their move to France. The peace of the atelier. The creation of tiny treasures. Not raising your head above the parapet.

I tried to explain all this to Annie on our walk by the Seine, but I noticed my usually cheerful friend growing quieter as I gabbled on.

When at last, I stopped to draw breath, she frowned. "Can I ask you a question?" I could tell she was going to anyway. "When did you last hear the birds singing?"

I stopped in my tracks to see if I could hear the familiar trill of a chaffinch or blackbird.

"You don't hear them any more – have you noticed?" Annie insisted.

It was true, I realised: the city was much quieter than it used to be – fewer birds, less traffic, its inhabitants relying on bicycles and the Métro. The silence was one of the many unnerving changes.

Another was the way people with whom we used to exchange cheerful greetings in the street now avoided my mother's smiles. Or crossed the road when they saw us coming. It wasn't peace. It was the silence of fear, of waiting to see what would happen next.

"The birds were killed by the smoke when the Nazis arrived," Annie said. "Don't you see? The time for art, just for the joy of it, is over. We need to make ourselves useful."

"I don't know," I said again. I thought of my mother crying for my father at night after she'd gone to bed. A muffled, suffocating sound as she pressed her face into the pillow. It was different for Annie: her family were far away; her family were safe.

"Aren't you furious at what is happening?" Annie's question cut through my thoughts. "To your father? Your city? About this new law?" She meant the Statut of Juifs – the first of the anti-Semitic legislation, which had been passed in France that October. "How can you spend your days in queues? Hiding at home? Doing nothing." She spat the last word out with some contempt.

"I'm not as brave as you," I said helplessly. I could feel whatever there had been between us slipping away. Had I always known that it would come to this? That someone like Annie would see through me in the end? "I'm better in the shadows – I always have been. That's why I work as an usherette, and you're on the stage."

"It has nothing to do with that," she said bitterly. "I'm not as good at words as you, so it's not something I can explain in language. But it's a feeling in my body, that I have to do something. And if you can't understand that – if you don't feel it too – then I don't know if..."

She didn't finish her sentence, but she walked away, her arms folded furiously over her chest. I stared down at the churning river and, later, wept on Lili, who stroked my hair. "Annie won't stay angry for long," she said. "She never does."

When I'd calmed down, Lili reached for her bag. "Do you want to see something?"

She reached for her old school satchel and pulled out a stash of photographs – German soldiers marching outside the cinema.

"I don't know what to do with them," she said shyly. "But maybe Annie or her friends could use them in some way?"

"How did you take these?" I asked, sifting through the photos.

She touched a tear in her satchel. "I made a hole in my bag and I lined up the lens there."

"But that's so dangerous."

She flashed me a grin. "No one suspects someone who looks like a schoolgirl." She was barely out of school. Just sixteen.

"I don't know," I said. "I'd rather you didn't get involved. And Ima..."

"Ima doesn't need to know." She took my hand and gave it a squeeze. "And I'm already involved. Aren't we all?"

What was wrong with me? I thought in the queue. I'd always identified with wild spirits like Colette and Emily Brontë, but when it came down to it, maybe I was more dully law-abiding than I thought. The queue shifted forward a fraction. It began to drizzle. The woman in front of me sighed heavily. "It'll be mangel-wurzels for supper again."

"Mademoiselle?" A gendarme tapped me on the shoulder. A young man with thick dark eyebrows, sleepy eyes and soft boyish lips. I have no idea how he found me – maybe he'd asked around the neighbourhood. "She asked me to give you this." He slipped a note into my hand and disappeared before I could respond.

Esther, They've come for me. Please tell my family if I don't return. Sandrini has my details. With love, Annie.

I could feel the curiosity of the queue, gazes flicking towards me and then nervously away.

"Is it bad news?" The woman in front of me asked at last.

Ignoring the question, I left the queue and the shifting glances of the other women. I made my way across the city to Annie's apartment. There, I asked one of her neighbours, an old woman who lived in the apartment below, if she'd heard anything.

"They came for her in the morning," she told me. "It was

the French police – following orders, no doubt."

"Do you know where they took her?"

"To the police station. And from there, I don't know."
She shrugged. Better to keep your head down, to mind your
own business; better not to ask questions – to thank God it
wasn't your family they were coming for.

I spent the day pacing the city, finding out all I could
about what had happened to Annie. An avuncular man,
who worked at her local boulangerie, told me to go home,
to leave the matter alone. It wasn't any of my business –
they were only taking foreigners. Crasseuses immigrées.

The last person I spoke to that day was Lili. I waited for
her outside the darkroom at the Tabarin, which Sandrini
had allowed her to keep. Knowing better than to step in
while she was at work, I imagined her deft movements
on the other side of the door. Her purposeful step as she
moved the film from tank to tank. When she came out, she
smelled of those strange chemicals she used for developing
and fixing.

"Did you ever get in touch with those friends of
Annie's?" I asked. "The ones who might be interested in
your photographs?"

"My snooping, you mean?" She managed a small smile.

"Investigative work," I corrected. The restless rage that
had been with me all day pushed me forward. "Could you
introduce me to them?"

31

December 1940

Dear Esther,

I don't know whether this will ever reach you – it would be far too dangerous to send it – but I thought it might help to write it down. I must hide it somewhere they could never find it.

Perhaps you could use it in one of your stories.

I thought of my mother this morning when they came for me – how she told us to be prepared. To keep a bag packed by the door. And yet when it happened, I wasn't ready; I wasn't even awake.

He arrived at six. I answered the door in my dressing gown. As you know, I took Sandrini's advice and never registered. But, of course, there are people who are aware of my secret. At the Tabarin – and maybe beyond.

"Annie Mayer?" The gendarme glanced at his notes. "You're Canadian, non?"

I nodded, shivering. He told me to pack a bag and come with him. It seemed that I was being detained as a citizen of an Allied country and not for any other reason. But he didn't seem to know my secret, and he had a kind face, was patient and gentle as I packed. And that was enough to convince me I might be safe to scribble a note to you.

As I climbed the stairs to my apartment, I could sense my neighbours, stirring, breathing, listening on the other side of their closed doors. Once I'd packed, I followed his flashlight out of the apartment and was taken to the nearest police station. There was a brief interview with a bored-looking bureaucrat who, again, confirmed I was being detained as a Canadian and not for any other reason.

After that, I was taken to the Gare de l'Est on a requisitioned bus. The train station was chaotic – crammed with women and a few frail old men, all from Britain, Canada, Australia and South Africa. All now considered enemy aliens like me. Many clutched babies or the hands of children; a few had brought forlorn-looking dogs.

German soldiers barked orders in terrible French, arranging and rearranging us: first we must get into groups of four, then according to age, then with mothers and children separate from the rest. The rules kept on changing. Rumours flew around the crowd – that we were being taken to a camp; that our internment was revenge for what was happening to Germans in Britain.

Eventually, frozen and exhausted, we were herded on to a train guarded by German soldiers carrying guns. We were packed in – ten or eleven people to each old third-class carriage, all perched on uncomfortable slatted wooden seats. An old man next to me, hunched and balding, started to shiver so hard I asked one of the guards if he could have a hot drink.

"What do you think this is?" he barked. "The Orient-Express?"

On my other side, a nun began to murmur a prayer under her breath.

A blonde, heavily pregnant woman opposite me snapped to attention.

"Get him a hot drink." She had a crisp British accent. "And one for me too. This is barbaric – I'm pregnant, for God's sake."

The guard – the same one who sneered at me just moments before – looked cowed. "I'll see what I can do." It took him a long time but he returned, eventually, with a cup of chalky pea soup.

"Do people always do what you say?" I asked.

"Usually." The woman nodded. With her brisk air of authority, she reminded me of my first ballet teacher. "Are you a dancer?"

"Yes," I said. "How could you tell?"

"It's the deportment." The woman had piercing blue eyes, a no-nonsense gaze. "I'm Margaret," she said, "but everyone calls me Bluebell."   Of course, I'd heard of the Bluebell Girls, Margaret Kelly's troupe of dancers at the Folies Bergère.

Bluebell struck me as one of those people who'd never started a fight she couldn't win. Sounds familiar, you're thinking. But it was different for her – she was Irish Catholic, she didn't have so much to lose, I thought. And yet, I quickly learned that Bluebell did have something – or someone – to lose: her Jewish husband, the musician Marcel Leibovici.

"I always thought they'd come for Marcel," she murmured to me when the guards were out of earshot. "Thank God he's safe – he managed to evade the register. Our son would have been classified as a mischling, because he's a quarter Jewish."

We were locked into our carriages. From where I was sitting, I could see a guard winding barbed wire around the handles of the door. My heart began to beat wildly. There were stories about camps, but only vague whispers. We had no idea of our destination.

Progress was slow, navigating the labyrinthine way out of Paris. The train was unheated and there was no electric lighting. We picked up speed in the open countryside, but, even then, halted often for other trains packed with soldiers clutching weapons, their faces unsmiling.

Esther, it was awful.

When we stopped for a signal, a mother of a young boy in our carriage asked if anyone had any paper and I tore a page from my book and lent the woman my pen. She scratched out a note to her family in silence, while the rest of us looked away to give her some privacy, then she wrapped it around a five-franc piece and dropped it out of the window. A couple of the others did the same, but I'd already sent my message to you. I thought of Antoine then – do you think that's very soppy? I'm sorry about our harsh words, Esther, the last time I saw you. I know it was your fear stopping you from taking action. I understand that better now.

At one stop, we were given more pea soup by the Red Cross and some mouldy bread, which no one could face. I offered the others the little food I had, and the nuns shared some cheese and ham. The young mother passed around eau de toilette for us all to sprinkle on ourselves to ward off the increasing stink of the toilet. But then one of the nuns spilt the whole bottle, making the carriage reek "like a tart's boudoir", claimed Bluebell, which made us all giggle. Even the nuns.

It was snowing hard when the train arrived at Besançon. Bluebell, who's travelled a lot, pointed out the Swiss mountains in the distance. We were close to the border. On the platform, the guards began to unwind the barbed wire from the handles.

Outside the station, army vehicles were waiting for us and we clambered in. Those sitting nearest the back of the trucks were the first to glimpse, through the canvas flaps, the walls of the huge, grey barracks a few kilometres outside the town. Caserne Vauban. My new home.

The blocks are four storeys high, with cold stone floors and small high windows. We were taken to our dormitories and each given an iron bedstead. The walls and straw mattresses here are infested with crawling creatures – fleas, I think, and lice. The mattresses are thin and decaying, and the rooms are littered with old military coats, shoes and helmets, and smeared with urine and shit.

"It's like boarding school," one of the Brits joked, but nobody laughed.

A young nun asked if we had arrived in hell.

As soon as the lights went off tonight, insects dropped from the ceiling and crawled out of the walls in the dark. They're buzzing around my lampe de poche as I write this. I don't know how long the light will last, but I can't sleep for the coughing and the creaking of the women around me.

In the bunk above, an elegant Parisienne, who's here for the crime of being married to a Brit, is wrapped in her fur coat, sobbing herself to sleep.

I can't stop thinking of my family. Of my childhood spent under those huge Canadian skies, running barefoot through the market where my parents worked. How far away it all is now. I can't stop thinking about that ripped-up ticket home. About our foolishness in saying we didn't want a safe life. I can't stop thinking of how now I'm living in a camp under the rule of a German Kommandant.

But none of these thoughts bring me any comfort. Maybe, to help me sleep, I'll run through pieces of choreography I know instead. The Dying Swan. The Rose Adagio. Odile's thirty-two fouettés. My arms and legs twitch even at the thought of them.

I might have abandoned dancing, but maybe dancing will never abandon me.

With love, Annie

32

"So the good news is – I've found my dance," Mim tells Lucky as they wander along the brownstone-lined street after the class.

"I knew it." Lucky grins, taking her into his arms for a celebratory jig. "There is a dance for everyone. Even the most stubborn of students."

"What does that say about my personality?" Mim sneaks a glance at him, as she catches her breath. "If I tick the tango box in the quiz, does that make me a drama queen?"

"I would never suggest such a thing," he teases. "You're a lady of taste."

They are quiet for a moment, listening to the sounds of the city. A block or two away, someone leans on their horn, shouts an expletive. In the distance, there's the thrum of music; further still, a siren.

"Where shall we go now?" Mim asks. The afternoon stretches ahead of them, full of possibility.

"I don't care, as long as it's got aircon." Lucky pulls out a handkerchief and mops his brow.

Mim stops next to him. She is aware of how dry her mouth is. She swallows, feels the anticipatory flutter in her belly. "My flat has aircon," she says eventually.

Lucky gives her a careful look. "Are you sure?"

"It definitely does," Mim laughs. "But I can't promise I have complete control over it."

They're standing as close to each other as when they were dancing earlier, but the energy between them is different, crackling with anticipation.

"I like you," Mim says. "I like dancing with you; I like being with you; I hate the way I was the other night."

"I like you too," he says.

They kiss: a slow, sober, steamy afternoon kiss that leaves Mim fidgety with desire.

"You lead the way," Lucky says.

As they weave, hand in hand, through the streets back towards Brooklyn Heights, Mim finds that she's walking with a spring to her step, beaming at everyone they pass. It's exactly this feeling, she realises, that made Gene Kelly's character swing from lamp-posts in Singin' in the Rain. All the usual nagging voices in her head are silent. She's noticed they're quieter around Lucky.

When they reach the flat, Mim is embarrassed, for a moment, at how grand the apartment block is. It's not the kind of place she could have afforded herself. She gives the receptionist a shy nod as if she's breaking some kind of rule about having guests.

"What a place," Lucky says in the lift, but there's no sly edge to his words.

"Esther's plays never made much money, but she worked on Hollywood scripts. Particularly films set in the Second World War, which makes more sense." Mim pauses. "She and my grandmother always said they'd left Europe before the Occupation."

"Why do you think they said that?"

"I'm still not sure." She considers telling him about Lili and then decides against it; she hasn't even discussed it with her mum yet.

She's shy again as she unlocks the door to Esther's apartment, but Lucky makes it easy.

"What a view." He strides towards the panorama from Esther's bedroom. "I bet that's inspiring to look out at every day."

Mim shrugs, feels herself shrinking, as usual, at the sight of the water. But Lucky wraps his arms around her and, with the warmth of him next to her, it's not so bad.

"I've never done it sober before," she admits. It's easier to say it while they're not looking at each other.

"I hope it won't be a terrible disappointment," he teases, kissing her cheek. "But would it be weird if I asked if I could shower? It's just so hot out there and I want to be fresh for you."

She laughs. "You're already fresh for me, but sure."

"Come in with me?" He grins.

In the bathroom, Lucky takes his clothes off in a straightforward way, not showing off, but not ashamed either. It's weird to stand naked next to him in broad daylight. Mim knows the feel of Lucky's body under clothes – his triceps under her hand in the Lindy hop, his hip pressed against hers in the waltz, holding each other in a close abrazo in the tango. But this is different. There's no pretending or performing; there's nowhere to hide. But maybe because of the dancing, Mim is a calmer version of herself. She feels as if her mind is at home in her body for once, not floating a few feet above it.

"What's this?" She runs a fingertip along a thick scar running down one of Lucky's legs.

He glances at it. "An old childhood wound – I cut it on a sprinkler in the garden."

"It looks nasty."

"It was – I can still remember the blood – so much of it. And I remember thinking just before I passed out – and this will make you laugh – 'My mum's going to kill me.'"

Mim smiles sadly. "I know exactly what you mean."

But Lucky doesn't pick up on any particular significance in her words. "Of course, my mum ran out of the house, absolutely petrified. It was the first time I saw her cry. I was in hospital for weeks."

"It sounds awful."

He shrugs. "Well, I was young. Children are resilient. I mainly hated having to lie still in that hospital bed, and I promised that when I got better I would spend every moment I could moving and dancing. I already loved to do that – I just hadn't taken it very seriously until that point. So I was lucky, really, in lots of ways. Lucky to survive, lucky to work out what I wanted to do so young, lucky to dance again."

"Like your name." Mim smiles.

"Can I ask about this?" he says, touching the quill on her right wrist. "It is because you're a writer."

"That's right." Mim nods and she kisses him. Maybe one

day, she thinks, she'll tell him the whole story.

There's not much room in the shower for the two of them, but it's delicious to feel the cool water running over her. Delicious, too, to embrace skin on skin, to taste the salty sweat of him as she kisses his chest. It quickly stops being strange or awkward to be naked with Lucky and starts to feel like the best decision she's ever made. They kiss and touch in the shower until it's too cold to stand there anymore, and then they stumble, wet and bedraggled, to the bedroom, where they don't even make it to the bed, but collapse, giggling, on their towels on the floor, finding the warmest parts of each other with mouths and hands, and staying there, in the bedroom, for most of the afternoon, until Lucky suggests showering again and getting some food.

In the wee small hours of the morning, Mim is woken with a jolt. The old dream is back, her arms pinned to her sides in a suffocating grip. She lies, drenched in sweat, waiting for her breathing to return to normal.

She looks over at Lucky sleeping. He is on his back with his arms thrown above his head. Mim gets up carefully, reluctantly. She makes her way to the bathroom to pee and glances after at her face, her glowing cheeks and dishevelled hair. She feels strangely alert. Maybe it's the new feeling she has of being in her body; maybe it's the dream. But she doesn't want to think about that now, doesn't want to return to that night. She has a beautiful man sleeping in her bed; she just needs to distract herself until he's awake again. In the kitchen, she pours herself a glass of water and tiptoes back to the bedroom. Retrieving Esther's book from the desk, she finds herself a spot, in a crack of light, in which to read.

33

April 1941

Esther,

You won't believe where I am now. Or who I've been with. Really you won't. It's good – don't worry – far better than Besançon. But I mustn't run ahead of myself...

First things first, I'm out of that terrible place. They let me go. As simple as that. I still can't believe it. They never found out the thing I daren't even write down.

I didn't argue, just packed as swiftly as I could, shrugging off the old military coat and boots that became my unofficial uniform there. I can't describe the relief. And I kept thinking: why was I freed? Why was I given another chance when others weren't? It's all frighteningly arbitrary.

A group of us were taken to the station and given our train tickets and some change to make a phone call when we reached Paris. All the way there, I thought about whom to call. I didn't have a number for you – and the Tabarin is still closed. Then I remembered Antoine – the number he'd given me. I know you'll laugh at that, but maybe it was because of the things I saw at Besançon. The cruelty and the dirt and the cold. Maybe it made me think I should grab every chance at happiness I had.

When I reached Paris, the Gare de l'Est was full of desperate souls, trying to escape the city. Fear has a smell, don't you think? A sour reek. In real life, it's different from the way we perform it on stage. It's an animal way of holding yourself: still and quiet and hunched, like a mouse I saw hiding under a costume rail, not wanting to draw Cancan's attention.

Luckily for me, I know about body language. The Nazis have an instinct for it too, so disembarking the train, I held my back straight and my gaze steady. I didn't smile – that would be unnatural in the circumstances – but I practised a look of benevolent calm, as if I had nothing and no one in the world to fear. It was acting, of course. I was starving and terrified like everybody else, but there was too much at stake not to pretend.

Still, despite everything, despite the frightened faces, all avoiding the gaze of the Wehrmacht at the station; despite not knowing where I would be sleeping that night, it was a relief to be away from the lice and the filth and peeling potatoes until my hands were red raw. Relief, really, is too small a word – maybe you can help me find a bigger one. We need bigger words for so many things these days.

When it came, the dreaded bark was so close it made me jump out of my skin. "Vos papiers, s'il vous plait."

I thought, just for a second, it had come for me. That,

having survived the camp, I was going to be found out as soon as I returned to Paris. But, instead, a couple of soldiers stopped a mother and a child nearby. I noticed the woman's thin, worried face, her hand tightening around her daughter's hand. A little girl with short bobbed hair and skinny legs, one knee grazed. It took everything in my power not to stare at them for too long, not to wonder if their secret was the same as mine. Not to give myself away.

All I could do was to force myself to keep putting one foot in front of another, until I reached the nearest telephone. I was so close I could hear the increasing intensity of the soldiers' questions. And I could feel the little girl's gaze on my back as I passed by. I wondered if she had her life mapped out in front of her, just as I did: if she had dreams of being a nurse. A teacher. A mother. A dancer.

There was a gasp and a flurry of movement and then they were taken away, as I knew they would be. But I would have given anything, in that moment, to do more than walk past. I would have given anything, in that moment, to do something. To help.

Antoine arrived in a car – God knows where he found the petrol – but he's the type to know someone who knows someone. He looked immaculate, as always. And handsome. Paris smelled of lilacs, of spring, and I was glad to be back. I don't know where I imagined we'd be going – I hadn't thought that far ahead, but we pulled up outside the Hôtel Le Bristol on rue du Faubourg Saint Honoré.

"You'll be safe here," Antoine said. "It's one of the few in the city that hasn't been occupied by the Germans – only Americans so far. Their embassy is here, and the place is full of them."

"It's too much," I said. "How can you afford it?"

"Don't worry, it's just for a night. Let's check you in – we'll have dinner and you can have a good night's sleep."

"Actually," I asked, "can I have a bath first? I want to wash that place off me."

In the bath, I finally cried. I wept for the place I'd left. The things I'd seen there. The filth and the suffering and the cold and the constant exhausting fear. I wept, of course, for the women I'd left behind.

And yet somehow I'd got away, through no skill or effort of my own. Just luck. And now I was in a hot bath in one of the most luxurious hotels in Paris. But why? I knew that Antoine had a soft spot for me. Still, it felt like too much. What did he want in return?

I'm a virgin, as you know, but I'm not stupid.

The sound of the bedroom door opening interrupted my thoughts. I sat up in the bath, my hands instinctively covering myself.

"Hello?" I called. "Who is it?"

The other person fell quiet in the bedroom. There was no movement towards the bathroom, but none away from it. I was acutely aware of how vulnerable I was. How naked. I stood up, the water dripping from me.

"Hello?" I said again more assertively.

"Just me," Antoine called from the room. "I wondered if you were ready. I'll meet you downstairs."

"OK," I shouted back, but I felt unsettled.

It was OK, I told myself as I got dressed. Nothing to worry about. Antoine wouldn't hurt me – he'd come to pick me up, after all, and he'd arranged the hotel room without asking for anything. But, then, I wondered again: why hadn't he asked for anything? It's not usual at the moment, is it? Everybody wants something. And a more sinister thought occurred to me: Antoine was the only person who knew where I was. And one of the few, too, who knew my secret. Could I really trust him?

I sat on the bed and went through my options. The eternal question: to stay or to go. The hotel bed was as soft as a cloud after those straw mattresses. I could have curled up on it and gone to sleep. But then I would have missed supper.

It was a shame to put on my old tired clothes after feeling clean for the first time in weeks. As I dressed, I longed for a little powder and lipstick. Even stockings would have been something. I wondered if I should draw a line up the back of my calves to feign their appearance, as some women did, but my stomach growled loudly. There were more important things to attend to.

In the restaurant, Antoine returned to his usual charming self, updating me on what everyone was up to. He confirmed that the Tabarin is still closed, but that Sandrini's show at the Lido has been a huge success.

"There's talk of him returning to the Tabarin," he told me. "I'm sure there'll be a job for you there."

I wasn't sure – and, if I'm honest, my meal distracted me. Esther, the meal! Beef bourguignon followed by crème caramel. The kind of food we dreamed of at the barracks. When I'd more or less scraped my plate clean, I told Antoine, I didn't want to return to dancing. I wanted to make myself useful.

"Maybe that's how you could make yourself useful," he said.

"Flashing my knickers for a Boche audience." I shook my head. "I don't think so. It's not exactly how I saw my life going. I should be dancing with the Ballet Russe right now."

"Paris is full of people who had other plans," Antoine said. "And a talent like yours shouldn't go to waste."

"I thought I had more to learn," I said pointedly. I hadn't forgotten his criticism, all those months before.

"We all have more to learn." Antoine shrugged. "But you had a breakthrough, I think, just before the Tabarin's closure."

I knew the night he meant. Just after the outbreak of war. The night I ripped up my father's ticket. But I didn't want to think about that evening. Not now. And with my belly full of food and wine for the first time in many weeks, I grew sleepy. There'd been no sign from Antoine that his intentions were anything but honourable. That was, until the end of the evening when he insisted on walking me to my bedroom.

"There's something I want to show you." He took my arm and steered us both up the Bristol's sweeping staircase. He nodded at a young couple making their way down to the dining room, their faces flushed, their whispers conspiratorial. To a stranger's eyes, Antoine and I would have looked like just another pair of lovers.

On the way upstairs, I imagined Gisy or Belle laughing at me for being so naïve, for thinking I could get anything for free. I remembered Belle stroking her new fox fur. Antoine is handsome and generous, I thought: it could be a lot worse. Still, my hand shook a little as I opened the door to the bedroom. I was good with pain, I thought, and physically strong: maybe the first time wouldn't hurt.

Inside the room, Antoine acted strangely, pulling the door carefully closed. He held a finger to his lips and cocked his head as if listening out for something. It was quiet on the second floor. He walked over to the windows and checked the blackout curtains were in place.

"I want you to look in the drawer of the bedside table," he said. "The left side."

I had no idea what to expect: carnations, lingerie, a bottle of wine? The drawer stuck a little as I went to open it. I could feel the weight of something in there, but it took a moment or two to respond to the item inside, despite the regularity with which I saw it.

"It's a gun," I said, like an idiot, needing to sit down on the bed.

Antoine took a seat next to me. "I want you to look after it," he said.

It looked small, almost innocuous, in his hands. "Why me?"

"Because no one would suspect you," he said. Up close, I realised Antoine didn't smell like everybody else: there wasn't that sour reek of fear. There was something different about him: a sense of purpose.

Of course, I knew the risk of being found carrying a gun. The warning is on posters everywhere. One of the many items that are verboten – on pain of death.

"We'd like you to look after it and then take it somewhere," Antoine said. "We'll let you know where."

"We?"

He gave her a knowing look.

"It's dangerous."

Antoine shrugged. "You know, you're a very beautiful

woman," he said, almost conversationally. "As well as a wonderful dancer. Perhaps we could team up one day?"

I rolled my eyes. Some men call you beautiful as if it's a ticket to something. But I mustn't think about tickets. Not tickets home, ripped up into tiny pieces. Useless.

I realised there was no getting out of this. I knew my answer – I'd known it since the moment I saw the gun.

"Don't roll your eyes," said Antoine, deadly serious, and I could tell that he didn't mean the compliment like the others, the men who hung around the stage door to fawn on us girls after a show. "I don't mean that way. Your beauty – even your dancing – we could use those things."

With love, Annie

34

In her new state of semi-freedom, Annie had to sign in every day at the local police station and she also had to give them an address. At first, she stayed in her old dressing room in the Tabarin. Dédée lent her Cancan, whose warm body was a comfort, stretched alongside her like a hot water bottle; less comforting was the terrier's habit of pricking up his ears at the sound of every creak, at times emitting a long, low growl.

Out in the city, other dogs whimpered and barked – I heard them from my own bed in the Pletzl, as Lili slept next to me – reacting to sinister visits made after dark. Curt demands in German. I thought of my father. Was he frightened, too, lying on his back on some bunk in a room full of men, all longing for their women, their families?

Occasionally, a sad little postcard reached us, saying, I am safe. Don't worry. So much he couldn't write, knowing his words would be read by hostile eyes. Was he safe still?

Did they know he was Jewish? Was he able to work in any way?

I hoped so. I pictured him running his callused hands over a piece of freshly cut timber, reading the grain and texture of it like Braille, communicating with us in that way somehow.

When Annie couldn't sleep, she rehearsed her journey to the police station the next day. She practised it in her mind, she told me, like her entrance on stage, taking care to place one foot in front of the other with elegance and poise: feet turned out, head alert, nothing to hide. However anxious Annie was beforehand – no matter what quarrel or discomfort, the rubbing of a toe shoe, the scratch of a hangover – she let it all slide away as she took up her position on the Tabarin stage.

It was the same on the walk to the police station. She let everything drop away – childhood visits to the synagogue with her family, their faces lit by the Shabbat candles, the fear at Besançon, the gun hidden deep under a pile of costumes at the Tabarin – until she became a woman with no past, no family, no secrets, just standing in the spotlight, existing only for the viewer. Nothing to fear, nothing to hide.

We were reunited not long after her return to the city – the first time she walked back into the meeting room and saw me there.

"Esther, you're here." She hugged me. "I knew you'd come round." Her greeting was so warm, so joyful, that the froideur between us melted away swiftly.

It was good to have her back, during those miserable months. The only faint glimmer on the horizon was the rumour that, after his success at the Lido, Sandrini had plans to return home to the Tabarin and reopen the theatre with a new show.

"Will you dance again?" I asked.

"I don't know." She paced a little in that cramped room, while I typed. She was often told off by Antoine or one of the others for this. We were meant to be as still and quiet as possible. "I used to feel it like an itch." She shook her head. "No, it was stronger than that. It was something I had to do every day, but it's not there any more in my body. It's disappeared – at least for now. How about you? How's your work?"

"I don't know – it feels enough to be writing these at the moment." I nodded at the pile of leaflets on my desk. I didn't add that, since our separation, I had felt less of an urge to write my own stories.

At the sound of footsteps out in the corridor, Annie brought a finger to her lips and we both fell silent, listening to the drip from a leaky pipe. The footsteps continued up the staircase past our room. Our meeting place had been secure so far but you could never be too careful.

"Did we do the right thing?" I whispered. "Staying in Paris?"

"Yes," she said. "We're useful here. What would you be doing in London? Hiding underground? Dodging the Luftwaffe? At least here you can help."

I was quiet. I wished I had her certainty. Things were difficult at home, with Rebecca and my mother sewing until their hands cramped, Lili and I sneaking out for our secret assignations, covering for each other. Just a night or two before, Rebecca had interrupted me while I typed away. She ripped the paper from my beloved Remington and glared at it, then at me.

"I thought as much," she said furiously. "You are putting all of us in danger."

"We're already in danger," I said.

My Resistance work had given me a sense of purpose; when I was typing the leaflets or articles, a kind of focus took over me.

"I think we should move." Rebecca crumpled the paper into a tight ball. "It's not safe for us to stay in the Pletzl."

The move was one thing we agreed on, but we'd have to persuade our mother, who didn't want to leave her friends, or the address to which my father sent his postcards. I could feel the rift between Rebecca and me deepen after that, almost hear the creak of the weight of it, as we pulled away from each other.

I stayed up that night after she destroyed my work, to rewrite my piece again. Most of it was stored in my memory. I dropped it off the next day, ashen-faced. There had been another cry that night. A woman's shriek of denial, as she was taken away. To hear that kind of suffering, and not to be able to do anything – I think it does something to you. Some kind of harm that can never be undone.

"Bad night?" Antoine asked, when he saw my face.

I nodded.

"Will you be seeing Annie later? I need to get a message to her."

I said I would.

"It's an address." He relayed the details to me.

I knew what it was for but I didn't tell him that; Annie never was very good at keeping secrets from me. In the weeks after her return, I started to jot them down, began to work at my own fragments again – I always found her story more compelling than mine. Or perhaps, as she observed, hers was a way into my own.

The address was on the other side of Paris. I helped Annie to pack her bicycle pannier, hiding the gun beneath brown paper packages.

"I wish I could come with you," I said.

"Well, that would just attract more attention," she said. "I'll be fine. I survived Besançon, I can cycle across Paris."

I watched her ride off – a little wobble and she was on her way. The journey went smoothly until she was a block or two from her destination and beginning to anticipate her arrival, to repeat the coded phrase she had to say. She may even have been mouthing the words to herself as the large black car pulled up next to her and wound down the window.

"Bonjour, Mademoiselle," said the German soldier in the passenger seat. He was a handsome man, Annie said, but his pleasant manner made her suspicious. "How are you on this fine day?"

"Ça va bien, merci," she tried to remember the expression of benevolent calm she used for the police station, but her face felt tight and strange.

"Where are you off to?"

"To see a friend," she replied. It was the first thing she thought of.

"On such a beautiful day," the soldier teased. "Perhaps it's a boyfriend you're meeting?"

"Perhaps." Annie made herself smile coquettishly and dropped her shoulders, which were hunched close to her ears.

"Lucky fellow." The solider began to wind up the window. "Tell me," he said, as an afterthought, "What's in that basket of yours?"

She didn't know where the answer came from, or if it was genius or suicide. Her mouth responded without her permission. "A gun."

Was there a moment of doubt in that handsome soldier's mind? Did he wonder if anyone transporting such a weapon would be bold or stupid enough to admit it? Or was he simply beguiled by Annie's pretty face and bare legs? Who can say? As I imagine the scene, I suspect there might have been an ice-cold second or two – though it must have felt longer to Annie – before the car of Germans burst out laughing.

"As if," cried one of them from the back. A face Annie could make out less clearly through the glass. "A pretty little thing like you?"

"A gun," the driver repeated, chuckling to himself, as if Annie had told a brilliant joke. And then they drove off.

Antoine was right, Annie realised, as she continued, sweating profusely, to her destination. Her gender and beauty weren't obstacles to this kind of work. They were weapons she could use.

On a high, after making the delivery, she came to find me in the meeting room, waiting until we were alone.

"I have a sudden urge," she said, "and you must promise not to say, 'I told you so.'"

"OK," I said.

"You promise?"

"Sure."

"I want to go dancing tonight." She paused, fidgeting.

"It's the only thing I know to do with this feeling."

I smiled, biting my tongue.

She examined her fingernails. "You promised," she said, correctly guessing at my thoughts.

"Sure. We can go dancing. I mean, I'm no Dot."

She beamed at me. "You'll do."

That night we went to a dancehall in Montmartre – a place I'd never been to before or since: crowded, smoky, a little rough around the edges. Full of artists and theatre folk and not a German solider in sight. Everyone dancing and drinking to forget. We found a tiny table in the corner and, as usual, I sat there like a sentinel while Annie was barely off the dancefloor all night – jumping up for dance after dance. She'd found something in that resistant act and, though it was a terrible time, and there was worse to come, I remember that evening with fondness. To dance and carouse, even to love, those things felt like acts of defiance.

The urge even took hold of me. Halfway through a Django Reinhardt number, I clambered to my feet, hoping to grab Annie for a dance. I elbowed my way through the bouncing crowd towards her, but, just as I reached her, two things happened: the band began to play the next song – and it wasn't a cheerful piece of gypsy jazz, it was a sultry tango.

The second thing was that I realised I wasn't alone in making my way to Annie, like a moth to candlelight, because standing opposite me was Antoine: his handsome face pale, his hair slicked back, his suit looking improbably immaculate in a place like that.

The song they played that night was "Por Una Cabeza" – a bittersweet tango about gambling and love. About how life's greatest joys and sorrows often come down to the narrowest of margins. Not a song I could dance to with Annie. I melted away, leaving my friend to Antoine. Wordlessly, they took up a tango hold.

A funny thing happened, though. Other people began to melt away when those two began to dance – all the crackle of their chemistry sizzling in every movement. Antoine's arm encircling Annie's waist, their faces pressed together, as if they were whispering each other secrets in bed. Antoine's dancing didn't have the polish of Annie's but he knew how to hold a moment, how to slow things down, and when to speed them up into a tangle of legs and intentions. None of us could tear our eyes away. A few other couples tried to keep up, but in the end they surrendered and joined the rest of us, captivated.

Even with Annie in her tired old dress, in that Montmartre dive, the pair of them radiated something we all still had inside us: sorrow and longing. I felt lucky to witness it. And yet it left me hungry for something of my own. When the song came to a close, Antoine dropped Annie into a deep back bend, his face brushing close to hers in an almost-kiss. The room burst into spontaneous applause.

Magnifique. I had the word ready for them in my head, all prepared for when they returned to the table. But they didn't come back, not straightway. Annie danced with everyone and anyone – and she was usually fair with her attention – but that night she partnered Antoine for song after song. However, Antoine hadn't arrived alone that night and his disgruntled partner made her way to our table soon enough.

"I see I'm not the only one suffering from tonight's

turn of events," Belle said, her white-blonde hair perfectly coiffured. "Can I join you?"

I stared at her stupidly. Belle always made me nervous.

Without waiting for an answer, she took Annie's seat and clicked for the attention of a waiter. "Some evening this has turned out to be." Her shoulders slumped for a moment in a rare sign of defeat.

"They're magnificent together." My eyes followed the pair around the room.

"Yes, even I can't deny that." Belle paused to light a cigarette. "And what about you?"

"I'm happy to watch." I dragged my gaze away from the dancers for a moment to look at her.

Belle gave an infuriating smile. "D'accord," she said, letting the subject drop.

"What happened to your boyfriend?" I asked.

"Which one?"

"The whiskery gentleman – one of the Tabarin regulars."

"He got bored." She shrugged. "Or I did. I forget which. He's gone to join his family in the Unoccupied Zone, but he's left me some guilt money, at least."

She offered to buy me a drink and I figured it was the least she could do. Over a bottle of gros rouge, she asked after my father and we caught up about mutual friends at the Tabarin. It was the first time I'd spoken to Belle properly and I found it difficult to align the person sitting next to me – generous, charming, attentive – with the individual I'd known at the Tabarin.

Maybe she read my mind; maybe one memory, in particular, hung between us, but halfway through the night she leaned over and whispered, "I want to say something."

Her breath was hot and boozy in my ear. "I wanted to apologise for what I said that day, to you and Annie."

I stayed silent.

"It was wrong," she continued. "And what is happening now is wrong too. I'm sorry."

I wondered whom she'd been spending time with: if they were her words or someone else's.

"I was just angry," she added. "About Annie telling my secret. About the decision I had to make about the baby." She sighed. "But who'd want to bring a child into a world like this?"

I couldn't disagree with her there, but she mixed up the timing. She'd insulted us months before she'd collapsed at the Tabarin. Yet, if I saw an opportunity, lying on the table between us, to put her right, to tell her Annie hadn't said a word about pregnancy, that it had been me, albeit accidentally, I didn't take it.

Belle remained with me, turning down offers of dances when they came and buying the drinks all night, even as my gaze followed my friend and Antoine around the dancefloor.

When Annie returned to our table to knock back a glass of water between dances, she gave me a look as if to say, What is she doing here? I responded with a shrug. Did she expect me to sit alone?

Correctly interpreting this wordless exchange, Belle slung an arm around my shoulder. "I've been keeping Esther company." She smiled in that feline way of hers. "Since you've been doing the same for Antoine."

"Antoine is free to do as he wishes." Annie tossed the remark lightly over her shoulder as she returned to the dancefloor, where the man in question was waiting for her, giving our table – and Belle, no doubt – a wide berth.

"Can I tell you a secret?" Belle leaned over to me. "I don't even mind – I get you all to myself." She slipped a hand under the table and began to stroke my leg, slowly and deliberately, the way you might smooth a cat's fur, first one way and then the other, to see how it would react.

Later, on the way to the toilet, I found my step was unsteady. I was full of liquor, flushed and tired, and filled with some nameless excitement that I knew was to do with Belle – her hot breath against my face, her slim fingers stroking my thigh. Someone was in the bathroom and, as I waited, I leaned against the wall, which seemed to bounce to the beat of the music. In the dark, dimly lit corridor, with Annie and Antoine whirling to the band, Belle came to find me.

"Dance with me," she murmured.

"What? Here?" I glanced around.

"Pourquoi pas?" She pulled me to her, entwining her arms around my neck. This wasn't like my cheery dance with Annie: it was something else entirely. I could feel the light silk of Belle's dress, the warmth of her body beneath it. It was a dance of seduction. At her touch, some part of me I hadn't even clearly known was there came alive. A desert flower on its first contact with rain.

35

Mim glances up from the pages. Her legs have gone to sleep, sitting on the floor. Belle must have been Esther's first love affair. Had Robbie been hers? Not really. Their relationship had begun in the rooms of cheap hotels and B&Bs – Brighton had enough of those. She couldn't bring him home, couldn't face seeing Frankie over morning coffee the next day. Not that Frankie liked Robbie in that way, she assured Mim of that: she just didn't approve of their relationship.

"He's not good for you," she said simply. "You're not yourself when you're around him."

"That's because it's all new," Mim said breezily. "We'll get there. It's early days." She tried in that moment to imagine Robbie and her as an ordinary couple at home together, drinking coffee. That was what ordinary couples did, wasn't it? Reading the Sunday papers. But the fantasy never seemed to develop further than that. It was a lifeless portrait.

"You've put him on a pedestal," Frankie said. "And you can bring him back here. There's no need to creep around."

"We're not creeping around." Mim laughed. But, only a few days before, they'd been sitting at a corner table in the Cricketers, one of Brighton's oldest and cosiest pubs, and Robbie, in a rare moment of affection, had raised her hand to his mouth to kiss it and then dropped it suddenly, as if he'd been holding something too hot. He disappeared to the loo and returned, sheepishly, a few minutes later.

"Sorry about that," he said. "I thought I saw one of Frida's mates." As if that explained it. "But I think we're safe."

"Was it Emma?" Mim nearly asked – she knew from her snooping on social media the name of Frida's best friend, the one who joined her for early-morning sea swims – but she stopped herself just in time. Mim had joined the group once herself. A dangerous move, though it was large enough for her not to be noticed.

"First time?" Frida gave her a friendly smile as she pulled a woolly hat over her white-blonde hair. Up close, her body was perfect, even in the unforgiving morning light. "You'll find it's addictive."

Mim never went back, but not because she didn't enjoy it. She was a strong swimmer – it was the only sport she liked at school. That day, she'd held back from the group so she could enjoy the experience on her own and, looking back at the land with a seal's view of the world, she had a rare moment of perspective. She realised she'd drifted off course.

Months ago, when she'd written the article, she'd mistaken the real reward – the fact she'd done a good piece of work – with the fake one: Robbie's praise. And it had been weeks – months, even – since she'd written something decent, throwing herself down the rabbit hole of her obsession with him. She began to swim back to shore alone. She needed to finish things with Robbie. It was no good. But then she caught his eye in the newsroom again, and he smiled at her, and she threw everything else away, as usual.

In the pub that day, she forced her voice to sound nonchalant, unbothered. "It's OK to see other people, isn't it? Now you're divorced?"

He chuckled affectionately. "We're not actually divorced yet – it'll take a few more weeks for even the decree nisi to come through."

All the signs were there, Mim realises now, picking at the memory like a scab. And maybe, she thinks, admiring Lucky's sleeping body in the morning light, maybe even the sex wasn't really worth it. It was exciting, sure, hiding it from people at work, catching secret glimpses of him in a meeting, locking eyes as he glanced up. Making him sweat a bit. Perhaps, now she thinks about it, Robbie was always in a rush, always half-there. Not like Lucky, who cares about what she likes, who touches her as if he means it. So why can't she let Robbie go? Did the pain bring its own sweetness? Or did it just feel familiar to her?

As if hearing her jangling thoughts, Lucky stirs and stretches. "What are you doing?" he asks sleepily, reaching for his glasses.

"Just reading." Mim closes Esther's book and pushes it into a drawer in the desk. She climbs into bed and curls up next to his warm body.

"What do you want to do today?" He spoons her,

wrapping his arms around her.

"More tango. Do you think we'll be able to find another class?"

"I'm sure there's always tango happening somewhere in New York," he murmurs into her hair. "What were you reading?"

"My great-aunt's memoir – the one I told you about."

"What's happening now?"

"A lot of dancing." She smiles. "Some sex too."

"Sounds like a bestseller."

"It's hard to imagine how frightened they must have been," Mim says, suddenly serious. "I don't know how people live through such things."

Lucky is silent for a moment. "I don't suppose they have much of a choice. My mother lost relatives in the Dirty War." He paused. "A lot of musicians and dancers fled Argentina at the time."

"How awful." Mim is glad he can't see her face. It's easier to talk this way somehow. "It makes me feel ashamed of the kinds of things I get upset about."

"What things?"

Mim swallows. "Oh, the usual." She traces a finger down the inside of his wrist, where the skin is paler, silky-soft. "Things I could have done differently," she says, aware of the evasion, of Frankie in her head, judging. "People I've lost."

"I beg you, I love you, I forgive you," Lucky says lightly. "All of that?"

"Not always easy to say to yourself." Mim turns her head on the pillow to face him.

"We're always toughest on ourselves." Lucky takes her

hand and kisses the quill tattoo gently. "It's easier to be nice to other people."

Mim nods.

"I beg you," Lucky kisses her, his mouth moving gently to her neck. "I implore you," he teases.

"Do you forgive me?" Mim asks. "For that thing with the phone?"

He stops kissing her, glances up at her face. "I do," he says, serious for a moment. "But do you forgive you?"

"Maybe I should try imploring you," she says, lightly changing the subject.

He grins at her. The day stretches out before them. "What would you like?"

36

My friend's eyes were glittering with excitement when we next met for coffee at a cosy bistro near her new apartment in the Latin quarter. And not just excitement at her new place, I suspected, which was tiny, with a low beamed ceiling, but still far better than sleeping in her dressing room. The owner of the bistro, Madame F, was charmed by Annie and served us real coffee when she could rather than the chicory imitation most places offered.

"You'll never guess what?" Annie said.

"What?" I asked obediently. She'd caught me daydreaming about Belle and I blushed furiously at the interruption.

"Antoine and I are teaming up."

"Teaming up?" I repeated.

"Yes, a ballroom partnership." She nodded. "We're going to debut at the Tabarin's new show, Dans Notre Miroir. Sandrini has promised us a starring spot – we'll be Paris's answer to Fred and Ginger."

"How exciting." I forced myself to smile. "You danced beautifully together." That much was true, of course, but I was still undecided about Antoine.

"You're not sure about him?" Annie guessed correctly.

"He's fine," I said.

"Tell me," she insisted.

I paused, trying to find the right words. "He's kind," I began. "And brave, too, with the work he does. But I think he has an eye for the ladies."

"You're not the only one to say that." She frowned. "But still," she added stubbornly, "I like him. I always have. And, if I'm honest," She sighed heavily. "Who could blame any of us for wanting a little love at the moment?"

I avoided her gaze. How could I start to tell her about Belle? About our stolen moments at her apartment or the kinds of places in Paris that welcomed lovers like us, or at least turned a blind eye. Annie's desires seemed straightforward compared with mine.

"I thought you were never going to dance again?" I teased, changing the subject.

"I don't think you ever really believed that, did you?" Annie smiled, and then her expression grew more serious. "The only thing is, even Sandrini can't stop the Germans coming. They go to all the other cabarets."

My jaw tensed at the thought of it. The Tabarin had always been a refuge for my family. And my father had now been taken by them... There had been a couple more notes from the stalag: They are keeping me busy. It is good to be working. I think of you all the time.

I was glad to hear he had the consolation of his work. A place where he could store his feelings. But Ima had deteriorated since he'd gone. Her eyes looked glazed and occasionally I would find her muttering to herself furiously as she worked, lost in another world. Usually so on top of things, she began to forget important tasks, to leave dresses unfinished or pans bubbling over on the stove. How would she feel about German soldiers being in the same building as her daughters?

The Bal Tabarin was such an intimate venue, with the audience's seats near enough to the stage that they could see the sweat on the dancers' skin, hear their breath strain or the occasional grunting effort of a move. It seemed indecent somehow that the Nazis would be able to get so close.

"Don't you mind?" I asked quietly.

"Of course I do. I mind all of it, but…" She was quiet for a moment, as if checking whether anyone close to us was listening. "In this new role, Antoine and I might be able to make ourselves useful."

"Useful how?"

"I don't know yet."

She sipped her coffee and pulled a face. It wasn't the good stuff that day. It was getting harder and harder to find. Things we'd taken for granted in peacetime – meat, butter, coffee – were disappearing. Even the leather went to make German boots, so the clippity-clop of wooden-soled shoes became one of the strange new sounds we all became accustomed to in those years – though not the worst of them.

Paris grew more tense by the day. The Commissariat général aux questions juives, the organisation responsible for coordinating anti-Semitic policy throughout France, had been established in March that year, run by Xavier Vallat, a vicious anti-Semite. More statutes against Jews were passed thick and fast: Jewish businesses had to register, and were monitored carefully. Eventually we seemed to be prevented from any profession at all.

My mother had been persuaded by Rebecca to move away from our neighbourhood, where everyone knew us, to a place in the Latin Quarter. Friends helped with the move and with work too. Sandrini sent repairs for the costumes, and Dédée sent her children's darning their way. There were other friends and supporters from our Tabarin days, and I will never forget their kindness. It took many people to keep a family in hiding during those days, and only one to betray them.

"Do you think your mother would make me a new dress?" Annie asked more cheerfully. "I was thinking of something like Ginger's in Swing Time."

"The one with all the ruffles?" I laughed. "It'll be difficult to get hold of enough fabric."

"No – the white dress she wears for 'Never Gonna Dance.'"

I knew the one she meant. A slinky gown cut on the bias that swirled like water around Rogers as she moved.

I nodded. "She loves dressing you – I'm sure she'll be back at the Tabarin like a shot."

"I hear Belle's returning too." Annie sighed.

I blew on my coffee loudly, even though it was already quite cool.

"You seemed to be getting very cosy the other night," she persisted. "Didn't she mention it?"

I'd seen Belle several times since, and I knew she was returning to the Tabarin as a dance captain. She'd apologised again for what she said that day at the Tabarin.

"It's not something I really believe," she said in a rare tender moment, gazing up at the ceiling. We were scrunched up together in the single bed in her tiny Montmartre apartment. She trailed a lazy finger down my arm. "Sometimes it feels like there's not enough to go round."

"Of what?"

"Love," she laughed. "Or anything, really."

I learned more about her in those snatched moments together, once her make-up had smudged off, her hair had lost its perfect curls. She told me how she'd left home at fourteen – her mother was a violent alcoholic. She'd barely known her father.

"I discovered early on," she said, painting her lips at her dressing table. "That men liked the way I moved. I knew I could make money from it too. But I didn't know how much dancing would come to mean to me, how you feel free up there. And powerful."

Her face softened when she talked about dance. "But, of course, my name had to change. No one was going to see plain old Jeanne do the cancan."

Her words made me think of Diaghilev scoffing "Who would pay to see Marks dance?" Everybody wanted to reinvent themselves, to leave something behind.

"Jeanne isn't so bad," I said loyally.

"Belle is better." Her lip-sticked mouth smiled at me in the mirror.

Of course, it made sense that a name that meant "beautiful" might be made up, adopted for the stage. I always felt a little sad when Belle reapplied her make-up. It signified her armour was on for the outside world, the end of our private time together. She only ever gave me glimpses of Jeanne. Belle was second nature to her by the time I knew her.

There are so many feelings I have about our affair, looking back: how clearly she saw me – more clearly than I saw myself. How she knew what I needed and wanted. Ours was a clandestine relationship, like so many in Paris in those years: our unexpected chemistry made all the more potent for its secrecy. Sometimes, during its course, she would catch my eye across a crowded room and smile in that catlike way, more to herself than to me. Perhaps she was thinking of something we'd done together and was reliving the memory. That's what I told myself, as I felt panic prickle at my skin: that she smiled because I excited her, rather than the fact, perhaps, that she'd taken for herself something that belonged to Annie.

I never said any of this to my friend in the café that day. But she seemed to pick up on something from my silence.

"I wouldn't trust her," Annie said. "You know what she's like."

"We all need to be careful," I said, pivoting the subject. "Including you."

She didn't correct me for once. "Do you think I should peroxide my hair?"

"I don't know." I chewed my cheek, I knew why she was asking. "Maybe it would look like you had something to hide?"

"They want me to change my name too."

"Who's they?"

"Sandrini. Bergé. Antoine."

"What do they want to change it to?"

"Something more glamorous," she said. "More French. And maybe not Hebrew in origin."

I nodded. The moment settled between us.

"They've suggested Amélie," she added.

"I like that," I told her. "It's almost as if your real name is hidden in there, if you say it quick enough. Annie Mayer. Amélie."

She nodded, a dreamy look on her face. "I do like him, you know. And I think perhaps he likes me too. But I've told him we won't do anything until after the first night, otherwise we might jinx it." She laughed. "I don't seem to be able to keep any secrets from you, do I?"

I laughed too, but my laughter was uneasy. I wish it had been the same for me. My secrets weighed heavy on me, and at night I dreamed of them spilling out, falling from my coat like the leaflets I wrote as soldiers shot me down as a traitor in the street.

37

The bustle at the Tabarin on the run-up to the new show almost resembled the old days, though I was keenly aware of the absence of my father. That delicious sawdusty smell of him as he pottered about the place serenely, while Ima hurried past with armfuls of costumes.

I was grateful that my mother had the distraction of making Annie's dress. Although she tried to hide it from us, she was in a bad way; desperate with worry, she'd grown very thin in the months since our father had been away. She missed our old neighbourhood and her friends there, the women who'd brought up their children side by side with her. In our new apartment, near Annie's in the Latin Quarter, we kept our heads down, avoided the gaze of our neighbours. Once, running an errand in the Pletzl, however, I'd caught my mother there too. Just standing outside our old apartment.

"What are you doing?" I asked.

"I wanted to see if there were any more letters from him." She looked at her feet, sorrow pressing down on her shoulders. I wondered if she felt the pull of the place – dark and dingy as it was, but our childhood home, nevertheless, where we'd learned to speak and walk and read and sew and love each other. Where my parents, in the early days of their marriage, had once felt safe, after fleeing Poland. I thought of the way Ima hummed wistful Gershwin songs when she was pregnant with Lili, the sunlight catching on her needle.

I remembered what my father had told me about the pogrom. "We'll keep you safe," I promised.

"But what if I can't keep you safe?" She couldn't look me in the eye. "What use am I?"

"Don't, Ima." I took her arm, as fragile as a wishbone beneath mine.

"You won't tell Rebecca?" she checked.

There weren't many secrets my mother kept from my sister. Flattery made me nod, but I extracted a promise from her, in turn, that she would avoid the Pletzl – as a neighbourhood full of Jewish immigrants it was a dangerous place to be now. "He's not going to come back," I told her sadly. "Not any time soon."

The last time I saw my mother smile was watching Annie try on her new dress. It was a work of art, fitting her like a glove around the bodice, while the skirt glided lightly over her slim hips and shimmered around her when she moved.

"It's perfect." Annie twirled in front of the mirror in her dressing room.

It had been such a long time since she'd had the chance to dress up for the stage. We all wore our clothes until they fell apart. Slipping into that shimmering silk must have felt like gliding into the ice-cold sea on a baking day.

I had another surprise for her. With the help of my mother's friends in the costume department, I'd bought a pair of shoes for Annie, which I thought would be perfect for that night. Though they were delicately made, silver and strappy, I'd asked the cobbler to make them as comfortable as possible, with a slightly flared heel and hidden cushioning in the sole. The perfect shoe for dancing.

I told Annie as much, when I gave them to her, and her eyes welled with emotion. "Esther," she said, "it's too much."

"I thought they could bring you luck."

As my friend did up the straps and twirled around the room in front of my mother and me, I smiled with pleasure. If the story of the Red Shoes pushed up through my thoughts like a weed, I did my best to pluck it from my mind.

When opening night finally arrived, I was nervous for Annie and Antoine, and for Lili, too, who had smuggled in her camera, ostensibly to take photographs of the new show, but in reality to document the more unwelcome members of our audience. Everyone was jittery that evening and even the good-natured Sandrini snapped at one of the callboys – something I'd never heard him do before. Dressed immaculately, he gathered the company around him for a brief pep talk not long before opening.

"We're back," he said. There were a few hoots of pleasure, a brief smattering of applause. "I know it's different now. But we're still going to put on a show. That is one thing we can do in Paris better than anywhere else in the world." He said the words pointedly. "Whatever else is going on, remember: big smiles and big performances, everyone.

Don't let them know what you are really thinking. You are safe out there on stage. You're the ones in the position of power, so never forget that."

"Chérie, I'm always in a position of power," drawled Gisy, wearing nothing but her usual peignoir. Everyone laughed, and it felt like the old days. Just briefly.

I was helping out as a dresser. Belle had requested me – I think she enjoyed the thrill of having me so close to her, right under Annie's nose. The plan was for me to attend to the pair of them, as the two most important dancers in the company.

It was a full house that night. We could hear it. Even backstage the theatre felt different, with footsteps and chatter vibrating through the building.

Dédée came to wish Annie luck. "Je te dis merde," she said with a smile. It was an old expression, from when spectators came to the theatre in horse-drawn carriages. The more shit there was back then, the better.

"That's no way to speak about our new audience members," Annie murmured. "Or maybe it is..."

I felt increasingly nervous in the countdown to curtain-up – "Amélie et Antoine" weren't on until almost the end of the night, so there was a long wait. I fidgeted around, while my mother made last-minute adjustments to the dress, my hand shaking as I tried to pin a gardenia into my friend's hair.

"Esther, you're making it worse." She took the flower from me and pinned it in herself.

"I'll find her something to do," Belle called cheerfully from next door. Once I was in there, she pushed the door closed – a sure sign to anyone paying attention that there was something going on between us. No one shut their dressing room without good reason. You might miss out on some gossip. Or a cue.

"How am I going to distract you until curtain-up?" she smiled naughtily, switching off the light and kissing me. "Say you love me," she said in the darkness. It was an act of madness to fool around like that, on the most important night of the year. "Say you'll never forget."

I said all the words she needed to hear.

Afterwards, Belle kept me busy, needing more powder, fresh lipstick, a lost earring to be found. On and on it went until, from backstage, we heard the curtain go up. From the volume of whoops and cheers, it sounded as if there was plenty of metaphorical manure out there. Paris was ready for a show, desperate for a distraction from daily life, to journey into the fantastical world created by Sandrini and Erté and their talented, plucky artists.

In the end, I almost missed my friend's debut. I heard Sandrini's voice announce them and rushed to the wings to watch, squeezing through the crush of people to claim a place next to my mother and Lili.

"What's going on with you and Belle?" my sister murmured in my ear as she raised her Leica ready to shoot the Tabarin's newest stars.

I glared at her. An impish smile curled on her lips.

"Snooping!" I hissed.

"Investigative work," she whispered back. "Don't worry – I'll never tell."

I don't think Lili did snoop on me, in reality. I think it was simply that she was the only person from whom I couldn't keep the secret of who I was. Fortunately for me, no one was paying any attention to whispers in the wings that night, not even Ima. All eyes were on the stage.

"Now for our newest act," Sandrini announced proudly, "France's answer to Fred and Ginger, but, dare I say it, more passionate than that famous pair, more elegant, more Parisian. The Tabarin is proud to present Amélie et Antoine…"

There was a cheer from the gallery, where most of the French members of the audience were sitting. It didn't matter that Annie wasn't French – never let the truth get in the way of a good story. A hush fell upon the house as the band began to play the opening bars of "Por Una Cabeza."

Annie performed that night with every part of her body. Not just her legs and feet, but her hands, her face, her fingers. She gave everything she had to Antoine, to all of us. And the tango made us yearn – yes, even the Germans, I think – for everything that had been lost: home and family and peace. It contained all the longing of everyone who watched and, when they finished, the audience leapt to their feet. The noise was deafening. I turned to Ima, who was gripping my arm so tightly her knuckles went white.

"Sometimes, it's worth it," she said quietly, her eyes on the dress she'd made. I think she meant not just her own handiwork but those brief moments in the theatre when we could escape ourselves. Her face was wet with tears. I knew she would be thinking of my father, of the way his hand caressed the surface of an item he'd carved and smoothed and made his own. "I don't think a piece of wood ever stops being a living thing," he'd whisper.

I wondered if my mother felt the same about the dress she'd made. "It's even more beautiful than Ginger Rogers' gown," I told her.

"I know," she said, quietly satisfied.

What was it like to be Annie that night? I'll never know, of course, but she told me that, as she walked on to the stage, she did her usual trick of letting everything drop away from her. There's a timelessness in moments of creation, which any artist will recognise, and Annie lost herself as she performed. But the second they stopped to take a bow, the world returned in a rush. She hadn't anticipated so strong a reaction and it almost unmasked her. She remembered, in that moment, who was in the audience.

A pair of German officers sat at a table very close to the stage. One had a thin face and glasses that reflected the stage lights, so that you couldn't see his eyes. He seemed to gaze at Annie with a penetrating stare.

She was shaking with adrenaline as she made her way off stage.

"You were incredible," I said, hugging her. I could feel her trembling beneath my embrace.

She leaned over to me and whispered in my ear. "I think one of them knows."

"Knows?" I couldn't guess at what she was talking about for a minute. "Something about the way he looked at me," she said. "I should have dyed my hair."

"Annie," I said. "Amélie, I mean. Think of the police station: you have to let all of that drop away."

"You're right," she murmured. There were other people pressing all around us, keen to congratulate the new stars of the Tabarin. "I'm Amélie now. And she doesn't have anything to hide."

38

May – July 1941

My friend was true to her word. She began calling herself Amélie that night, and, as long as I knew her, she never went back. Backstage, she and Antoine pushed through the clamour of people congratulating them. They made their way to her dressing room and, like Belle and I not so long before, they pushed the door closed.

Shaking with adrenaline, they fell upon each other like long-separated lovers, but even as Amélie kissed him, she told me later, she couldn't shake the fear of the man in the audience, staring at her – her and not Antoine– a predatory look on his face.

A knock at the door made them jump apart. Amélie wiped her lipstick from Antoine's cheek and ran a hand over her hair.

Outside, the bespectacled solider was waiting for her, as she had somehow known he would be. He was there with a friend – a large, avuncular man. It was against the house rules for audience members to visit the dressing rooms, but these two had slipped through.

"Mademoiselle," the officer with glasses began politely; the soldiers often had beautiful manners. "My compliments on your dancing." He presented her with a bunch of carnations.

Amélie tilted her head a little as she accepted the flowers. A subtle thing – something she'd learned in ballet class. Revealing a little neck, showing she was listening, but giving nothing away.

"I wonder, if…" The officer looked from her to Antoine, and Amélie realised she was making him every bit as nervous as he was making her.

"My friend here would like you to join him for dinner," interrupted his larger companion, in heavily accented French. He clapped a hand on the shoulder of his colleague.

Amélie swallowed. "I can't… which is to say." She glanced at Antoine, and perhaps it was then that the penny dropped.

"Are you sure?" insisted the larger officer, his cheeks ruddy with vin rouge. "We'd make it well worth your while."

I can't, Amélie thought. I won't. She wanted to drop the flowers on the floor and stamp on them.

But the bespectacled solider was more sensitive than his companion. "Forgive me – I should have understood. A performance like that…" He sighed wistfully. "I knew a girl back in Berlin who could dance as beautifully as you."

And they saw a tiny glimpse of his life, then, like a door left open. Just ajar. He kissed Amélie's hand and shook Antoine's, and hurried his more bullish friend away from them.

Their encounter with their first fan was an uncertain thing – delicate, frightening. Up close, you could see they were just people too. But I don't know if that makes it any better.

*

Of course, Amélie hadn't lied. She had been Antoine's ever since their first conversation. Not long afterwards, they consummated their partnership.

She and Antoine became stars overnight. There were more glamorous gowns – designed by Erté and Jeanne Lanvin. The flowers in Amélie's hair grew bigger, her accessories more excessive. The camera loved her and Antoine.

There were so many pictures taken by Lili, or press photographers attending their latest show: Antoine in tails, Amélie in glittering gowns, always with a sleek bias cut, sculpted to her body, the skirts liquid-smooth as she cut through the air. In their lifts, Amélie flew like a bird: photos caught her suspended, perfectly still as her dress billowed behind her.

"I always was better at the light than the dark," she said, almost ruefully, as we looked through their latest batch of publicity pictures.

"But what light," I said. "You look like a swan up there. Pavlova herself would be impressed."

"It's funny because I always thought I would find fame dancing with the Ballet Russe," she murmured. "Not tangoing in a music hall."

They shared their success generously with the rest of us. Antoine was friends with some Polish farmers who supplied the black market, and he ensured his friends never went hungry. Amélie hosted suppers, feeding as many of us as she could cram into her tiny apartment in the Latin Quarter. Briefly, on those nights, life would not seem so very bad. As long as we didn't think too much about who was paying for the best seats in the Tabarin.

As everyone predicted, the romance didn't last. It was Belle who told me, as we shared an illicit cigarette in her dressing room. Tobacco was scarce, and women couldn't buy it during the war, but men were allowed one packet a week and Belle had admirers devoted enough to indulge her habit. She shared her spoils with me when she could.

Was it love? I never got over my essential distrust of her, never knew how far things went with the men who fluttered around her outside the stage door after a performance. I never asked. I just took what I was given and waited until I was summoned. That's the way it could be with performers: I always knew the difference between us and them.

"If I was able to tell you something about Antoine, would you want to know?" Belle passed me the cigarette, leaving a scarlet smear on the stub.

"A new woman?" It wasn't hard to guess.

"Touché."

"Not you?" I asked carefully. I didn't want her to know that I cared.

She laughed. "Mon Dieu, non. Marguerite." She named a slight, pretty dancer in the ensemble. "I thought your friend might want to know."

She avoided saying Amélie's name – she was always "the Canadian" or "your friend". I wondered if she called her "La Juive" to other people. I also wondered, despite her apologies, if that's what she called me.

By the time I spoke to Amélie, someone else had got

there first. I found her in her dressing room, redoing her eye make-up.

She glanced at me. "You've heard."

"I'm sorry." I joined her in front of the mirror, put a comforting hand on her shoulder.

"And now I have to go on stage and pretend we're still in love."

Outside, we could hear the footfall and bustle of the theatre filling up.

"You'll be able to do that." I gave her shoulder a squeeze. "You've had lots of practice at pretending."

Amélie bit her lip; I could see her eyes filling with tears, which she brushed away furiously.

"I felt secure when I was with him." She sighed. "Some nights, after leaving here, I couldn't be sure I'd get home safely."

I knew what that was like: stumbling through the streets in blackout after the curfew, hearing footsteps coming towards you and feeling your heart tighten, barely breathing until you discerned the identity of the person approaching, or heard the steps change direction.

"I know who he is," she said, returning to the job of cleaning up her eye make-up. "I know what people say. But there's a good heart in there – I'm sure of it. And he made me feel safe."

"But you're not safe," I wanted to say. "None of us is."

39

While the rest of the world is watching the Olympics in London, Mim and Lucky dance their way through New York. They find tango classes and milongas, returning to the group they saw in Central Park. As they dance, at this milonga and others, the first sentences of stories – the very beginnings of things – start to form in Mim's head. She jots them down in a notebook, on receipts, napkins, any paper she has to hand, and pretends she can't see Lucky gazing at her fondly as she does.

All the dancing and loving have brought back her appetite. Her mother has stopped asking if she's eating, perhaps she can see from the glow in Mim's cheeks that she is – tucking into pizza and sushi and burritos and all the delicious food that New York has to offer. And sometimes, especially if she's in one of New York's Parisian-style bistros like Pastis, tucking into eggs Benedict, she thinks about how fortunate she is to eat so well, without fretting, in the way that Esther and her family did, about where the next meal might come from.

She never thought of herself as lucky before, but maybe she is – to be alive now, to be alive at all. Her limbs feel different – less heavy and stiff with grief. Now, with a little more flesh on her bones and a bloom to her cheeks, when she catches sight of herself in the glint of a Fifth Avenue shop window, she barely recognises the woman she sees.

One morning they bump into Bibi, who swiftly senses a kindred spirit in Lucky. "Come up and see me," she coos like the old screen siren she is.

"You don't have to," Mim tells him later in bed, her sticky cheek against his chest, listening to the beat of his heart. "Visit Bibi, I mean."

"Why not?" he says. "She seems right up my street."

And he appears to be genuinely delighted with Bibi's company the next day, partaking in her afternoon martinis and grilling her about all the old movie stars in her photos in a way, Mim never has. He helps Bibi to take each picture carefully from the wall as she sits with it in her lap, telling the story behind it.

"Frank and Ava," she sighs. "That was a pickle." Or, "Marlene – she made a move once, but I was spoken for at the time."

"You never told me you were staying below a living legend," Lucky tells Mim.

"Oh, I don't know about that," Bibi laughs. "I always just played the kooky friend."

"Maybe I wanted to keep her to myself." Mim sticks her tongue out at Lucky.

"Ha, too late," he laughs. "You won't be able to get rid

of me," he tells Bibi. "Now," he asks, "did you ever meet
Fred Astaire?"

Bibi claps her hands with delight. "That's a story. I was
lucky enough to dance with him – just the once, mind, at
the Stork Club…"

"What?" Lucky jumps to his feet. "When? And, you
know, now I'm obliged to dance with you, so I can say I've
partnered the woman who partnered Astaire."

"Partnered, ha," Bibi laughs.

"Mim, play us a tune on your phone," Lucky says.

"Oh, I think we can do better than that." Bibi nods at a
record player housed in a polished walnut cabinet next to
her drinks table.

Mim riffles through the records and grins when she find
a copy of Ella Fitzgerald and Louis Armstrong singing
"Cheek To Cheek."

As the music starts, Lucky gives a little bow. "May I have
the pleasure of your next foxtrot?"

"Let me check." Bibi scans an imaginary dance card.
"You're in luck – this one's free."

Lucky offers his hand and Bibi gets to her feet. She is a
good dancer, following his lead with ease, her feet shuffling
in tiny steps, her shoulders shimmying expressively. Mim
sits on the floor by the record player, watching them and
listening to those decades-old lyrics with new ears. About
being in heaven, about your cares disappearing.

"The body never forgets," Bibi tells Mim proudly, when
the pair of them return, flushed, to the seats – she to her
chair, Lucky next to Mim on the floor.

"You're a born dancer," Lucky says. "You both are."

He takes Mim's hand and kisses her cheek. Mim flushes

with pleasure. She's not had much experience in being on the receiving end of public displays of affection from a guy. She likes it.

"Are you still going through Esther's papers?" Bibi checks.

"A little," Mim admits. She can't lie in front of Lucky.

"I wake sometimes to her sitting on the floor, reading," he says. "She's a terrible insomniac. But she's started writing, too. Did you know that?"

"I thought I was getting better," Mim says quickly. "At sleeping."

She doesn't want to talk about her own jottings. It's early days. She's keen not to jinx it. The sleeplessness is one part of her life that's still not working. Sometimes, in those lonely hours, her happiness feels like a brittle thing: as she watches Lucky sleep, she worries that she's waiting as much as she is watching. Waiting for it all to go wrong again. She still dreads the recurring nightmare, the pinning down of her arms. Lucky held her like that once in bed, playfully. Just for a moment.

"Don't do that," she said urgently. "I hate being held like that."

And he stopped straight away. "I'm sorry – do you want to talk about it?"

She hadn't.

"Why are you reading in bed with this gorgeous man next to you?"

Mim shrugs and smiles at her tipsy friend.

"She's a strange young lady," Bibi whispers conspiratorially. "A bit melancholic at times, but I've grown rather fond of her."

"She's the bee's knees," Lucky whispers back, grinning at Mim.

Still perspiring from the dancing, Bibi pushes up the sleeve of her pink cardigan and Mim notices, for the first time, a five-digit number inked on her left arm. She tries not stare, but she can't get it out of her mind.

Taking herself to the bathroom, Mim perches on the tub, perturbed by Bibi's tattoo. She remembers a Holocaust survivor coming to speak to them at school, but this is different: Bibi is a friend, someone she has grown close to. And yet someone who, despite her warmth, still has her guard up. Mim wants to know more, but she can't ask today. Not with Lucky around.

A blister on her foot from all the dancing is beginning to rub and she opens the bathroom cabinet to look for a plaster. Inside is a huge bottle of Chanel No 5. A tub of the hand lotion too. Mim takes it out and gives it a sniff. It's a scent that takes her back to duty-free with her mother picking up another bottle for Esther.

"It reminds her of home, I think," her mum used to say.

Good friends often share similar tastes, Mim thinks. She and Frankie would share everything – books, clothes, make-up. Never men, though. They had different types. And Frankie wouldn't, she told herself. Kept telling herself.

The problem was hers – not her friend's – she just never got over that feeling that she was second best. It nagged at her when Robbie eventually began to stay over. She would find herself watching his face, trying to read how much he looked at Frankie, how loudly he laughed at her jokes. At the end of the night, as the three of them headed to bed, she would sometimes wonder if he would rather be in the other bedroom with Frankie. She splashes her face with cold water as if it could rinse her memories away.

When she returns to the others, Lucky is seated in one of the armchairs next to Bibi. FeeFee is on his lap, looking up with utter adoration.

"We were just saying we should go on a day trip," he says. "Go to the beach. Take a picnic."

Mim feels unsettled, conscious of the swelling of unhappiness that started in the bathroom. It's not only Lucky's suggestion, though she doesn't like it, or the tipsiness of her companions, but some incomplete thought she can't identify.

"Maybe something else." She glances around the room for her key. The party is over for her. "I don't like the beach."

She can feel the other two exchange looks behind her back – the kinds of looks Abi and her mother swap. Maybe it's near its end – this good thing with Lucky. Maybe if she ruins it herself, she won't have to worry about losing it some other way.

40

"How's Belle?" Lili asked one morning, as we lay next to each other, under the tattered patchwork quilt we shared.

"Fouineuse," I said. Snooper.

"It's OK." She seemed to sense my anxiety, my shame. "You can talk to me," she insisted. "I'm not a baby any more."

I glanced at her. It was true – she'd just turned eighteen and, though still slight of build like our mother, with the same light, quick footstep, she'd lost the puppyish look of childhood. Her girlish plaits were gone, too. She'd recently convinced someone at the Tabarin to cut her hair. Our mother picked up the plait-ends from the floor and tucking them into a bag. Now, Lili wore her hair in a neat bob, pinned in a side parting. There was a natural wave to it, though she didn't spend time fussing around with it as other girls did. Too busy patrolling the streets with her camera.

"I met a man in London." I lay on my side, picking at the

peeling wallpaper in that dank room, a repeating pattern of cherries. "A man who liked men." I thought then of Ambrose, with his varnished fingernails; I hoped, wherever he was, that he was OK. "He said I would know when I found my person. Her, he said, when I found her."

"Do you think it's Belle?" Lili asked.

I shook my head. "We have fun, but…"

Hearing a muffled shout in the street below, we both fell silent, our ears alert to any disturbance. It was nothing in the end – a rare moment of exuberance. "Is it Amélie?" Lili asked quietly.

One of the cherries tore off too quickly under my fingers. Staring at it, I was tempted to call my sister a snoop again. "No," I said at last. "She's something else to me. My friend. My muse."

"But you'd hate to be on stage." Lili jumped out of bed and poured water into the washstand, splashing her face and patting it dry.

"It's not that. It's just she's never been afraid to pursue something she wants. I think too much about everything. I worry; I'm a coward.

"You're not," Lili said, pulling yesterday's skirt from the back of a chair. "Not everyone's brave in the same way. Amélie and I are…"

"Impulsive?" I teased. "Nosy?"

Lili shrugged off the jibes. "You're just waiting for your moment." She fastened the buttons on her blouse. "I think he was right: that she is out there for you." She threw me a grin. "Will you tell me when you meet her?"

"Of course." I swung my legs off the bed, moving more slowly than Lili, as usual. "And will you tell me when you've met someone?"

"Maybe." She stuck her tongue at me and turned to the blackout curtain. Shreds of morning light frayed at its edges. "Come on," she said impatiently. "We're wasting it."

In June 1942, it became mandatory for Jews over the age of six in occupied France to wear the yellow star, with the word Juif in black. My family and Amélie hadn't registered, so we didn't wear them, but we came across people we knew with those hateful badges on. It was impossible to know how to react – impossible to look at them and impossible not to. Sometimes I told myself to harden my heart. It was a phrase I began to repeat in my head in those years when I saw something terrible. I'd instruct that organ, as if it could listen, to toughen up. And I would imagine a protective layer growing around it. I don't think it ever worked.

I remember walking with Amélie along one of the narrow, cobbled streets of the Latin Quarter. We were arm in arm, laughing at something, and we saw an old woman walking towards us – small, white-haired with a tired coat, the yellow star on it. We fell quiet as we passed her, stopped laughing at whatever silly thing it was. She met our gaze proudly, sensing our shame. She stared us down.

Once we'd passed her, Amélie said, "Do you think she's a good cook?"

"What?" I asked, confused.

"Or a wonderful seamstress, like your mother? Or a former teacher? Or a mother? A grandmother? Do you think she has a favourite artist? Or a favourite song?"

I shook my head. "We don't know her."

"I can't remember the last time I set foot inside a synagogue," Amélie said. "Probably when I was back home.

To me, being Jewish isn't the most important fact about me. Being a dancer is. But the Nazis don't care about that – the yellow star reduces you to a single thing."

I was quiet. "Do you feel like we should be wearing them?"

"Esther," Amélie said, "nobody should be wearing them."

We started to hear rumours of a rafle, a round-up, that summer – the warnings came via our friends. Antoine, Sandrini and others repeated them. As a family, we discussed leaving Paris, but where would we go? What would we do? People had already started to disappear. People we knew.

At the Tabarin, we'd found Gisy weeping, not long before her cue to go on stage. Her lover, the Jewish doctor Gilbert Doukan, had been arrested and taken to Drancy internment camp on the outskirts of Paris. "But all he does is heal people," she told us helplessly. "Why would anyone hurt him?"

We couldn't decide whether the Tabarin or our apartment might be safer, but whenever we needed to travel between the two, Amélie offered to walk with us. She took her bicycle – glad, I think, of a prop – and, wheeling it along, she wore her expression of benevolent calm. Her confidence and her poise were such that you would never know she was a Jewish dancer, accompanying a Jewish family, all hiding in plain sight.

I think it was because we were dividing our time between two places that it went wrong. That day, all of us had been at the Tabarin, hidden mostly in a back room that was usually used for storage. But the intense heat and various chores of the day pulled us out from time to time, and we didn't keep track of each other. When the news of the round-up arrived at the theatre, white faces repeating stories of the vicious arrests taking place across the city, no one knew where Ima was.

Amélie and I raced back to the apartment, but it was empty. We had to be careful, as we checked every room, to keep the panic from our voices so the neighbours didn't hear.

"She might have gone back to the Pletzl," I said to my sisters when we all reconvened at the Tabarin.

"Why would she have done that?" Rebecca asked.

"I found her there once, looking for Papa."

The silence between us was as heavy as a greatcoat in that cloying heat.

"And you never thought to say?" Rebecca's voice was ice.

"She made me promise." My own sounded choked. "And I told her never to go back."

"But she wasn't well." Rebecca began to pace.

"We shouldn't have let her out of our sight," Lili said quietly.

We stayed awake all night in that stuffy Tabarin back room, waiting for our mother's quick step, for her exasperated exclamation: "Girls! What are you doing?" We waited all night, but she never came.

At that most dangerous time, our mother just walked out of the theatre and back to her old neighbourhood. I still don't know what she was thinking. I imagine her in her summer dress, a hat on, a tight belt around her tiny waist, always respectable, always immaculate, picking her way through the baking streets towards her death.

Why? Why would she leave a place of relative safety to venture out on a day like that? It was unbearably hot, it was true, and there was a kind of madness in the air – like the crackle before a storm. A strange silence preceded the knocking on the doors, punctuated by the occasional bleating cry of a child from a cellar or some other secret place.

I suspect she'd never stopped returning to our old apartment, despite her promise to me. I understand the pull of places: I feel the magnetic tug of Paris, even now, strong enough for it to cause a twinge of pain at night. I wake bolt upright and think, I must go back – how have I come so far from home? And then I remember the thing that I long for is gone. The people I loved, gone. The Bal Tabarin razed to the ground. The young girl who mooned and smoked and laughed at other people's jokes – she has gone too, and there is an old lady in her place, older than my mother, as she was back then, but never as brave or foolish as her, as she walked across Paris in July 1942, back to her old neighbourhood. A suicide mission.

Maybe she wanted to be with her friends. Maybe she wanted to check my father hadn't come home. To see if she hadn't missed one of his postcards. Maybe she was just bone tired of waiting and hiding, hiding and waiting. Maybe she thought it would be simpler to walk out like a dancer, head high, chin up and say, "Here I am."

They picked her up, of course. The French police, not the Germans, as we originally heard. She and the others were taken in buses to the Vélodrome d'Hiver, and we travelled as close as we dared to that dreadful place. The noise of it was terrible. And the stench. I imagined our mother in her white summer dress in that unbearable heat. I thought of the things she'd carried in her handbag: mints, my father's photograph, a darning mushroom, a needle and thread.

We planned how we might rescue her, what we might do, how we might do it. We came up with implausible ideas – to bribe the nurses going in or dress up as nurses ourselves. Anything to get her out.

"I'll go," Lili said. "Let me do it. No one ever suspects me."

"No," Rebecca and I both snapped.

Shortly after, we were ordered to leave the area.

Here are some things that happened: they shot gendarmes who'd warned people to escape. Parents gassed themselves and their children to prevent them from being taken away. One woman threw her babies from a roof to save them from an unknown death. Our mother walked across the city to the place where she'd loved her husband and brought up her children, where she sat in the window and sewed and hummed and made challah and danced, always moving, always alert to the next attack. She walked across the city and she never came back.

41

July 1942 – August 1943

They kept thirteen thousand people in the Vélodrome d'Hiver for five days in the baking heat, with almost no water, food or adequate sanitation. Then they were moved to internment camps, before being sent by train to Auschwitz. I can't imagine what that journey back to Poland must have been like for our fragile mother. I still can't bear to think of it. I don't know how we got through those days, or how those on stage performed at night to the German soldiers. I don't know how any of Paris kept going at all.

There was the time before we lost our mother and there was the time after. She was everywhere in the apartment, in the Tabarin. I was haunted by the sound of her quick, lively footstep, her idiosyncratic expressions, half-French, half-Yiddish, the chug of her sewing machine.

We never recovered from the loss and, in practical terms, we started to go under too, struggling to pay rent on the apartment. There was never enough money, never enough to eat. We were terrified, all the time, that we might be discovered. There was a price on our heads – a hundred francs for anyone who betrayed a Jewish neighbour to the authorities. I heard somewhere that more than a thousand letters of denunciation were sent to the authorities a day.

After giving up our apartment, we slept at the Tabarin, adjusting to the creaks of the building, the occasional step of a nightwatchman. He was a friend, we'd been assured, but it was difficult to trust anyone.

A note she must have scribbled in those days at the Vélodrome d'Hiver found its way to us.

My girls, Look after each other. Keep the stitches between you strong until we meet again.

Until we meet again. Life became more difficult for everyone in Paris after the Vél d'Hiv round-up. The atmosphere at the Tabarin changed too. There was less laughter. We all got thinner in the bitter winter that followed. Our shared suppers became rarer and less exuberant.

One night, at such a dinner the following year, Amélie and Antoine told us all that they'd been invited to perform on a tour of prisoner-of-war camps in Germany.

"You won't go," said Bluebell, Annie's friend from Besançon, who was there that evening. "They asked me too and I said absolutely not. I wouldn't dream of taking my dancers to that place."

Things were difficult for Bluebell, with so many mouths to feed, and Marcel, her Jewish husband, still in hiding. There had been some terrifying times for them, but, like all of us, she carried on. Marcel lived alone at that time in a sixth-floor attic on rue de la Bûcherie, which a friend of his rented for him.

As it happened, the apartment was just across the street from a Prefecture of Police, but somehow the gendarmes missed the musician in hiding on their doorstep. The redoubtable Bluebell managed to run two households – one in secret – procuring food for Marcel and ensuring his washing and darning were done, even providing him with paper and reading material for the long, tedious hours. Marcel, it was said, was desperate for a piano, but, at that, his wife drew the line. Live music would attract interest they didn't need.

At Bluebell's outburst, Amélie and Antoine exchanged a look. Their romance was long over by then – and Antoine was still with Marguerite – but there was still a strong bond between the dance partners.

"Edith Piaf is going," Antoine said. "Charles Trenet. I've heard rumours about Maurice Chevalier joining us too."

"In that case, you must," snapped Rebecca. "If stars of that size are going."

She got up to leave.

"It's not the kind of thing you say no to," Antoine said quietly.

"She did." Rebecca gestured appreciatively in Bluebell's direction. "She managed it."

"It's different for her – she's English," said Antoine.

"Irish," Bluebell corrected him tartly. "And she's right – I don't see why you must go."

"They say they're going to release five hundred prisoners," Amélie said quietly. She'd been silent until then. "But I don't believe them."

"So why go?" Rebecca insisted.

"What if we saw your father?" Amélie asked. "What if

we could take some kind of message?"

"There's a slim chance of that," My sister said huffily. But I could tell, like me, she was thinking the matter over.

None of us had returned to the Pletzl since the round-up, but we heard our old neighbourhood had been emptied. We'd lost all contact with our father.

"Aren't you frightened?" I asked, from my usual place next to her. Amélie had been a huge source of strength to me since Ima's departure, knowing instinctively how to comfort me.

"Here," she said, picking the dress my mother had made for her first performance. "Hold this." I sat with it on my lap, stroking the silk, as if some essence of Ima were contained within the fibres.

Amélie shrugged. "I'm frightened all the time. We all are, aren't we?"

"Yes. But to be in Germany…"

"There's nothing we can say." Bluebell stood up to go. "They've clearly made up their minds."

Bluebell was right, as usual. Amélie and Antoine were joining the tour and there was nothing anybody could do about it. But not so long after that dinner, Bluebell needed her own favour from Amélie.

The office of the friend who rented Marcel's flat for him was raided and the address of the hideout seized by the authorities. The friend rang Bluebell in a panic at six in the morning, and she, remembering that Amélie lived near Marcel in the Latin Quarter, called on her in turn.

She got straight to the point. "Marcel needs a dance partner." You never knew who was listening.

"A dance partner?" Amélie didn't understand at first.

"Yes." Bluebell insisted. "It's a difficult pas de deux – one I can't do any more because of the children. But a young woman like you, who I know has those particular skills," she added, "might accompany him."

The penny dropped and Amélie agreed to the task – a dangerous one. Taking Marcel to a new hiding place. A couple was less likely to attract attention than a man on his own.

When the time came, there was only one hair-raising moment, passing a gendarme on the street, who gazed at the pair with some interest. Amélie felt the warning signs in her body – a tightening of the shoulders, a prickling sensation running down her arms. She forced herself to look back at the gendarme. To avoid his gaze would be a betrayal of her fear. Their eyes met for a moment and Amélie realised she recognised him. It was the young man who'd knocked on her door the morning she'd been taken to Besançon. She remembered his kindness and flashed him a quick smile. He nodded in return, gazed from her to Marcel and passed them by. Her heart slowed a little and she realised how tightly she'd been gripping Marcel's arm.

"We live to dance another day," she murmured. But, like all of us, she felt sure it would catch up with her. No one was that lucky.

I went over to her apartment as she packed for the German tour. I brought a letter for my father, just in case. She hid it in the lining of her suitcase.

She paused, stooped over the case, staring at those silver shoes. "Am I like Giselle?" she asked. "Is dancing going to kill me?"

"Don't be silly," I reassured her.

"Maybe it's unnatural for a woman," she said. "To love something so much – something that's not a husband and children. Maybe there's something wrong with me."

"You're just nervous about the tour," I said. "It'll be all right." But I was as worried as the rest of them.

42

After putting Esther's book away, Mim lies awake, her mind racing, her thoughts circling around what happened to her great-grandmother, of what it must have been like for her daughters. And she's still only seeing part of the story. What happened to Lili? She still has no idea. And she's unwilling to bring it up with her mum again, can't bear the prospect of more evasion.

But in the days that follow she struggles to shake the tightening sense of dread deep in her belly. And the tango, which previously struck her as the answer to everything, doesn't seem to be able to maintain its trick of soothing her. At a milonga, she gets into a fight with an older man, who steers her around the dancefloor like a wheelbarrow.

You never knew what might happen in a tanda – the set of three or four songs during which you had to stick to the same partner. A handsome guy like Lucky could be surprisingly tender rather than arrogant; a fragile old man wearing a cravat could have a nasty streak; a slight woman could offer the strongest lead.

With the wheelbarrow guy, Mim wanted to show off some of her new moves – a gancho or boleo – but he simply trots her around the room leaned up against his plump belly. When she complains to him, he tells her that she doesn't know anything about anything.

After she storms off, she expects Lucky to take her side as usual, but he says instead, as if she has betrayed some sacred law, "You never break off a tanda."

He, meanwhile, has been dancing with the most beautiful woman in the room – an elegant Argentinian with a sheet of pristine dark hair, which Lucky's hand caressed in the tango hold. They make a striking pair – dark-haired, long legged – stalking across the room together like big sexy cats.

"Why don't you go back to her?" Mim needles. "Dance with her again."

"I don't want to dance with Maria." He took her hand. "I'd rather spend time with my girlfriend."

Mim wakes early, pondering it all crossly. She loves New York, but sometimes she feels so far from home. She wants to tell someone – Frankie – about the awful Maria. How dare she be so elegant and so – Mim searches for the word – chic. She spits it out in her head like an insult.

What a bitch. She can hear Frankie's laughter in her head. Elegant and chic.

What do you think? Mim asks her friend, as she watches Lucky sleeping.

I think he's gorgeous, Frankie says. But she sounds wistful, as if she's looking at an old photograph of him. She's holding something back – Mim can tell.

What is it? she asks. Do you have psychic powers wherever you are?

Hardly, Frankie chuckles. Where I am is in your head.

Mim finds she can't say anything to that.

I was just going to say – Frankie continues wearily in the tone of a ghost that is tired of delivering accurate premonitions – that he's nice. And it's a shame you're going to fuck it up.

"I won't," Mim snaps. "You don't know that."

But she realises, too late, that she's said the words out loud, and Lucky has started to stir. How dare Frankie come along and ruin things for her, like she always does. Like she always did.

"Are you OK?" Lucky murmurs.

Mim stares at the ceiling. "I've been reading about my great-grandmother."

She can feel him listening, waiting for her to say more.

"And there are other things I can't stop thinking about." She hesitates, unsure whether to confide in him. "My grandmother and Esther had a sister they never talked about. Lili."

"Did she die in the war too?"

Mim shakes her head. "I don't know. They never spoke about her. Silence is golden – that's what my grandmother used to say."

"That's a big secret to keep." He takes her hand.

"Exactly."

"Does your mum know?"

She thinks of his mother, envying their closeness. The bubble of two they seem to share. "I don't know." She props herself up on one elbow. "I haven't spoken to her about it, really. I want to finish Esther's story first."

"Why don't you read it all in one go?" he asks. "Just get it done? I could stay with you, if you'd like. So I'd be here if you needed me." He mimes zipping his mouth shut.

She laughs. "A fidget like you?"

Grinning, he mimes a hand jive. "Well, I could always go upstairs and dance with Bibi."

"No, it's OK." Mim picks up his hand, examining his palm. "I'd never get you back."

43

October 1943

Dear Esther,

Where to start? First, I like Piaf very much. Perhaps it was inevitable that two little street kids like us might see eye to eye. She is petite, elegant, a potent bottle of charisma. On stage, she cuts a fragile figure – as tiny as the sparrow she is named after – and then she opens her mouth and unleashes a voice of such raw power that it always casts a spell on the room.

It was Antoine, of course, who first caught her eye on the train to Germany. She checked with me first. "You wouldn't mind if he and I went to bed together, would you?"

"Antoine is free to do as he wishes," I replied. A line I can trot out breezily these days, as you know.

Anyway, Antoine wasn't interested, and her affections have moved on to one of the members of Fred Adison's band. I'm relieved about that. It might have been difficult to see them together, up close. She is generous with us – a kindred spirit – and I know she has her own Jewish friends and lovers back at home.

Everyone on tour has someone to protect. Something to hide. Charles Trenet, who sings "Douce France" to French prisoners every night, has his own secrets, of course.

"The pair of us here at a time like this," he said to me once. "What are we thinking?"

"As if we have a choice," I replied. It was the first and only indication that he knew what I might be hiding.

It is a strange time for me and harder than I could have imagined. The endless beaming and posing – me in my glittering gowns and Antoine in his tails – as we dance for an audience of skinny prisoners, who don't know what tomorrow will bring. They surround us after our shows, offering cigarettes and other small gifts. It is almost unbearable.

But I prefer their attention to the German soldiers at the Tabarin. I don't mind that some of them stare at me, perhaps imagine themselves in Antoine's place. I steal my own glimpses of them in return, always keeping my eyes peeled for any sign of your father.

I thought I saw him once. I stared for too long at an older man's face. It was the same shape as your father's and he had the same greying hair and thick dark eyebrows. For a moment, I felt all hot and cold and excited that it might be him. But it wasn't, Esther. I'm so sorry.

The man I'd been looking at came to find me afterwards. He asked shyly, "Mademoiselle, are you married?"

Castigating myself for leading him on with lingering

looks, I said I wasn't – and he asked then if I would do something for him. Sometimes the younger men asked for a kiss. And sometimes, well, I give them what they want. I wondered if it might be something like that, but he asked if I would take a letter for him. A letter for his wife.

"It won't take me any time to prepare it," he promised. "I write to her in my head every night. I know the words exactly." He gave a shy smile. "They are not very original – they are what we would all say: 'I love you, I carry the memory of you in my heart. It is what keeps me going. It is a gift I unwrap every day that I never tire of.' No matter what they steal from us, they can never take that, can they? You can destroy a human body but you can't destroy love. I want her to know that."

I blinked away tears and agreed to take the letter. Pretty soon Antoine and I were inundated with requests from other prisoners to do the same for them. We gave away many of our belongings at that stalag and filled an empty suitcase with the letters.

When we left, it was like carrying a bomb. Something that could kill every single member of the party if the circumstances conspired against us. Imagine: no more Piaf, no more Trenet. Think of the songs we might miss in the future.

We carried the suitcase through Berlin almost without incident, and then, just before we reached the train station, the air-raid siren began to scream. At the sound of it, we all piled into the nearest bunker, squashed up like children playing sardines. I locked eyes with a tall man in the distinctive blue-grey uniform of the Luftwaffe. He had a neatly trimmed moustache and grey eyes that seemed to take in everything at a glance. It made me nervous. As I sat on my precious suitcase, I murmured something about how a lady likes to keep her treasures close.

"Not just the ladies," he said in perfect French, nodding at the musicians still carrying their instruments.

Outside, bombs began to fall, shaking the bunker's walls. The lights flickered out. Next to me, Edith began to mutter a prayer to Saint Thérèse, whose medal she always wears around her neck. To cheer her up, her lover began to play the first bars of "L'Accordéoniste", a song by the Jewish composer Michel Emer, on his guitar. The other musicians joined in. Piaf's astounding voice sang a few tremulous notes. For a minute or two, there was comfort in the familiar song.

"How can you?" A woman shrieked through the noise. "How can you play music when they are trying to kill us?"

"We know whose side the French are really on," boomed another, a man's voice this time. "If I could see, I would smash your instruments over your head."

It went very quiet then and I was scared even to take a breath. I was acutely aware of what I was sitting on. The Luftwaffe officer was so close I could have touched him.

The lights flickered on again and everyone glanced carefully about themselves, trying to work out who had been shouting what in the dark. Slowly, almost insolently, Edith's guitarist began to strum again and, one by one, the other musicians joined in.

It was far too cramped to dance, but Antoine and I started to clap along to the music in solidarity, and Edith began to sing. It was the most intimate gig you could imagine with France's Little Sparrow, but not every member of the audience appreciated it.

A woman stood up, towering over the seated musicians, her face tight with rage. "How can you just sit here? Insulting us? Playing music?" There followed a list of curses in German. A few others clambered to their feet and joined in, shrieking in a mixture of German and French.

The last one to stand was that Luftwaffe officer: you could tell by the way he held himself that he was accustomed to taking control of a room. He stood up slowly, as if this squabble was beneath him. His grey eyes lingered on my face. I sat with all my weight on the suitcase. I know how to hold myself, to make myself as light as air in lifts, but I also know how to do the opposite – and I pressed my weight down on the suitcase as if my life depended on it.

"This is life during a war." He addressed the woman who had started the shrieking. "There is always someone dying somewhere." He paused. "I think they are brave to make music here underground, surrounded by the enemy. We don't know how much life we have left," he continued. "We could all die like rats in this bunker, buried underground, and wouldn't it be nicer to do that listening to some music, enjoying the company of beautiful women?" And he smiled warmly at me and Piaf.

An uneasy peace settled. The officer and some of his countrymen even joined in with the clapping and singing, though the furious woman, who had started the ruckus, folded her arms and sank deep into herself. Who knows of her suffering, of whom she'd lost? Everybody has their own story to tell.

I suppose the point is: you don't always know who'll be on your side. Sometimes friends arrive dressed like an enemy. And sometimes, I suppose, the opposite might be true.

With love, Amélie

PS I won't put this in the suitcase with the other letters – you'll never guess where I'll hide it. I have the perfect place, thanks to you.

44

Lucky has been planning some kind of surprise for her today. Mim hasn't had the heart to tell him there's nothing she likes less.

"Give me a clue," she asked yesterday. "Do I need to pack anything? What should I wear?"

"Just something cool, as usual," he said. "Shorts and a T-shirt. Maybe take sunscreen. I'll pack the rest."

Before they leave, he dashes up to Bibi's and returns carrying an old-fashioned picnic basket. He insists on stopping at her favourite deli and filling it with expensive treats, almost bouncing with excitement as he enjoys some kind of banter with the shop assistant.

Mim waits for him outside, trying to imagine she's someone else. Someone without a past. She thinks of the way Amélie could let all her history drop away from her as she walked on to stage or accompanied Jewish friends to safety. If only Mim could do that; if only she could do it forever.

They walk hand in hand to the subway station, without saying much. Lucky's silence seems to crackle with anticipation for the day ahead, but Mim's is darker. She can't get Esther's story out of her head, and her mood has been spiralling. It's still early but the heat is settling already. At Jay Street–MetroTech, there's the buzz of festival excitement, despite the early start. Everyone's dressed for the beach – women in summer dresses, candy-apple reds, lemon-sherbet yellows.

"This feels like a trip," Mim says suspiciously.

"Nothing gets past you, does it?" Lucky laughs.

"Are we going to the beach?" she checks.

He continues his bouncing stride towards the platform. "Can't you just give my surprise a chance?"

"I don't know if I can," she says.

His hopeful face just fills her with dread. I can't do this, Mim thinks. She stops in her tracks.

"Mim, come on." Lucky reaches out to her but she pulls back. A woman passing by in a gingham sundress throws them a sharp glance.

"Are you going to make me swim?" She's aware that she sounds like a child. "I told you I don't do that. I told you I don't like the beach."

"I thought maybe you were just resistant – like you were to dancing."

"No." Mim shakes her head. "It's different." She feels a shiver of cold pass through her. He hasn't listened to her. He hasn't understood anything. "Where are we going?"

"Coney Island." Lucky places the picnic basket on the ground. "We don't have to – it's just an idea."

Everything disappears in the end, Mim thinks. Everything is taken away, like in Esther's play about the woman who loses all her belongings, one by one, until she is alone in an empty room. She's going to lose Lucky, she knows it in her bones. He's standing there with his picnic basket and he looks so sweet and he looks so stupid. She thinks of Giselle miming "I," "you", but what is the third word? Love? Beg? Forgive?

"I can't do this," she says. "Any of this. Planning trips. Starting again. It's not working any more."

"What's not?"

"Dancing. Escaping myself."

"Maybe you don't need to escape yourself." He looks around helplessly. "It was a stupid idea – forget it."

"You just don't understand," she says furiously, unable to let it go.

"Then tell me." He turns his hands palms up. A gesture of invitation. As if he is asking her to dance. "Tell me everything."

My best friend drowned, she says in her head. But she still can't do it: say what happened out loud. Explain her part in it.

"I just ruin things," she says instead. "It's what I do."

She needs to free him, she needs to let him go, allow him to be with some woman like Maria, who is elegant and chic, who will just glide in his arms across the dancefloor and ask nothing of him. Or a woman like Frankie: strong and kind and independent, who never seemed to need anybody. Who'd never pull him under like a drowning woman clings to a lifeguard.

"I can't do this," she says again. "I can't go to the beach with you. I can't do anything else with you. It's been nice but…"

"Tell me what you're stuck on," he says in a low, urgent voice. "The reason you can't forgive yourself."

And there it is. Even though he's put his finger on it, she can't go there. She is still ice-brittle. Furious. Terrified. She is crying loudly now: heaving, gulping sobs.

"I'm going to walk away now," she tells him. "Don't follow me. Go to the beach with someone else."

She needs to get out. She doesn't know where she's going. Just away from him. She knows she has crushed him again; that she will continue flattening him until all his boyish bounce is gone.

She needs to keep walking. She mustn't turn round, she mustn't look back at him. He'll be OK. It'll all be OK. But Mim doesn't know when or how.

45

Winter 1943

There was a brief flurry of excitement when Amélie and Antoine returned to the Tabarin, but the response to their trip was mixed. Even though we knew they hadn't had much of a choice, none of us felt comfortable with it. When I asked, Amélie was quick to change the subject; besides, she was preoccupied with the delivery of the letters she'd brought back.

At the Tabarin, things started to sour. The German soldiers still came and sat in the best seats in the house, but they smiled less and muttered things between themselves. There was a shortage of soap, and everyone smelled bad crammed up close to each other in that intimate space.

Once or twice, a fight broke out between a solider and another member of the audience. On his part, Sandrini forbade the Germans from going backstage to visit the dancers, but that didn't stop nasty skirmishes. One evening, when Belle cancan-kicked a newspaper out of the hand of a tipsy Frenchman, he made a playful grab for her ankle. In turn, a German officer – Schmitz, the large, ruddy-cheeked man who'd accompanied Amélie's first fan backstage – smashed the butt of his pistol into the Frenchman's face, breaking his nose.

"Sometimes, I get sick of this work," Gisy told Belle and me after the show. "Taking my clothes off for angry men."

Her light seemed dimmed since the arrest of her beloved doctor. Sometimes I'd pass her dressing room and catch her sitting on her own, gazing into the distance, a lit cigarette still burning in her hand.

Belle shrugged. The bad behaviour of men rarely fazed her. I wondered about her childhood – something she rarely spoke of, though she shared, in passing, glimpses of her early life, the kind of company her mother kept.

Sometimes, I felt bad for Belle, who didn't seem to have anyone in the world to love her; guilty that I didn't care for her more. But she didn't let me in. Once, I teasingly called her Jeanne – her childhood name – but she stopped me. "You mustn't," she said. "Jeanne's gone. She let people hurt her, but I never would."

By the end of 1943, the Nazis were suffering serious losses – the Allies were fighting their way through Italy, and the Russians were advancing. In Paris, the Resistance became bolder, sabotaging factories, warehouses and railways, but air raids on the city also grew fiercer – though the most common targets were the industrial plants on its outskirts. Action had replaced words. My essay-writing skills became surplus to requirements.

My sisters and I slept in a tiny back room at the Tabarin, next to Lili's darkroom, on a couple of single mattresses. Lili and I were used to sharing, but she was often out at night, on her secret assignations, locking herself in the darkroom afterwards, where she pegged her photos out to dry like tiny clothes on a washing line. She'd started to work with a group that was hiding Jewish children, with the help of convents and Catholic orphanages; she presented herself as a young schoolteacher taking them on day trips. "It's hard to escort them on and off the Métro," she told me. "Trains have taken away everyone they loved."

Though she started the war as a schoolgirl, my little sister blossomed into womanhood during those years. Chiselled, poised, determined, she'd found a surety though her work – and not only her work. Once, as she watched the band rehearse from the first-floor balcony, she beckoned me over.

"There he is." She pointed at the pianist, a quiet redhead with a dry sense of humour.

"Who?"

She shot me a sidelong glance. "My person," she said. "I promised I'd say, didn't I? Now you must tell me when you meet yours."

I stared at the pianist, realising I'd had no idea. I'd passed him and Lili chatting, but she spoke to everyone in the Tabarin. "Does he know?"

A quick smile. "I think so."

"Well, this proves I'm not as nosy as you, because I never guessed." I pinched her arm lightly. "And it's not just because you want somewhere better to sleep at night?"

She shook her head. "It's more than that."

I watched that night when the pianist played "Lili Marlene" – a favourite of the soldiers on both sides – and followed his gaze to his own Lili in the wings. She returned his smile, then closed her eyes, swaying gently, her arms wrapped around her, taken to a secret place.

46

My affair with Belle had slowed down, so it surprised me to discover she still had the power to wound me. I came across her one night outside the stage door, whispering sweet nothings with the awful Schmitz. I hadn't forgotten how he'd broken the man's nose with the butt of his pistol. I stormed past, muttering a choice word or two. Traitor, idiot, schlemiel. And worse.

"Who was that?" I heard Schmitz ask as I stormed away.

The next day, Belle called to me from her dressing room. "I have cigarettes to share."

I paused, glaring at her. "Where did they come from?"

"I think you can guess." She lit a Gitanes and offered it to me.

I thought of how the man with the broken nose had been dragged away by the Germans. How we could hear his howls, even above the noise of the cancan. How the soldiers crept back to their seats, wiping their hands on their trousers, ordering another round. There had been other incidents like it since. So many missing by that point: my mother, my father, all our childhood friends from the Pletzl, countless artists and performers from across Paris. And who was left? Not the best of us. Just those who survived: it was only a matter of chance.

"I shouldn't have taken any from you before," I said. "And I never should have kissed you, either."

"You wanted me to kiss you." Belle blew out an angry little puff of smoke. "You were just too pathetic to ask."

I knew her by then – I knew that under her tough exterior was a person as terrified and fragile as the rest of us, but I said the words anyway. Words as old as the female body. "That was before I knew where your mouth had been."

I shut the door of the dressing room after me but I heard the ashtray smash against it as I left.

"What happened between you and Belle?" Lili asked.

"Nothing," I lied. "I just don't like her choice in company."

I could usually count on Lili to get riled up on my behalf, but instead she said, "Poor Belle. She's only trying to survive."

She had a dreamy look in her eyes that day I hadn't spotted before. She took my hand and placed it on her belly, firm and round beneath my touch. How had I missed it?

"It'll be over soon," she said. "That's what I hear from my networks. The Allies will land and Paris will be free again. My child will grow up in the Tabarin, just like we did. Life will be good again."

"Lili." Tears pricked at my eyes. She was nearly twenty, but she would always be my little sister. I imagined her child's heart beating beneath my fingers. A tiny thrumming of hope.

My sister's pregnancy didn't stop her Resistance work; if anything, she became more filled with purpose. Her neat little bump set a few tongues wagging at the Tabarin, but she didn't care. She had more important things to be thinking about.

When she told Rebecca, our sister's eyes filled with tears just as mine had and, though the three of us wept together in that back room for our parents and what they were missing, I was reminded of how the birth of a child can unite a family, just as Lili's arrival had.

A few days later, Lili was out when Rebecca and I received a visit from Sandrini in our backroom home. We got to our feet, Rebecca started dusting down her skirt and glanced around the room nervously, as if assessing how the place needed tidying up. Sandrini had Amélie with him and they looked sombre.

"Girls." The director's voice was heavy and I felt very cold all of a sudden. "Someone has informed on you: we need to get you out as soon as possible." He sighed, brushed a hand through his immaculate hair. "I'm sorry I couldn't protect you."

Rebecca and I exchanged a worried glance.

Sandrini looked at my friend. "Amélie has offered to hide you at her apartment until we decide what to do next."

Rebecca was thanking him, like the grown-up she was, but I felt a burning rage sweep through me. "Who informed on us?" I demanded. "Do you know?"

Sandrini shook his head. "There is so much of it around."

"Belle." I exhaled.

Rebecca put a restraining hand on my arm, but I barely

felt it. "Esther, we don't know that."

"I do."

Fury pulsed through me, sweeping me up in its certainty. A rage aimed not just at Belle, but at myself, for my weakness, for all the hours I had lain in her arms, for the secret part of myself I had allowed someone so hateful to see.

"Belle can be spiky," Sandrini said uncertainly. "But there is a good heart in there, I think. It could have come from anywhere. There are German soldiers in here every night, to my great shame." He rubbed his face. "I wish it could be different – I wish I could have turned them away. Especially after what happened to your mother. I wish more than anything that I could stop them, but I can't."

My fury was a tidal wave. I started marching to Belle's dressing room, with my sister and Amélie trying to keep up behind me.

She wasn't in, but the release was briefly delicious: swiping off the make-up from her dressing table, ripping up her photographs into tiny pieces, stamping on her precious cigarettes. By the time I made for her cancan petticoats, lovingly made by my mother's own hand, Amélie pulled me away, her grip on my arm surprisingly strong.

"We don't have time for this," she murmured. "You must calm down – we need to get you out of here."

She and I stood in front of Belle's dressing room mirror. I glanced at myself, dishevelled and wild-eyed, just as Belle wandered in, eyebrows raised at the mess I'd made.

"Did you tell him?" I would have flown for her physically, had Amélie not still been holding my wrist.

"Who?" She did a great impression of confusion.

"Your German boyfriend?" I glared at her. "Did you tell

him we were here?"

"I don't know what you're talking about." Belle went pale, looking from my face to those of the others, as if trying to work out who was most likely to believe her.

"Someone has informed on Esther and her family," Amélie said quietly. "We need to get them out of here."

My mind leapt to Lili. I hadn't seen her since that morning. "Where's Lili?" I asked the others desperately. "Has anyone seen her?"

My fury made me stupid and blind that day, especially to my own role. I was so busy blaming Belle that I didn't realise the person who'd betrayed us was looking back at me in the mirror. It was another failure to protect my sisters. The second of my major crimes. Jamais deux sans trois.

47

Amélie walked Rebecca and me from the Tabarin to her apartment in the Latin Quarter at dusk. She took her bicycle with her and chatted away, just as she'd accompanied Bluebell's husband, Marcel. Rebecca and I could barely manage a word, staring at our feet as we cut through the Tuileries Garden and passed over the Pont Royal to the Left Bank.

Amélie lived on a narrow street leading away from the river, where the tall townhouses seemed to tilt so closely together their foreheads almost touched. She left us at the apartment with a little food for supper. There wasn't much – a small onion and a couple of potatoes.   Rebecca began to prepare a meal in angry silence.

"You directed your fury at Belle," she said eventually, "but I don't know how Lili could be so careless. We don't even know where she is."

"Belle was the one who gave us away."

"You really don't know that." She sighed. "The three of you – putting all of our lives at risk."

"At least we've been doing something."

"I've been doing something." She held the knife in the air for a moment. "I've been doing everything – working, supporting us, preparing the food. All of it. While Amélie and Lili go gallivanting."

"Risking their lives, you mean?" I stood up, the chair scraping against the floor. "Risking their lives for other people?"

"Risking all of our lives." Rebecca's voice was getting louder. "You think if Lili were found out, they wouldn't come after me? At least Amélie's relatives are far away."

"You can't say that." I began to pace. I knew I should offer to help her, but I was too cross. "You can't say anything about her. The risk she has taken – for complete strangers."

"How do you know it wasn't her who said something? She's the one who has just come back from Germany."

"She would never do that," I said in a low, furious voice. "She has as much to lose as any of us."

"Not Lili." Rebecca sighed. "She has the most to lose, and she's acting like it's nothing at all."

I wondered then, for the first time, if Rebecca was envious of Lili. She was the oldest of us, the most maternal. Had she always thought she might be the first to have children?"

"Why do I get the least love?" My sister started to chop the potatoes into angry chunks. "The least indulgence. Must I always be the sensible one?"

"Rebecca." I stopped pacing. "I'm so sorry."

"We mustn't quarrel." She brushed the back of her hand across her forehead. "And we mustn't make too much noise here, either. God knows who's listening."

After a weak potato broth, we waited for them in the kitchen, jumping at every unexpected sound. At last, we heard light footsteps. One person or two – we couldn't tell. The door creaked open and Amélie appeared – and then Lili. Rebecca and I scrambled to our feet and the four of us hugged each other tightly.

"I think we need some wine," Amélie pulled a bottle from her bag. "But we mustn't make too much noise."

Everything we did in hiding had to be done in silence or near silence. It was easier for Rebecca, with her sewing, and me with my books, but Lili found it impossible, pacing the small apartment with her camera around her neck like a caged safari tourist.

"I can't bear this," she'd hiss at us. "How can you bear it?"

"We have to." Rebecca didn't look up from her stitching. "We don't have a choice. Stop moving around – we need to be quiet."

But there were tender moments, too, when we were briefly stitched together: Lili lying on the double-bed enveloped by Rebecca and me. A squeal when she felt her baby kick.

"What is it?" I asked.

"She kicked me," Lili said. She was convinced it was a girl.

"Let me feel." I placed my hand on her belly, Rebecca did too.

"Do it again," I pleaded.

Nothing. "Stage fright," Lili laughed.

The three of us lay there, feeling the rise and fall of Lili's breath under our hands. In a low voice, Rebecca began to sing a few Gershwin numbers, old favourites of our mother's. In the middle of "Someone to Watch Over Me," my older sister gasped. "I felt it that time."

"Let me, let me." I moved my hand near hers.

"Keep singing," Lili smiled.

Rebecca kept going. Our niece loved "I Got Rhythm," kicking up her feet as if in time to the music.

"Maybe she's going to be a cancan dancer," I murmured.

"Oh, I hope not," Lili laughed.

"I can't wait to make clothes for her," Rebecca said. "Do you think she'll be petite, like you?"

Lili squeezed her hand. "She'll be the best dressed baby in le tout-Paris."

"Have you thought about names?" I asked.

"I thought I'd name her Abigail, after Ima."

None of us said anything for a few moments. "She will love that," Rebecca said quietly. "When she comes back."

There hadn't been a word from our mother since the note that had found its way to us from the Vélodrome d'Hiver.

At night, we slept badly, waking abruptly with every slammed door, every heavy footstep, waiting, in my case, for Amélie's return, when she would whisper any news. The Gestapo had come looking for us at the Tabarin. They'd searched the whole place, but found no trace of us. Our mattresses and other belongings had been tidied away by speedy hands.

"Belle didn't come into work today," Amélie added, as if it was something she'd been debating whether to share with me.

"Because she is feeling guilty," I said dully.

"I don't know." Amélie shook her head. She and Belle

had never been friends, but Amélie wasn't one to gloat.

"Thank you," I said. "For hiding us like this."

"Of course," she said.

"Do you think we'll be all right?"

"I hope so." She sighed. We both knew she couldn't promise more than that.

48

One evening, I woke before Amélie's return from the Tabarin. The bedroom felt different, though I couldn't say how. I had been napping in a chair, while Rebecca and Lili slept in the bed. I lit the oil lamp. The electricity kept failing in those last months of Occupation.

"What is it?" Rebecca asked softly.

"I don't know," I replied. "Maybe I heard something."

We stayed quiet for a few moments. "Lili?" I whispered. "Are you OK?"

There was no reply.

"Lili?" Rebecca went to shake her, but our sister wasn't in bed. We got up as quietly as we could and searched the apartment, but she wasn't there.

"She must have gone out." I started pulling on clothes.

"No," Rebecca said firmly. "What are we going to do out there? Traverse the streets looking for her? She'll come back. She knows where we are. We should stay here."

"But what if something happens?"

She folded her arms. "What can we do?"

I squeezed past her to find my coat, slung over one of the kitchen chairs. "That's so like you," I snapped. "Not to do anything." In my rush, I knocked Colette's La Vagabonde from the kitchen table. I'd been rereading it for comfort. The sketch of Amélie that had been hidden in its pages fluttered down to the ground.

Rebecca stooped to pick it up, glancing at the drawing as she did so. She passed it back to me without saying a word. "And it's so like you," she said, "to follow someone else – Lili, Amélie, whoever it is – without thinking a thing through. Wherever she has gone, Lili will come back."

Embarrassed by her discovery, I agreed to wait until Amélie returned from the Tabarin. We sat in the darkness in furious silence until the familiar sound of my friend's footsteps made their way up the stairs.

"What's going on?" Amélie asked when she found us both sitting at the kitchen table, not speaking to each other.

"Lili's gone." I got to my feet, relieved to see her.

"Gone?"

"She's not here – we don't know where she is."

"I'll go and find her." Amélie turned on her heels and made for the door again.

"I want to come too," I insisted.

"No," Rebecca snapped.

"You mustn't," Amélie agreed.

There was more painful waiting for Rebecca and me. It was so quiet between us I could hear her darning, the sound of the needle entering the fabric, coming out the other side. There was the occasional mutter under her breath when she had to redo a stitch.

"Do you think Ima misses sewing?" I asked.

"I would say she misses us more." Rebecca said more gently.

"They will release her when the Allies win," I said. "And they will win, I'm sure of it."

My sister didn't say anything in response to that, but her silence filled me with dread.

Not long after, the quiet was broken by an arrival. People entering the building. As usual, we held our breath until we heard a key slip into the door. We fell on Lili and Amélie when they came through.

"Lili," I said, shaking her slightly, "where were you?"

My sister didn't have a chance to answer before being swept up into Rebecca's embrace. "It's not just you anymore." Rebecca put a protective hand on her bump. "It's our nephew or niece."

"OK, you crazy aunties." Lili laughed, pulling away from our flapping around her. "My child will be a fighter like me – she'll understand."

"Seriously," I insisted, "where were you?"

"Helping a friend move some of the children into hiding. They thought, as a pregnant woman, I was less likely to be stopped." She allowed herself a small smile of satisfaction. "And they were right. I got them safely to a convent – they can stay at an orphanage nearby, among the Catholic children."

We slept that night three to a bed, with Lili in the middle so there was no way she could get out again. Sometimes when I woke I reached out and touched her to check she was still there, until she told me to stop it. If I'd known it would be the last time the three of us slept in a room together.

The next day, we were querulous, still squabbling about the night before. Amélie went for a walk by the river to clear her head. She paused on the Pont Saint-Michel and stared down into the water below. "Movement," she said to me once. "It was always movement that helped me, even the motion of water."

She was so deep in her thoughts that she didn't notice the gendarme approaching, taking his place next to her on the bridge, his gaze also focused on the water.

Amélie glanced sharply at him, but his stance stayed steady. It was the same gendarme she knew.

"Mademoiselle," he said quietly. "Don't be alarmed" – although, of course, few things are more likely to cause alarm than such words. "And don't make any sudden movements – you never know who's watching."

Amélie held herself as still as a spring. She wondered if it was worth running. She reminded herself to breathe.

"You're hiding someone in your apartment," he continued. "Your landlady has reported them to the authorities. There will be someone coming tomorrow, so it would be a good idea to get them out tonight."

"Merci." She didn't know what else to say.

He nodded. For a moment, she thought he was going to leave it at that. "I saw you dance once," he said. "An unforgettable experience."

She thanked him again.

"We never had this conversation."

She agreed that they hadn't. And then he was gone.

Amélie returned to the apartment, placing one foot

in front of another very calmly. She knew from years of working in a theatre how quickly nerves can jump like fleas from one person to another. She also knew that she couldn't take us back to the Tabarin – she needed to find somewhere else, and then she remembered the convent Lili had mentioned the night before.

Amélie was preternaturally calm when she reached us, almost scarily so. I could tell from her face that something had changed.

"I don't want you to panic," she said in a low voice, "but we need to move you tonight."

"What has happened?" Rebecca said. "What have you heard?"

"Why wait?" Lili said. "We could go now."

"We must be careful," Amélie whispered, glancing at the door. "My landlady might still be listening. Lili, can you let me know the name of the convent you took the children to yesterday? I can go and talk to someone today, to see if they can help us." Lili nodded and went to find some paper to scribble out the address. "What I need you to do is to get your things together and stay very quiet today," Amélie continued. "Be alert for any sudden noises. But don't panic – we'll get you out."

Our instinct, of course, was to fly. To run out into the streets. But where could we go?

"Look," Amélie said sternly, "I'll tell you what I learned in Germany – over and over again and never more than in that dreadful bunker. You can't show fear – you have to hold yourself together." She touched her lower belly with her hand. "Otherwise, you fall apart like a sack of potatoes."

She glanced at our faces, her gaze lingering on mine.

Later, I wondered if she was trying to memorise it, in case it was the last time we saw each other.

49

We were accustomed to waiting by then, but no wait was like the one we had to endure that day. It didn't take long to pack, I remember that much. We had few belongings left. There was Lili's camera, some baby clothes that Rebecca had started to make for her. She'd begun a tiny cancan dress from Tabarin scraps. I had a couple of my exercise books, my copy of La Vagabonde with the sketch of Amélie folded inside.

We became acutely aware of the noises of the outside world, listening for booted feet in the streets, flinching as a neighbour's footstep made it up the creaking wooden stairs, always seeming to slow outside Amélie's door before moving on.

Occasionally, one of us would say to the others, "Do you think we should just go?"

And sometimes one of us might agree, but never the three of us, and somehow we'd decided that a consensus was required. The seconds ticked through the night. We sat in cold darkness, the other two at the kitchen table, me on the floor, leaning my head against Lili's leg, ensuring, in the way that a dog might, that if I fell asleep and she moved, I'd be able to keep track of her.

Meanwhile, at the Tabarin, though I didn't learn it until later, Amélie's return was delayed by the appearance of Schmitz at the stage door. Maybe he missed Belle since her disappearance; maybe he just fancied a change, but the grip of his fleshy hand on Amélie's wrist was tight, his gaze hungry and mean. "Come out for supper with me, pretty dancer."

"I can't. My boyfriend." She glanced around for Antoine but, in the worst possible timing, he appeared moments later with Marguerite on his arm.

Would going out with Schmitz help her at all? Distract him, in any way, from what she was about to do? But, no, if she went out for supper with him, much as she could do with the food, he would want more. As Amélie glared down at his hand closed over her wrist, as she saw the glisten of hungry sweat on his forehead, she hated this man as much as she'd hated anyone in her life.

Maybe she couldn't hide her feelings, for once, because he dropped her wrist. "Putain," he spat, letting her go. "You promise everything on stage, you know that?"

She walked away from him as quickly as she could, without looking back. When she was sure no one was following her, she came home to us and said, "It's time."

It's time. Strange to think, as I write this in New York, overlooking the Statue of Liberty, that I can walk freely through the city. An old woman, sure, a little stiff, a little hunched, but I can move from block to block and passersby don't even look tat me. I can move unnoticed in the world. Who would have thought that would be the greatest blessing? Or that the biggest danger for us, as four Jewish women, could simply be to pass through a city at night?

We moved as quietly as we could, weaving through the cobbled streets of the Latin Quarter, moving as one animal with eight legs, as united as Amélie and Antoine when they danced the tango. Breathing together, our feet in unison. Five of us, really. Not four. A tiny heart beating deep in Lili's belly. Did her child sense the danger and silence that night? Did it tell its own heart to beat more quietly, lest its enemies might hear it?

Once or twice, other footsteps. Once or twice, glances shared between us, a tightening in the shoal formation.

Finally, with Lili's murmured instructions, the convent was in sight. Our place of safety. We could see the arched doorway opposite us, but there was something going on in the same square. A commotion. Noise.

We froze in the shadows, instinctively reaching for each other's hands. The orphanage Lili had mentioned was across the square from the convent. It was where Jewish children had been hidden and delivered by her just the evening before.

Despite the blackout and the time of night, lights poured out from the second and third storeys of the building. Raised German voices echoed across the square. We heard the word, "Inspektion." One, shriller than the others, demanded that the children should say their prayers. A test.

Lili had told us how the nuns would teach Jewish children the Catholic prayers to help them survive, but at least one child hadn't been there long enough to learn them. We heard her as she cried, "Je ne peux pas." I can't.

There were scuffles and a scream that echoed across the square. A woman shrieking. Perhaps a nun or a teacher. From where we were standing we could only hear a dull thud and then momentary silence. There was the scrape of moved furniture, and then arms outstretched holding a girl of four or five out of a third-storey window, her legs kicking beneath her.

"No," Lili murmured. I could feel her shaking violently. I tightened my grip on her hand.

"We can't," Rebecca said. There was devastation in her voice.

A moment of silence before the soldier let go. The child called for her mother as she fell. A thin, pitiful sound. And then the crying stopped.

"Wo ist das nächste Kind?" he asked. Where is the next child?

I don't want to pass on to another human being everything we heard and saw in those few minutes. Whatever I do, whatever I have done, part of me will always be there. I tried to block out the noise. I tried to harden my heart. I have tried every day of my life to forget. But it always finds me.

We began to edge gradually towards the arched doorway of the convent. A chain of us in the shadows. There was so much dreadful noise in the square that they didn't see us, our backs pressed against the wall, moving forward inch by inch.

Four women, linked by their hands. I don't know how but we finally reached the door. We slipped through one by one: Rebecca then Amélie then me.

Lili murmured "No" again. So quietly only I could hear. She couldn't tear her gaze away. The soldier held a little boy then, with tubby baby cheeks, barely old enough to say any kind of prayers.

"We can't," I whispered.

We can't do anything. We can't help, we can't save them, we can't stop this. If we want to live, we have to do nothing. That is the choice: to witness it and be forever damaged, or to sacrifice yourself.

Did I feel her grip on my hand loosen? Could I have tightened my own? When did she decide? Moments before or only once the three of us were out of danger? Who can know another person's heart?

Lili. Who was good at keeping secrets, though I could never guess at hers. Whose footstep was light like our mother's. Whose heart was big like Papa's. Whose nosiness was never really nosiness, but something else. Something bound up in how much she cared for the world. Something closer to love.

I didn't catch her in time. I didn't stop her. She said "No" a third time, but this time as a shriek. A blur across the square, running. I don't think she had a plan. I think she just needed to say "No" loud enough for the whole world to hear it.

Rebecca and I said, "We can't," but Lili said, "No." Her ending was swift. A shot to the head from a solider standing guard at the orphanage door. An execution. Everything in my body strained to join her, but Amélie's response was faster and stronger than mine. I could feel the line of her from the tips of her fingers and up through her arm. A body worked to full strength through a lifetime of physical exertion. How could something so delicate contain so much fight?

She held me back, she stopped me, she dragged me from the gates. I never got to see my sister lying on her back, looking up at the sky. Looking, perhaps, at freedom. A freedom I would never get to taste for myself, even though I lived for many decades longer. Lili was able to escape that square, that sight, that scene, those noises, but however long I live, however far I come, however much I write, I'm never free to leave.

50

Mim sits for a very long time with Esther's book open in her lap. She thinks of Lili lying on her back, a single gunshot at the centre of her head, but she knows that idea has come from films, that the reality was likely to be much messier. She doesn't know how long she sits there for, thinking and not thinking. A third girl. The youngest, like Mim. Was that why Esther always had a soft spot for her?

Lili. All the things she would never get to do again – walk those Parisian streets she knew so well. Ride on her bicycle down the Champs-Élysées. Sit with Esther in the shadows of the Tabarin, watching the shows together from the wings. She never would have seen Paris liberated. She never became a famous photographer. She never got to meet her child.

Mim had suffered. She had lost things, lost the people she loved the most in the world. Frankie. Her father. But her life hadn't been stolen from her – more than that, on the night she came close, she had been given a second opportunity, and what had she done with it since? Squandered it on self-pity.

Was Lili the reason Esther and Rebecca fell out? The sisters must have revisited that night countless times, together or alone. Or perhaps they couldn't bear to. Mim just doesn't know. It's still very early in New York. She messages her mum, telling her she needs to talk about Lili. Surely her mother will stop evading the subject now.

When she calls, a few restless hours later, her mum is sitting at the kitchen table. She looks as if she's been crying. "I have Abi here," she begins. "I've told her about Lili."

She directs the laptop screen to her sister's tear-stained face. Abi raises a hand but looks too upset to speak.

So she didn't know. Her sister hadn't kept the secret from her, after all.

"Did you know Lili was pregnant?" Mim asks.

Her mum nods. "My mother did say something about that, yes, but she was confused towards the end, so I never knew how..." She folds her arms, holding herself together. "She kept talking about going back to Paris," she says softly. "Just one more time. But it was too late then."

The three of them are quiet for a minute or two. "I'm so sorry, Mum," Mim says. "It must have been terrible for you to find out like that." She swallows. "What did Grandma tell you?"

"That they witnessed something unspeakable. That Lili was shot." Her mother wipes her face with her hand. "It must have been unimaginable for my mother," she says. "For both of them."

Mim nods.

"I never felt like I could complain about anything," her mum says quietly. "Growing up. Because nothing could compare with what my mother had been through."

"Why did she and Esther fall out?" Mim asks.

"I don't know." Her mum gets up to fetch some kitchen roll and passes a piece to Abi. "They were always two very different people, but the strain of living through that can't have helped."

Mim watches her sister, sitting at the table, tearing the kitchen roll into tiny shreds. "Abi, I'm sorry," she says eventually.

"What for?" Her sister starts to tidy the shredded paper into a pile.

"For everything." Mim sighs. "For not appreciating you. For that time when you were staying with Frankie and me – when you came in and we were talking about Ben... That wasn't kind."

A flicker of something passes over Abi's face. Something moving on. "It's OK," she says, without hesitation. "I forgive you." Just like that.

"I wish I could say sorry to Frankie too." Mim begins to cry. "I can't ask her to forgive me. I'll never know if she does."

Her mum and sister sit side by side, united, Mim realises, not in exasperation but in their love for her. When she finally stops, Abi is still there. "All you can do is forgive yourself, Mim," she says. "Like Esther and Rebecca had to."

"But what if they didn't?" Mim asks. "What if they couldn't?"

After speaking to her mother and Abi, Mim takes the elevator up to Bibi's flat. She hammers on her friend's door, but the apartment is oddly silent. There's no music or television chatter, no familiar bark or scuffle from FeeFee. A kind of restlessness nags at her. She needs to get out.

On impulse, she decides to go and see an old friend – someone she'd been watching for a long time from a distance. She doesn't let herself think about it for too long – she'll just talk herself out of it, and she needs all of her strength to tackle the queues and the water.

The New York heat is so strong that there are fewer people waiting at Battery Park than she expected. No one pays much attention to her, except for the ticket seller who coos over her British accent. She picks a seat in the middle of the boat and closes her eyes as the engine starts.

When she reopens them, she sees Manhattan's skyline receding on her right. Ahead, that famous silhouette, as tiny as a chess piece, begins to grow incrementally. Couples and families and friends arrange themselves in clusters in front of the railing, taking endless pictures. Mim watches two friends, flushed cheeks pressed together, cackling as they're photographed.

Are you here? she asks Frankie.

They'd been drinking that night two years ago, all three of them. It was Robbie's birthday – one of those hot summer days that brings a kind of madness with it. The Brighton pubs spilled out into the streets – noses and shoulders and tattooed arms pinkened in the afternoon sun. Colleagues leaned conspiratorially towards each other and said, "Shall we have one more?"

"Frankie's broken up with her fella, so we need to cheer her up," Mim told Robbie, and he grinned at them both and said, "We can do that, no problem."

He bought the drinks that night. "The decree nisi came through today," he told the girls cheerfully. "Isn't that the best birthday present?"

"That's great," Mim beamed, taking great care not to catch Frankie's eye.

"So fuck her, eh? That Swedish bitch." Robbie drank deeply from his pint, while Mim did everything in her power to mentally erase what she'd just heard.

"So either he's a jerk," Frankie said, while Robbie was in the bathroom. "Or, you know, he's still in love with his ex."

"He's just letting off steam – it'll be fine."

Frankie took her hand. "I think it's a bad idea – you and him. I really do. You're not yourself when you're around him. I think – don't you? – that maybe some of this stuff is about your dad."

Mim pulled her hand away. "Are you saying I have a Daddy complex?"

Frankie shrugged helplessly. "It wouldn't be the worst thing."

"I'm in love with him," Mim glared at her.

"I don't think you are. I think you're just looking for a plaster to stick over your pain. And you can do that through your work – you were doing it until Robbie came along."

"Shush," Mim hissed. "He's coming back now."

Robbie drank like a man on a mission, and the pair of them kept up with him, drink for drink. Back at the girls' flat, they opened a bottle of tequila and took turns to pick songs to play on Frankie's turntable until a neighbour knocked on their door to tell them to shut up.

There was a kind of crackle to Robbie that night. "You know," he said, towards the end of the evening, "the best birthday present for me would be to see you two kiss."

A weird silence fell. Would it be so bad? Mim thought in that moment. She always thought Frankie was beautiful – but then, she reminded herself, this was Frankie who'd seen her at her worst, who'd held her hair back when she vomited, who was the one person she couldn't hide a single thought from. How would it be to be weird with Frankie in the morning?

Her friend saved her from having to make the decision. Frankie pulled a face. "No, thanks, I don't see you that way, Mim, and even if I did, I wouldn't be doing it for your titillation." She threw Robbie a look. A look that said, I see through you and you disgust me. A look that said, My friend could do so much better. A look that said, I'm about to say something that could ruin this evening for everyone.

Mim had to rescue things. She wanted to row back to a few minutes earlier when they were leaping around the room to OutKast. She needed to say something. Something to break the tension, to distract her from the furious way Frankie was glaring at Robbie and the hungry way he was gazing back at her friend.

"We should go swimming," she blurted.

The others looked at her.

"It's a beautiful night. Why not?"

"Because we have drunk all the alcohol?" Frankie's gaze took in the detritus of bottles and ashtrays and records around them. "Because we have work tomorrow? No, Mim – it's a terrible idea."

"It'll clear our heads," Mim said. "Just a quick dip. Why not?"

Maybe, she thought, she could be outdoorsy and athletic,

like Robbie's wife. Maybe she genuinely fancied a swim. Maybe she just wanted to do anything she could to stop noticing the way Robbie looked at Frankie. She couldn't remember now – all she knew was that she would give everything she had to go back to that night and keep those words, "We should go swimming," in her head. Nothing that could have happened next – if she and Frankie had kissed, if Robbie and Frankie had, if he'd left her and she'd never seen him again – would have been more unbearable than what actually happened.

51

"Watch your step, watch your step. And welcome to Liberty Island," says a chirpy woman in a red vest, whom Mim passes as she makes her way, on unsteady legs, off the boat.

She's surprised at the wave of emotion she feels at being so close to the statue. Esther always spoke of the relief at seeing her when she and Rebecca arrived in New York, but Mim now knows the other things Esther would have been feeling. Only two sisters out of three making it to safety. Three fifths of their childhood family gone. The baby lost too.

It comes back to her then: Abi's drawn face, her hair still in plaits. Abi driving through the night to comfort her the night of the accident. She thinks of what it would have been like for her sister if she'd died too; she thinks of what it would have been like if she'd lost Abi. That was the reality Esther had faced.

She wanders aimlessly for a while, with the statue on

her left and the water on her right. Everyone around her is taking pictures, but she's not here as a tourist. It feels like something else. She needs to get away from the crowds, from the constant photography, from the chatter and noise of other people. Perhaps, she thinks now, this is the wrong place to have come for solitude. But then it's not solitude she's after exactly. She leans on the railing and takes a deep breath. A seagull lands nearby and eyeballs her. And she moves on.

She follows the crowd for a while, putting off the inevitable. She needs to go back. She needs to remember.

We should go swimming. That's how it started. Frankie said no, but Robbie seemed more enthusiastic. Thinking, perhaps, of the girls in bikinis. But Mim doesn't remember clearly what came next. There are gaps. We should go swimming. Then some kind of argument with Frankie. Her friend insisting it was a terrible idea. Mim snapping, You don't have to come. The fight almost curdled into nastiness as Mim stormed to her bedroom to grab her swimming stuff. Not wanting to lose the moment. Not wanting to lose Robbie's attention. Standing on one leg in there, as she tried to pull on her bikini bottoms, she crashed to the floor. A brief moment of clarity: I'm too drunk for this. And then she pushed that thought away.

When she came out of the bedroom, Frankie was waiting in the living room with a towel, her bikini on underneath her dress. I can't let you go on your own, you idiot. A resigned smile that told her she didn't trust Robbie to look out for Mim. That the only person who could do that was Frankie. It's her last certain memory of her friend.

Mim doesn't remember the short walk to the beach, or

scrambling out of her clothes, or plunging into the freezing water, the cold of it smacking her in the chest, making her gasp. She can imagine it, but those are old memories infecting this one.

She remembers Robbie kissing her urgently, trying to have sex, and thinking, We can't, not here, not with Frankie nearby. And then pulling away. And then something tugging at her, something too strong to resist – and her limbs not working. Simply not working. And her body's alarm system had warned her, had said to her, You're too drunk for this. But she had overridden it, like the selfish bitch she was, dragging Frankie with her.

She had no idea what had happened to the others, because now she was fighting for her life. Kicking with everything to stay afloat. And then there were waves and waves and waves, and they were coming too soon, too often, and she was swallowing salt water and it was sickening her and she was going to die out there in the Brighton sea, a stone's throw from her own flat. The flat at the top of the rickety townhouse where she and Frankie scrambled on tiptoes on a chair for the tiniest glimpse of their sea view. She wouldn't go back there. She wouldn't see all her things – her books and her clothes and the photos of her family – because she was stupid and vain and insecure. Because she had decided to love someone she didn't even love, who didn't love her back, and now she was going to die, and someone would have to tell the people who really loved her – her mother and sister – that she was dead. And her mother was going to kill her for this, she really would. For being so stupid. It was her last idiotic thought: that her mother was going to kill her for dying.

And then, suddenly, there was a light in the darkness. A familiar orange boat. Voices, arms – strong arms – pulling her out. Another figure in the boat. They're pulling an orange bin bag over the figure's shoulders. Frankie. Mim's heart leapt in gratitude, but the figure looked towards her and it wasn't Frankie, it was Robbie.

Someone screaming Frankie's name. Over and over. A terrible discombobulated shrieking. She is all in parts. Purple lips, jelly legs, belly full of water. She needs to get back into the sea. And someone is holding her back. Someone wearing a crunchy yellow suit. Men in uniform – she wants to make a joke about how fit they are, but she's got the wrong audience, because Frankie is the only one who will find it funny.

"It was my idea," she explained to the crunchy-suited man, who pinned her arms to her sides, preventing her from returning to the water. "It was my idea to do this. She only came in because of me. I need to get back into the water to find her."

Because it wasn't possible that they wouldn't rescue her. It wasn't possible; Mim wouldn't have it. Because, otherwise, who was going to call Frankie's mother and explain what she had done?

52

When Frankie's body eventually washed up on the beach, Mim wanted to see it. Her mum and Abi didn't think it was a good idea, but she insisted. Her family checked with Frankie's mum and there was some back and forth.

"Can I speak to her?" Mim asked. "Can I explain?"

They didn't think it was a good idea. Abi took Mim's phone, her mother found her a sedative. When she slept, after days of sleeplessness, she dreamed of Frankie on the boat with her.

"You're here," Mim said, clinging to her friend. "You made it. You're OK."

But Frankie looked unspeakably sad. "You never knew what was real or not," she told Mim.

When she finally saw her friend's body, it wasn't Frankie any more. Her face was bloated and unrecognisable. The only thing that really felt like Frankie was the quill tattoo on her left wrist, matching the one on Mim's right. She held hers next to Frankie's for the last time. Ink sisters.

At the funeral, Frankie's family seemed to keep some distance from Mim. Her friend's brothers pressed protectively around their mother. Mim's mum and sister stood, guarding her. Some friends from journalism college were there, a couple of Frankie's colleagues, her ex from the tattoo parlour, who wept huge, splashing tears.

Mim didn't cry at all. She was as rigid as a block of ice. People came up to her and talked, shared memories of Frankie, cried, touched her, even tried to extend their own forgiveness. But she wished they wouldn't. Their words, their emotions, their energy exhausted her. Back at their flat, she drank a neat glass of tequila and climbed into bed with all her clothes on. Abi got in next to her.

"Who's with Evie?" she asked.

"Boring Ben." Abi wrapped her arms around her sister.

"He's not that boring," Mim said.

"He can be," Abi sighed.

At Ellis Island, Mim wanders around numbly, thinking again of Esther and Rebecca's arrival. How lost they must have felt. It occurs to her, not for the first time, that she has been so wrapped up in her own problems that she has missed huge chunks of the lives of the people around her. Without thinking about it too much, she gets out her phone and sends a message to Lucky.

I'm so sorry about the other day. Can we talk? x

His reply comes quickly.

I'm going to salsa tonight. I could meet you at Club Cache before class?

He's keeping her in a public place, so she doesn't behave like a mad woman. But that's fair enough. She has time to freshen up a little before she goes to meet him.

Back at home, Mim has a cool shower and a long drink of water, but, still, she is nervous as she enters the club. Lucky is standing at the bar with a glass of water. He doesn't kiss or hug her when he sees her. His face doesn't light up, even a little; he doesn't stride towards her with his bouncy gait. Something in him has dulled and she's responsible for that. They sit at the bar, sipping iced water.

"The first thing I wanted to say is: I'm sorry," Mim begins.

"You already said that." Lucky takes a sip of water and places his glass on the coaster.

Mim is quiet. She thought this might be easier.

"It's OK," Lucky says after a minute or two. "If that's what you need, it's OK. I know you've got stuff going on. And I might have helped you through it..."

And it's his use of the past tense that makes Mim realise how much she doesn't want to lose this.

"I think you're swell," he says softly. "The cat's pyjamas." But there's no sparkle in his eyes now. "But you keep pushing me away. And I have to look after myself too," he adds. "I have to look after my heart."

Mim nods. She feels a prickle of emotion at her nose and eyes, but she mustn't cry, mustn't make it about her.

"I know you've had your heart broken, Mim. I have too. Everyone in this world has, or will have. That's just part of it."

She nods again, unable to speak for a few moments, but if she doesn't say it now, she never will. "My best friend died in a drowning accident," she begins. "The person I danced the 'Macarena' with in Casablancas. My main person, really. It was my idea to go swimming that night.

She was only in the water because of me. To make sure I was all right." She pauses. "I suggested it to impress a man I liked. And she drowned – he and I came back from it – but she didn't." She wants Lucky to touch her, but he doesn't.

"I'm sorry," he says instead. "It sounds awful."

"The thing is," Mim says, her voice cracking a little, "I couldn't save her. I couldn't get back into the water to save her."

Lucky reaches out and squeezes her hand. Then he takes it away again. "I wish I could mend your heart." He glances down at the bar. "But you have to do that, Mim."

There are things she wants to say to him, but she doesn't know where to begin. Salsa music starts to play in the background. She doesn't want to say goodbye; she doesn't want to think about the days ahead without Lucky. He gets carefully to his feet and she can see his sadness too. It was always there. She was just too preoccupied with her own.

"I'm not going to stay for the class."

"I get it," he says.

There are more people arriving but his eyes are on her face. It has not been very long, but it doesn't need to be – his offering her a tissue, watching Singin' in the Rain by her side, promising he would find the dance for her, holding her in the tango, kissing her quill tattoo, dancing with Bibi. Happy in his body, not trying to escape it. Content with himself. What a skill that is, what a remarkable thing.

"Do you have time for a last dance?" He holds out his hand.

For a few minutes, it's just the two of them and, even though they're dancing the salsa, it feels as sad as a final tango.

53

By the time Mim reaches Bibi's apartment, she is all cried out and has reached a kind of calm. The mood is sombre – even FeeFee is subdued in her greeting. Bibi glances at Mim's face.

"I think you have finished Esther's story."

Mim nods. She finds her way to her usual chair, drawing her legs up to her. "Did you know about Lili? And what happened to her?"

"Yes." Bibi looks away, out at the water.

"Did Esther speak about her much?"

"Not really. I don't know that we're much of a talking generation. But I know that Lili was with Esther until the moment she died."

Mim sighs. "I don't understand why she never spoke of her. Or her parents, either."

"It was a difficult time," Bibi says. "Even after the liberation of Paris. I know that Esther and Rebecca went every day to the Hôtel Lutetia. It had been used as a base by the German military intelligence and, afterwards, when Paris was freed, it became a centre for returning deportees. Relatives of the missing came to check the lists there every day to see if their loved ones had shown up. That's what Esther and Rebecca were doing. Looking for their parents. Everyone was looking for someone. Their hope was unbearable – we couldn't face them."

"We?"

"Those of us who returned from the camps," Bibi says. She pauses. "I think, if you don't mind, I'm going to make myself a drink."

Afterwards, when she's settled in her chair, she continues. "We think we must have been at the hotel at the same time – Esther and I talked about it later. Long before we met. Strange to think we were both in that building, both looking for people we'd lost. I was less hopeful, I think, because of where I'd been." She sighs. "The hotel beds were too soft for us – we slept curled up on the floor." Her gaze shifts away to the river.

"What happened to your family?"

Bibi sighs. "I was the baby, the youngest of five – I was born in 1929, just ten when the war started, fifteen when it ended. It stole my childhood and every single member of my family."

Mim is reminded again of how unremarkable her own pain is. "How did you keep on living?"

"You do it day by day, but it never goes away. You just build a life around it. I dug ditches for the dead. I sifted through their belongings. I took out any crumb of food and I ate it for myself. I wore their clothes. Everyone was compromised in some way."

"You didn't have a choice."

"As far as I could, I chose to stay alive," Bibi says quietly. She is silent for a moment or two. "Esther found it hard to forgive herself for what happened to Lili," she continues. "She believed she was responsible. Perhaps that's something she thought you could understand."

Mim feels Bibi's gaze on her, unsure of how much she knows. "I've been thinking of Frankie a lot today," she says. "Trying to talk to her, trying to let her go."

"Did it help?"

"I don't know. A little."

"It won't happen all at once. A little motion, and then a little more. That's how something moves along."

"Like dancing?"

"Yes, that's what that lovely man of yours would say."

Mim looks at her hands. "I think he's done with me."

"Well," Bibi tips FeeFee gently off her lap and gets to her feet, "maybe it's not the end of that story. Would you like a glass of water?"

While Bibi is in the kitchen, Mim uses the bathroom. When she returns, Bibi is waiting for her in the living room. There's something nagging at Mim, that slips in and out of her mind. It comes to her then.

"Esther's story seemed to end with Lili's death," she begins. "But do you know if she was still working on it? Did she ever write about how they left France and came to America? And did she ever see Amélie again?"

Bibi looks at Mim's face as if weighing something up, before making her way to a bureau, which she unlocks with a delicate key. She passes Mim a battered blue exercise book

NICOLA RAYNER

– the same kind that Esther used.

"She wanted me to give you this."

Mim opens the book carefully. Tucked into the front of it is a photograph of Esther and Rebecca. They must be in their twenties, with their arms around another young woman standing between them. A woman who's instantly familiar – wild wavy hair, an impish face, smaller and slighter in build than both of her sisters. The photograph answers a question Mim has wondered all her life – why had she always been Esther's favourite?

"Darling, you're in my sun." Her grandmother always batted Mim and her questions away, but Esther did the opposite. Esther held her close, whispered advice in her ear, mentored her writing – eventually, after many years, told her the truth.

Esther loved Mim the best because maybe her great-niece had given her a second chance. Because, in the strange way of families, a close resemblance seemed to have skipped a generation: Lili is the spitting image of Mim. Or perhaps, Mim realises now, it had always been the other way round.

54

May 1944 – August 1944

Please forgive me for telling the story this way. If you've got this far, I know you will have found Bibi. I asked her to keep an eye on you. I imagine the two of you will get on well. I'm sorry I'm not around to see it. Or maybe I am. I won't know until it's too late.

By now, you will have read about Lili. I wanted to explain in person. I wanted to smooth out my story, to tell you more gently, but in the end there wasn't enough time. There never is, you know. Even if you live to your nineties.

After the night we lost Lili, it was clear the Gestapo knew about Amélie too. Her eyesight was always sharp, excellent at picking a spot in the distance on which to focus for her turns. She glimpsed them entering the Tabarin before they caught sight of her and she swiftly made herself scarce.

She went into hiding in a place Antoine knew on the outskirts of Paris, where Bluebell and Marcel were also staying, until the city was liberated. I found all this out later, and heard of Amélie's final act of resistance, accompanying her old friend Gilbert Doukan, who had escaped from Drancy, to the train station, just as she had done for Marcel and for us. I like to think he headed straight back into Gisy's arms, before fighting for the Resistance in those last days of the Occupation.

Rebecca and I made our way to Marseille. They were quiet, painful months. We also went into hiding, kept safe only by the kindness of strangers, who put a roof over our heads. Rebecca picked up work quickly, as usual, and I did any odd jobs I could. I stopped writing, though, and I more or less stopped speaking too. I think my mind broke a little after Lili's death and, despite Rebecca's warnings and tears, I found myself wandering into the streets during the Battle of Marseille in August 1944, almost hoping someone would shoot me down. I didn't mind which side. No such luck.

We returned to Paris as soon as we could and, though we were too late to witness Resistance fighters chase Nazi cars out of the city, or to see the tricolore raised again from the Eiffel Tower, or Charles de Gaulle make his triumphant entry, the celebrations could still be seen and heard from every corner.

It was at that time that I caught my last glimpse of Amélie in Paris. Dancing with an American soldier outside Notre-Dame, she looked as lively and cheerful as I'd ever seen her. How could she do it? I wondered, as I watched her through a parting in the crowd. She danced with such absorption, such delight; it reminded me of the way a bird seems to take pleasure in its flight, with no thought for what has gone before or after.

I pushed through the throng and tapped her on the

shoulder. Her face said all kinds of things in a moment or two, like weather passing quickly through the sky. Recognition, affection, confusion, even defiance.

"How can you?" I said. "You're dancing."

"Esther," she said, "Paris is free. Is there a better time to dance?"

I glared at her. "You think I can dance after what happened to Lili?" I demanded. "You think I can write? You think I can do anything pleasurable?"

"I'm so sorry about Lili," she said. "But there was nothing we could have done – we didn't have time to stop her." She was very still for a moment, as if she was remembering it. And I was glad that she was. That I had ruined her day, if only briefly. "There wasn't time," she said quietly.

"You shouldn't have held me back," I continued. Still not done. Not saving Lili was the last and worst of my crimes: it was myself I could never forgive. But of course I didn't make that clear.

I saw the old fire in Amélie's eyes then. The small girl who snapped a cane in half when it hit her. "I hope one day you realise how wrong you are," she said. "I hope one day you regret saying that."

Another soldier tapped her on the shoulder for a dance. She nodded brightly and didn't look back at me.

Returning to the Pletzl in a fury, I found my sister at a street party close to home. She was celebrating in a very Rebecca, restrained kind of way, standing outside with the sun on her face. She'd padded out the shoulders of an old jacket and wore a vibrant turban. She, and others like her, saw it as their duty to show the world, as it arrived in Paris, that the city's women hadn't lost their sense of style.

"What on earth is wrong?" she asked, when she saw my face.

"I just saw Amélie dancing in the street," I said. "As happy as a bird."

"And why shouldn't she?"

This was not the response I wanted.

"France has been liberated," my sister said. "We have survived when so many haven't. And Amélie helped us."

"How can you two let go so easily?" I asked. "How can you forget?"

She tutted at me then, ever the older sister. "No one is forgetting anything," she said. "Or anyone. We will carry what we've lost forever. But today is a day for celebration."

"I'll never forgive her for stopping me. I could have gone after Lili – I could have been at her side."

"And I would never have forgiven you if you'd gone," Rebecca snapped. "I might be standing here as the only remaining member of our family." There was still no word of either of our parents. "Is that what you would want? Look," she bit her lip, "I know I was never your favourite. I know you didn't love me best, but I'm all you have now."

"Rebecca." I reached out to her but she stepped away from me.

"I will be grateful to Amélie for the rest of my life," my sister said. "And one day you might feel the same."

I didn't understand how two women, so different in personality, could be so closely aligned against me. The thing about righteous anger, though, is that it can be a comfort blanket – easier to wallow beneath it than face the things we've lost. At home, I shut the shutters and got into bed. I couldn't sleep, couldn't rest, couldn't celebrate. I covered

my head with a pillow to block out the sound of music in
the streets.

55

In the weeks that followed, I didn't go back to the Tabarin, taking circuitous routes through Pigalle to avoid it. If I ever saw an old acquaintance heading towards me, I ducked into a grocery store or hid behind a market stand. If I could have stopped breathing, I would have done, but we don't get a choice in these matters.

After the initial elation of liberation, the mood in Paris darkened. They called it the épuration sauvage – the wild purge – the punishment of suspected collaborators. A wave of executions, assaults and public humiliations. It was an ugly time – the darkest side of human nature revealing itself. Women had the worst of it, as usual.

An enduring image from that time is of girls who were accused of collaboration horizontale – sleeping with a German – being paraded through the streets, their heads shorn, swastikas drawn on their faces, their clothes all but torn off. I spotted a familiar face, once, at the centre of a sickening gathering in Place de la Concorde. Each of Belle's arms was held roughly by a man, while a third shaved her head, a burning cigarette hanging out of his mouth as he did so. I watched, feeling sick to my belly, but I couldn't turn away.

Belle held my gaze for a long time. Her beautiful white-blonde hair, of which she was so proud, fell away in clumps. I would like to say that compassion made me recall the way she warmed me on those cold nights in the Tabarin, the words we whispered, the part of me only she knew. But I just felt numb. She kept her gaze steady on me, as those men shaved her. Eventually I glanced away.

"Look at me," she said in a steady voice. "You're no better than them – at least, they do it out in the open. I remember what you did at the Tabarin, trashing my room when I wasn't there."

"You betrayed us," I replied unsteadily. "Lili died because of you."

One of the men shaving her heard me and spat on her head. She ignored him. "I'm sorry about your sister," she said. "But I never said a word." A moment of silence, as if debating to say more. "It was your jealous outburst by the stage door that night that gave you away."

"Liar," I said, but my heart began to race, replaying the night when I had caught her outside the stagedoor. Schlemiel. I'd used that Yiddish word, hadn't I? Drawn attention to myself. "Liar," I repeated more loudly. "You're lying." And yet the weary way in which Belle spoke had the ring of truth about it.

Other people began to join in with my shouts: "Liar! Menteuse!" Another person spat on her. A father lifted his child above the heads in front of him to teach her a life lesson about what happens to treacherous women.

The thing was, as I stumbled away through the Tuileries Garden, I couldn't conjure my memory of that night with any accuracy. I'd been starving and terrified. It wasn't impossible that I'd said something to give myself away. Had Lili's death been my fault? I scratched and scratched at the memory until it bled.

Shame prevented me from saying a word to Rebecca. I stopped sleeping, I stopped eating. I looked back at my crimes over the years. I had stolen Amélie's picture. I had told Belle's secret to Dédée and let Amélie take the blame. I had risked the lives of my sisters by returning to Paris from London. I'd had an affair with Belle, a probable anti-Semite, who'd never even liked me very much. I had it got wrong at every turn, and in the end I couldn't protect the person I loved the most in the world.

Unable to bear the contents of my head any longer, I decided to end it all. I would throw myself off the Pont au Change, wearing my heaviest clothes. I felt bad, fleetingly, for my sister, but Rebecca would cope, I told myself. I was only a burden to her – perhaps she could move on to a new life without me.

After I'd made the decision to do it, I slept well for the first time in months. Years, perhaps. I woke early in the morning, feeling deeply rested for once, to the sight of Lili next to me on the bed, her face just inches away from mine.

"What are you doing?" she asked, as if she could read my intentions.

I was too ashamed to reply.

"Esther." She sighed. She turned from her side to her

back, staring up at the ceiling. She seemed far sadder than the Lili I'd known. "You're wasting it."

"Wasting what?"

She glared at me. "You know what."

"I miss you," I told her.

But she had already gone.

I joined Rebecca in the kitchen, where she was making coffee. She smiled at me.

"I dreamed of Lili," I told her. "She was just here."

Rebecca passed me a cup. "What did she say?"

I sighed and tried to take a sip, even though it was still too hot. "She said I was wasting it – the way she used to."

"Well, she might be right about that," Rebecca said. She was always better than me at refusing to wallow, at simply getting on with things.

"There was a German solider at the Tabarin," I said slowly. "And I think he guessed I was Jewish. I was so sure of myself – blaming Belle – but I think I was the one who gave us away. I think I'm the reason Lili died."

There was a silence between us as Rebecca seemed to turn over what I'd said in her head. When she eventually spoke, she did so slowly and with care. "You're not perfect, Esther. None of us is. But you're not the reason Lili died."

We ate breakfast together for the first time in ages. I realised how hungry I was as I tore into the bread and cheese. I kept rediscovering Lili's message like a gem in my pocket. You're wasting it. Maybe I didn't want to be dead after all.

56

1945–1948

After the war ended, the official documents found us eventually, confirming the death of our parents. Brief, impersonal, containing nothing of Ima and Papa in them – the smell of them, the touch of their hands, callused from work, the memories of our tiny apartment in the Pletzl. Rebecca and I looked at those letters for a long time and then we folded them away, along with everything else.

I don't know why it took me so long to return to the Tabarin – more than two years after the end of the war. Maybe it was the memory of them. Maybe some time had to pass. But Lili's words haunted me; they pushed me through the days. You're wasting it. I finally made it early one afternoon when the place was a ghost ship, except for Monsieur Bergé, rehearsing with a couple of dancers I didn't know.

"Are you looking for Amélie?" he asked.

I nodded. I hadn't known, until that point, that I was. I

hadn't formulated my apology, but I knew in my bones that I owed her one.

"You're too late," he said shortly. And I wondered how much he knew of our story. "She's gone. Antoine too."

"Gone?"

"To America." He rolled his eyes. "Like everyone else."

I didn't know that it would be the last time I would set foot in the theatre where I'd grown up. That I would never again hear gossip emanating from the dressing rooms, the thrumming of the cancan dancers' feet, the knock of a callboy. I'd never again feel Sandrini's hand on my shoulder, his low voice asking for an opinion, or hear the click of Dédée's heels, accompanied by Cancan's toenails. I'd never again see my parents bustling around the place, Lili hovering below the stage with her camera, or Amélie leaping into le grand écart.

Maybe I thought I'd be back. Maybe I thought there would be more time. But in 1949 Sandrini was killed in a car accident, at the wheel of his beloved sports car, and Dédée, bereft, couldn't manage the place alone. She sold it to the owners of the Moulin Rouge in 1953. By 1966, the whole place was razed to the ground. But, of course, I didn't know any of that then. I turned my back on my old haunt and sprinted through the streets to reach Rebecca and tell her that we needed to go to America.

In the end, my sister didn't take much persuading.

"Yes," she said, her sad face more lined than it should have been at almost thirty. "We need this. Something different."

"And you don't think it's a hare-brained scheme? Following my friend across the world?"

"Maybe," she shrugged. "I don't have any better ideas. Maybe it will help you to start writing again."

It was strange to realise, so late in my life, how much Rebecca loved me. How had I missed it?

*

As the ship pulled in to New York, Rebecca and I had elbowed our way to the front of the railings to take in the city's jagged skyline. I might never have thought it possible that I could so easily leave the land of my parents, the Tabarin, Colette. But I hadn't realised how much we needed to escape the continent that was soaked with the blood of our family. I slipped my arm through Rebecca's and she squeezed it.

We struggled in those early days – we lived in a cramped apartment with a rat problem. Rebecca quickly found work in the Garment District and, between odd jobs, I started my search for Amélie, making a list of the city's theatres. I became an expert at schmoozing with the box office or chatting to the stage doormen, asking if they'd seen her.

"Pretty. Slim. A talented dancer. You've described every girl who comes through our door," said one dismissively.

"I haven't met her," said another. "But I'd like to."

"She can do thirty-two fouettés and le grand écart," I told a third.

He shrugged. "I'm sorry, ma'am, I don't speak French."

I also thought of Lili, in that bright new city – the things she would have photographed. The buildings shooting up, the new UN headquarters, the glittering shop windows, white sheets criss-crossing between the tenement buildings. I saw them through her eyes and very gradually I began to jot down a few words about these images.

Sometimes I thought I spotted one of them. Lili or Amélie. I was haunted by them both. I might see a brunette girl ahead of me, with Amélie's lively gait, and trot after her, desperate to catch a glimpse of her face. But it was never my friend. Rebecca looked too, knowing what it meant for me, and I thought she'd seen her one night in a Lower East Side bar, when we were enjoying the rare treat of a drink after a long working week.

Rebecca's face went pale. "I can't believe it," she muttered.

For a moment, my heart leapt. This time it would be her. But when I turned, it was just another handsome sailor. New York was full of them. They've never been to my taste, but my sister – usually so restrained, so ladylike – flew across the room, before I could say a word, leaping into the man's arms.

His face lit up like Times Square and they kissed in the manner of one of those post-war photographs. A swooping Hollywood embrace. It took my brain a few moments to catch up. A night in London. A tiny piece of embroidery. Forget-me-not. If I squinted a little, he looked like Jimmy Stewart. After all we'd lost, my sister had finally found something instead.

57

He was Lieutenant Commander Matthew Simon, a British naval officer who grew up in Wiltshire. His ship was docked for a stint in Brooklyn Navy Yard. If I'd tried to come up with a better match for my sister, I don't think I could have. He was the oldest of three children too, the apple of his mother's eye. Responsible, ambitious and kind, he thought Rebecca was the most beautiful woman he had ever seen, and he never stopped thinking that until the day of his death, a decade before my sister's. I'm surprised she carried on without him for as long as she did. Perhaps the quality I'm most grateful for in my brother-in-law is that he had a sense of humour – Rebecca seemed lighter around him and he took away a little of the weight that had been pressing down on her shoulders for so long.

With a different person, an extra body staying so often in our tenement apartment might have felt oppressive, but Matthew made everything better. He spoiled Rebecca

– bought her new dresses and scent and a television set that made us the envy of all our neighbours. It was no surprise when one afternoon my sister came back with a glittering engagement ring from Tiffany's on her finger. And I was happy for her, I really was. Even though I knew it would only be a matter of months before she'd make the move to Great Britain, ending up in the country she'd never wanted to leave. Yet there were times, walking around the Lower East Side to give the pair of them privacy, that I felt my own loneliness like a nagging ache in my belly.

It was at an audition that I spotted her. A thin woman with wild red curls eyeing up a salt beef sandwich that one of the dancers had left unguarded on a chair during her audition. The redhead winked at me. Her scrawny hand shot out and nabbed it. Foolish, we both thought, to leave a sandwich unguarded. No one who'd survived Paris during the war would have done such a thing.

"You here to audition?" she asked cheekily.

I shook my head. Even after all my years in the theatre, I could be blindsided by charisma. "I'm looking for someone."

"Tout le monde cherche quelqu'un," she said, but her tone was sad this time. "Everyone's looking for someone these days."

"What about you?"

"I won't find them here." She got to her feet, still clutching the sandwich. "Shall we go and share this?"

And because she could speak French, because of the number I saw tattooed on her arm, because she had lost even more than me, but was still there, in New York, stealing sandwiches and going to auditions, I knew she was someone I needed to be friends with. So that afternoon, during our impromptu picnic in Central Park, I told her about Amélie.

"You loved her?" She looked at the pencil sketch, which I always carried folded tightly somewhere about my person.

"She was my muse," I said shyly, because I'd never spoken to anyone about this but Lili.

She took the paper from me and smoothed it out. "Lucky girl."

I didn't know if she meant me or Amélie.

Birgit Goldman had been born in Berlin in 1929, to a Jewish family who'd fled from Germany to Paris in 1933. She spoke four languages – German, French, English and Yiddish – and she and I quickly became a double-act. She'd audition and I'd scout the theatres for Amélie and, yes, when we saw them, we would steal sandwiches.

"Do you ever think about giving up?" she asked me once, as we sat on my bed together, so Rebecca and Matthew could enjoy some privacy in the other room.

I hadn't told her the whole story. I hadn't told her about what happened to Lili.

"No," I said. "I have to find her. She saved my life, and I never thanked her. What could be more important than that?"

I realised we were holding hands. A knock on the door made me jump.

"There's something you have to see," Rebecca said.

I don't know why but my idiot heart leapt at the thought that it might be Lili. Lili in New York. Back from the dead. Could it be possible? My mind was muddled by the realisation I had feelings for Birgit that were more than platonic. I had to remind myself of where I was. That Lili would never come back.

I don't know if Rebecca read my mind or not, but she said, "It's Amélie."

Again, there was a juddering hiccup as my brain caught up. "Where?" I asked after a moment.

I followed her to the living room, where Matthew was sitting very close to the television – a chunky cube of a thing with a tiny screen.

"There." Rebecca pointed at the TV. "The Amélie and Antoine Ballet," Rebecca said. "They're on the television."

I got as close to the screen as I could. There they were, Amélie and Antoine, dancing on The Ed Sullivan Show with two other couples. The routine didn't have the rawness from their Montmartre days when they danced that first tango together. It was swooningly elegant, with balletic lifts. My friend might not have made it to the Ballet Russe but there she was on American television, being watched by millions.

Overcome with emotion, I flung my arms around Birgit. She held me with a grip that was surprisingly strong. Our embrace felt like coming home.

Lili, I told my sister. I've found her. And I didn't mean Amélie, but the woman in my arms.

58

Birgit helped me to find her. She knew a stagehand who told her that Amélie and Antoine had a regular slot at the Copacabana nightclub on East 60th Street. With the help of Birgit, who befriended the doorman, I discovered when Amélie and Antoine would next be performing there and managed to slip into the nightclub during the day to watch the dancers rehearse.

I found a seat at the back of the club, watching Amélie, Antoine and the two other couples I'd seen on television. It was less sedate than the number I'd seen on screen – more jiggly and glittery. There was a gorgeous looseness to the way Amélie was dancing. Her movement had changed in a way I couldn't quite put my finger on. It was an ensemble piece, but I wanted to see more of her dancing alone.

When they finished, the other dancers stretched and rubbed their limbs. A couple of them disappeared into the wings. Amélie, Antoine and two others stayed on stage for a debrief. On impulse, I jumped to my feet and made my way to the stage, my heart thrumming. I stood below in the darkness, squinting up at them in the light.

"Annie." That old name of hers slipped out. I couldn't help suppress the joy in my voice. Despite everything – the distance, the years and the space between us – she was still my old friend who'd cartwheeled across the stage at the Bal Tabarin. I would never stop loving her.

The dancers on stage went silent. Antoine glanced at Amélie, his usual cockiness gone. What had she said about me? She gazed in my direction, as if she'd never seen me before. "It's Amélie," she said coolly.

My palms were itchy with sweat. "Can we talk?"

"I have nothing to say to you." Her tone was icy, unrecognisable from the voice I'd once known.

"Please?" I knew I looked desperate. Standing below the stage, begging. My humiliation complete.

"Esther," she said. "You really have to go – you are not welcome here."

I stumbled away, my cheeks burning, but not quickly enough to hear one of the other dancers ask, "Who was that?"

"An usherette I used to know," she said.

I put one foot in front of another in the way I'd been doing for years. I was just the girl in the bookshop. The girl who never fitted in. Who was never good enough for the glamorous creatures on stage. Had I always known that our friendship would be temporary? Had I always suspected it might end up like this? With me begging her for something, while she gazed imperiously at me from the stage?

Just before I reached the exit, I felt a hand on my arm. It

was Antoine. "Do you want to go for a coffee?"

A few minutes later, we were sitting in a neighbourhood diner with coffees in front of us.

"What did you think of our new stuff?"

"Très élégant," I said politely. I didn't want to be making small talk.

"It's not as good, is it?" said Antoine, with his instinct for the truth. "As we were in the war? We've lost some of our rawness. Still," he grinned, "it's good enough for the Americans. But Amélie," he gave a low whistle, "she's changed as an artist. She's the dancer I always knew she could be."

"I can't bear that she won't talk to me."

"You hurt her." He took a sip of coffee. "Do you think she sleeps well?" He sighed. "Do you think any one of us does? Aren't we all haunted by the people we didn't save?"

I started to cry, and Antoine, being Antoine, offered me an immaculate white handkerchief. He allowed me to weep. He didn't try and soothe me. We'd all been through too much for that.

"If you'd like my advice," he said, when I was done. "Try again. Speak to her on her own."

He returned with me to the Copacabana and accompanied me in, leaving me in a seat at the back of the club. It was quieter, and when Antoine left, I was sitting in the place alone, the lights down, a spotlight on Amélie on stage. A piece of recorded music began to play which, without warning, jolted me back to my past, to watching my friend from the wings of the Tabarin.

It was The Dying Swan, but it was like watching a different dance, a different dancer. She'd always rushed it a little before, I realised, had been preoccupied with showing how far she could extend, a look of theatrical anguish on her face. But this was something different. Her gestures weren't as overblown, but this time I believed she was someone who'd experienced a fight to the death. That she was someone who knew that that it was a battle you wouldn't always win. Antoine had been right all along: Amélie's job as an artist hadn't been to perform the most impressive grand écart or the largest number of fouettés – it had been to say something true.

Her dance took me back to a square in Paris, to a young girl lying supine, looking up at the sky. Gazing at something I couldn't see. Lili and her child who would never be twenty-nine. Or forty-three. Or seventy-two. Who would remain frozen as they were in those moments forever.

Amélie's dancing contained pain and sorrow right down to the tips of her fingers. She'd felt everything too – I'd been wrong about that – she just expressed it differently from me. She held it in her body, the instrument that could best express it. My face grew wet with tears and, when she finished, I saw that hers was too.

I clapped. A solitary round of applause echoing through the empty nightclub. She brushed her tears aside and looked out into the darkness.

"It's Esther," I called from my hiding place.

"Oh," she said flatly. "I thought you'd gone."

"No." I got to my feet. "Still here."

She came to join me in the shadows. For a moment or two, we sat side by side, looking up at the empty stage.

"I've never seen you dance like that," I said. "Not even with Antoine."

She nodded as if she already knew.

"You did it," I said. "You became a great artist."

As she smiled in response – a slow, sad smile – I realised the dance she'd performed wasn't the kind of thing you'd usually see at the Copacabana. It was a dance for nobody else but her.

"Esther," she said, "I'm getting married."

"Congratulations." I gave her hand a squeeze, anticipating the same slight sadness I'd experienced when Rebecca had told me she was engaged. The lonely child in me terrified of being left behind. But it didn't come. I experienced a novel feeling: genuine happiness for another.

"His name is Victor," she said. "He runs a dance school, where I teach." She smiled. "No canes, though."

"I've found someone too," I said.

"What's she like?" Amélie asked. And I realised she'd always known.

"She is full of life," I said truthfully. "Despite living through the worst of times. I can't imagine what I would do without her now."

Amélie nodded and we were quiet for a few moments, our gaze still focused on the stage.

"I had a thing with Belle," I confessed at last.

"I knew," Amélie said. "We all knew."

I realised I hadn't said what I planned – I hadn't told her it wasn't her fault about Lili. But then perhaps she already knew that too.

"Antoine is going to train up Marguerite as his new Amélie," she said. "She'll be the one going on tour with him. He said" – she paused for a moment – "I might have another Amélie, but I'll never have another Annie."

"How can you leave it?" I asked. "Now all of this is starting – now that you can dance like that?"

"I suppose I got where I needed to get."

"But no one has seen it."

"You've seen it," she said. And I wondered then if she had missed me in the way I'd missed her. "And, more important, I have seen it. I know I'm capable of it. And so does Antoine. There's nothing like making a point – even if it takes a decade. After we're married, I'm going to teach at Victor's school full-time," she added cheerfully. "His students – they're poor kids like I was, facing a life of discrimination and poverty. Maybe some of us aren't meant to be stars – perhaps some of us are meant to create them."

"You were meant to be one."

"No, Esther," she sighed. "I was one. I was one of the stars of the Bal Tabarin – I know what that is like: the wild applause, people waiting for you at the stage door, flowers, champagne. It didn't make me happy." She paused. "Wait there." She got up and disappeared backstage. When she returned, she passed me a shoe bag.

I peered in and saw her silver tango shoes.

"I want you to have them."

"What will I do with these?" I smiled sadly. "I don't wear heels."

"It's what's inside them," she told me.

I pulled one of the shoes out and examined the sole. There was a faint crunch of paper under my fingers – something tucked into the toe of the shoe. I carefully extracted a few sheets, folded many times over, their edges worn with age.

"A few letters I never delivered," she said. "Addressed to you. Maybe you'll write about me one day."

We were silent for a moment or two, and my thoughts returned, as they always did, to that night in the square. "Do you still go back there?" I asked. "To what happened at the convent?"

"Every day." Amélie kept her eyes fixed on the stage. "Every night."

"I'll see you there some time." I looked at her face for a few long minutes and noticed the lines and sadness that had aged it. Somehow, I knew it would be the last time I'd see her.

"I'll never let you go," she said. "However many times we go back. I'll never let go of your hand. You'll be glad of it one day."

I nodded. "Thank you," I said. "I'm grateful. I am. It's just…" I swallowed, unable to speak for a while. "I should have held on to her more tightly," I said in the end.

Amélie got to her feet and held me – not one of her exuberant hugs of old, where she'd briefly fling her arms around my neck and then move swiftly on to the next thing. She held me as if to say: give your pain to me, I can take it from you. I felt everything in that embrace – all her courage, all her sorrow, all our years of friendship, all the lies I'd told, all the shame I'd experienced. I felt her say goodbye, too, in that hug. I felt a deep sadness that there wouldn't be cocktails and parties and laughs for us in the years to come; that whatever we had been to each other we wouldn't be that any more. We would have to make new stories with new people.

"You can loosen your grip on her now," Amélie said, as she released me from her embrace. "It's OK. Lili will always be with you. You can't lose her again."

59

Shaking with emotion as she finishes reading, Mim gets up to wash her face. In the weeks and months after, she started calling Frankie's mum at various times, during the day and night. Usually, but not always, hanging up before she answered the phone. Occasionally, Mim wouldn't be quick enough and she would catch the grieving woman, her voice deader, quieter than usual, drained of her lively expressiveness. The worst was the first time, in the early days.

"Frankie," her friend's mum whispered. "Is that you?"

That should have been enough to shame Mim to stop, but she didn't. She hung up, then slapped herself across the face until her cheeks were raw. Her mother caught her once, pinned her arms to her side like the coastguard had.

"I wish I'd died," Mim wept. "I wish it had been me."

Her mother started to cry. "You have to stop this."

And it had become a little easier since those early days

355

of madness – the days of hitting herself in the bathroom, refusing to eat, calling Frankie's mother so much that her phone was taken away from her. There had been Valium and temazepam and sitting opposite a kind woman, her mum's age, who asked her what she was going to do with all the love she had for Frankie.

She'd tried going back to work many months later. Someone was at her old desk. Robbie was still there, thinner and paler.

"He's a lifer," Frankie had said once. "He is so ordinary."

He tried to speak to her, but she shut him down. And they never again saw each other outside of work. Mim stopped socialising, gave up smoking and drinking. It wasn't for her health so much as the fact that nothing gave her any pleasure any more, even her work. She stared at the screen during the day, trying to shape the sentences in front of her, but it was too hard. When she did manage to finish an article, it came out as lifeless as she was. She couldn't remember how to do it. She knew they were keeping her on out of pity.

He'd got back with his wife. That Swedish bitch. There was a baby on the way. When it was born, the pair of them brought it in to be admired. He didn't look at Mim at all that day. Everyone else cooed, while Mim stood on the periphery, like a ghost. She never knew how to act at these gatherings, even in normal circumstances.

She walked away that afternoon, her computer still sleeping, her work shoes left under the desk, and she never went back. She ignored some calls from HR and then received a formal letter. She slept for ten days in Frankie's bed, barely leaving the flat until her mother and Abi turned up to pack everything away, to help her hand in her notice. She was a little girl again. The one sitting under the table at her father's funeral while everyone told Abi to look after her mother.

Now, she glances at her phone. Is it worth trying Frankie's mum just one more time? In the sober light of day? To her surprise, there is an answer after just a couple of rings.

"Miriam," she says heavily. She sounds exhausted.

"I wasn't expecting you to answer."

"I nearly didn't," she sighs. "You're lucky it wasn't one of my sons."

"That's fair," Mim says. She tries to remember the speech she has rehearsed in her head so many times.

"What do you want from me?"

Mim imagines the other woman sitting heavily into a chair. "I don't know." She strains to recall the words. She should start with "sorry". But it will never be enough. She makes an attempt at it. It doesn't go very well. There is a long awkward silence between them.

"If you want to know," the other woman says, almost conversationally, "I'll always wish that it was Frankie who climbed into the lifeboat and not you. If it came down to it, if it could only be one of you, I would choose her."

Mim sits at Esther's desk, her feet planted on the floor. She thinks of Amélie dancing The Dying Swan. The words she has always dreaded from Frankie's mum aren't so bad in the end. In fact, it's a relief to hear them. "There have been many times when I wished that too," she says at last.

"And if Frankie had survived and you hadn't," her friend's mum says, "your mother would feel exactly the same." She exhales, almost like a laugh, though not quite.

"But she might not have said it."

"It's OK," says Mim. Because it is.

They are both quiet for a moment.

"Frankie never did anything she didn't want to do." The other woman's voice is a little softer. "She wouldn't have got into the water if she didn't want to."

Mim exhales. Something in her shifts. "Thank you," she whispers.

After hanging up, the sense of relief lingers. Frankie's mum said the worst thing, and Mim endured it. Frankie died, and she survived her grief. She lost Esther too, and her grandmother, and her father, and yet here she is. She is still alive. Young, or youngish, and free and in New York City with the afternoon stretching out in front of her. What is she going to do with it?

She begins by running upstairs and knocking on Bibi's door, but her friend doesn't answer. Maybe she is napping. She'll try her again later. Mim looks at her watch. Eduardo and Felipe's afternoon milonga will be starting soon. She needs something to do with this wired restlessness.

It's not because Lucky might be there, she tells herself, as she pops downstairs to pick up Amélie's shoes. It's not because she misses him. It's not because she hopes that seeing her again at the place where their romantic relationship started might rekindle things. It's not because of that.

And, in the end, it doesn't matter, because he's not there anyway. As luck would have it, the first person she recognises once she's arrived is Maria, looking all elegant and chic, her hair swinging neatly down her back. Unflustered, she gives Mim a polite nod and is then swept away into the arms of the most handsome man in the room.

Mim tries not to spend the next couple of hours straining to see the door from wherever she is on the dancefloor, her heart leaping at the sight of any tall dark-haired man with glasses. She manages to forget him briefly as she dances with other people, losing herself in the embrace, in the music, in the meditative journey around the room.

It is just as she's taking off her shoes that Maria asks her to dance. "I'm practising leading," she says, as they take up the hold. But her lead is so smooth, so strong, Mim is pretty sure she's already mastered it.

"You're Lucky's girlfriend, aren't you?" Maria asks between songs in the tanda.

"Not really," she says. "Not any more."

"Oh," Maria's face falls a little, Mim is sure of it. "I imagine he's very sad about that."

"I'm the one who has reason to be sad." Mim tries to smile, but it doesn't really work.

The next song begins to play.

"How about you?" Mim asks. "Who do you have your eye on?"

"I'm just dancing for myself." Maria smiles.

The same words exactly that Frankie once used. A little sign, if Mim chooses to take it that way. Her heart almost stops beating. You're still with me, she thinks.

Of course I am, says Frankie. And, for the rest of the song, Mim is dancing with Maria – not the rival, as it turns out, she thought she was – but she is also dancing with Frankie.

60

At Bibi's door, Mim feels her friend's gaze on her face and she nods in response.

"I've finished."

"Let's sit down," Bibi says gently.

With the clocks ticking around her, the slight rasp of Bibi's breath, Mim stares out at the water. "Is Amélie still alive?" she asks.

"I don't know," Bibi says. "It was years since they saw each other."

Mim swallows before she checks her phone. There it is: an obituary in the New York Times. She reads it out to Bibi.

"She died so recently," she says quietly, afterwards, "while I was here in New York. Just six months after Esther." She sighs. "If only I'd known…" But then she stops herself. She wants to be done with If onlys.

"Do you think you'll take up her story?" Bibi asks. "Do something with it?"

"Maybe." Mim stares at the phone screen. The New York Times has led with the photograph of Amélie with Antoine and Edith Piaf.

"Or perhaps you'll do something of your own?"

"I don't know." A thought occurs to her. "Perhaps I could even combine the two?"

"I miss her, you know. Esther." Bibi rubs her hands, which are swollen in the heat, and for the first time Mim notices she is wearing a wedding ring.

Has that been there all along? Perhaps it is another sign of Mim's blindness. But not any more: she knows so little about Bibi's life, and it has been extraordinary; she needs to pay more attention.

"Bibi," she asks, "when did you lose your husband?"

But, even as she says the words, she realises how truly blind she has been.

Two flats, sharing the same view. One directly above the other. Bibi travelling with Esther to Paris to stand at the spot where the Bal Tabarin once stood. Bibi – who was Birgit, of course – searching for Amélie in all the New York theatres. Bibi, who wore Chanel No 5, when, in fact, Esther never had, Mim realises. She'd only accepted it as a gift and passed it on to someone who would use it. Someone who was with her when she died.

"I've been so stupid," she says quietly.

Bibi's gaze is kind, but she doesn't correct her. "We never lived together." She strokes FeeFee's coat slowly as she speaks. "It didn't suit our temperaments. And I had to give her cats away – I'm allergic, you see, and FeeFee would never have put up with it." She glances at the beloved dog on her lap. "Co-habiting wasn't right for us. But we were happy. Esther learned to be, in the end. When she didn't have to hide who she was any more. Would you like to see a photograph of our wedding?"

Mim nods and waits as Bibi goes to the bedroom and returns with a framed photo. Bibi and Esther in Pastis. Bibi in a cascade of white ruffles, Esther in her usual slacks, looking frail. They are beaming.

"That was last year," Bibi says quietly. "One of her last days out. They changed the law just in time."

"Why didn't she tell the family about you?" Mim asks quietly. "We would have understood."

"Esther was convinced Rebecca might be frightfully old-fashioned about it," Bibi says. "But when she found out on a visit to New York, it turned out that what Rebecca was furious about was the secret." Bibi sighs. "I think poor Rebecca always wanted to be closer, but Esther held her away."

"Because she wasn't Lili?"

"Something like that."

"I do that to Abi sometimes too," Mim says. She thinks of her sister's face the night Frankie drowned. Poor darling girl. She had let her down time and time again.

"Ahh," says Bibi. "Well, at least it's not too late for you two." She hesitates. "There was a reconciliation," she says. "A meeting in Paris. On our trip out there."

"Grandma saw Esther?"

"Just briefly." Bibi nods. "They returned to the square where Lili died. And they found her name and their parents' inscribed on the wall outside the Shoah Memorial."

Mim's fingers curl and uncurl in her lap as she thinks of the sisters standing side by side again, after all those wasted years of silence.

They are quiet for a few moments. "Did Esther find peace?" she asks eventually.

"I don't know that any of us find true, permanent peace," says Bibi. "Especially people who have gone through the kinds of things that Esther and I endured. But she found something in her work. And in her cats. And in her life with me. I think she wanted you to know that it was possible to keep on living after you've lost everything; that we never really lose the people we love. We carry them with us; they become a part of who we are. Nothing could destroy the love she had for Lili. For her family. For Amélie. For me. And for you, my darling."

Mim gets to her feet to be closer to Bibi. She crouches on the thick pink carpet by the older woman's chair and the pair of them cry together for Esther, for Frankie and for everything they have both lost.

When they are done, Mim wipes her face. "Should I tell my mum? About you and Esther?"

"I'd like that. Perhaps she and Abi could come and see me too?" She nudges FeeFee gently off her lap. "Now, if I were you," Bibi squeezes her hand, surprising Mim again with her strength, "I'd give that handsome dancer of yours a call."

*

In Brooklyn Bridge Park, Mim looks across at the promise of the Manhattan skyline as the day's sunlight begins to soften. The evening stretches out in front of her.

Are you going to get in touch with him? Frankie asks.

You never give up, do you? Mim smiles. You're as bad as Bibi.

I like her.

Of course you do.

Mim fishes out her phone and writes the message quickly.

Please come dancing with me one more time. I beg you: please forgive me. I'm determined to become a better partner.

She is begging, but sometimes that's just what you have to do. She can see he's read the message and now he's typing something back. The dots dance across the screen. She can barely stand the waiting.

I have a good feeling about this, Frankie reassures her.

Mim nods. She still has Amélie's silver shoes in her bag, just in case. She can feel them under her arm, next to her notebook.

Frankie is quiet again, but Mim doesn't feel the panic she once would have done at her silence.

I'll always miss you, she tells her friend. I'll always love you.

I know that, Frankie replies. You can give it a break with the soppy stuff. Just take me out dancing. You don't want to waste it.

The phone buzzes. The light bouncing off the water makes it difficult to see the screen easily, so Mim has to shield it with her hand. Lucky has replied.

Where shall we go? X